SINCE WE FELL

A SECOND CHANCE ROMANCE

ANN GIMPEL

Edited by

KATE RICHARDS

Edited by

DIANE EAGLE KATAOKA

CONTENTS

SINCE WE FELL

Second Time Love is the Sweetest of All
A Romance Novel
By
Ann Gimpel

An idealistic woman.

A naïve man.

A life-shattering mistake.

Juliana is relentless, driven, focused. An archaeologist, she's clawed her way to the top of the heap. It's a lonely heap, but the only man she ever loved proved men aren't worthy of her time.

Discarded by the woman of his dreams midway through college, Brice never offered his heart again. A world-recognized expert on lung diseases, he has his work. Usually it's enough.

It's almost Christmas, and Juliana is called home from a dig to see her dying twin one last time. She and Brice are thrown together after a fifteen-year hiatus. She tells herself nothing's changed, but her heart sings a different song. If she listens to it, there's only one true love.

CHAPTER 1

*J*uliana Wray—Julie to her few friends—slumped against the padded back of a business-class seat, grateful no one was sitting too close to her. She'd been on the move for the last fifteen hours, and it would take nearly that before her over-the-Pole flight landed at Sea-Tac. She'd been unusually lucky securing a last-minute flight from Cairo to London, and she'd paid through the nose for the seat on her current plane.

She sucked dry, recycled air and tried not to think about what might be in it. Planes had notoriously poor filtration systems. Her eyes felt hot and gritty. Blinking only made it worse. When she glanced at her hands, she winced at how dirty they were. Once the captain turned off the "fasten seat belt" sign, she'd make a dive for the restroom and wash them. Never mind the water on airplanes rivaled the air for impurities.

Curling her hands into fists, she focused on inhaling deeply, blowing it out, and doing it again. Sleep would be a true luxury, but worry ate at her.

"Everything all right, miss?" A tall, buff flight attendant

leaned over her, solicitousness stamped into his Greek god good looks. Tawny hair fell just past his chin line, and his eyes were the shade of raw emeralds. He was so perfect, she wondered if she was hallucinating.

He consulted a roster in one hand, probably detailing his few business-class passengers. "Dr. Wray, correct?"

She managed a perfunctory smile. "Yes. That would be me."

He smiled back. "What kind of doctor are you?" Maybe his interest was part of a coffee, tea, or me gig he tried out on all his female travelers, but it gave her a momentary break from her worries.

"Not medical. If there's an emergency on this plane, you'll have to look beyond me, I'm afraid."

He angled his head to one side. "Okay. That's what kind of doctor you aren't, but it's not what I asked."

"I'm an archaeologist. Reason my clothes are so trashed is I came straight from a dig in northern Egypt."

"Sounds fascinating. Maybe when we're a bit further into the flight, you can tell me more."

"Maybe so," she murmured, aiming for a non-committal tone. The last thing she'd be doing is sharing details with anyone outside her immediate team about what was shaping up as the find of the twenty-first century.

He must have picked up on her withdrawal because his smile lost a few lumens. "What can I bring you from the drink tray?"

"Juice. Mineral water. Maybe something to eat." A dinging bell overlapped her words, and the "fasten seat belt" sign winked out. "If you'll excuse me, I'd like to wash up before I eat anything."

"Of course, Dr. Wray. I'll have a snack prepared for you by the time you return."

"That would be lovely. Thank you."

Juliana waited until he moved to the next passenger two rows back before unfastening her seat belt. She lurched upright and closed the short distance between her seat and the restroom. Once inside, she sluiced water over her hands. Dirt made tracks down the ivory porcelain sink, so she pumped extra soap and wished she had a brush to do a more thorough job scrubbing beneath her nails. Once her hands were as clean as they were likely to get, she went to work on her face. She'd tried to wash up on the Egypt Air flight, but the lavatory was so dirty she hadn't made it past the threshold.

One glance in the small mirror convinced her not to look again. Her dark hair hung in lank strands to the middle of her back. She'd scooped it into a ponytail somewhere between Cairo and London, but over half had escaped. Circles ringed her eyes, and she had the haggard look of someone who'd missed one too many meals, which wasn't far off the mark. She'd never acclimated to the food at the dig site, so she hadn't eaten much to stave off stomach problems.

"Thirty-five years old," she muttered. "If I look this bad now, where will I be at fifty?"

The question was rhetorical. She didn't bother answering it, but she did redo her ponytail before walking back to her seat. True to his word, the flight attendant—Richard, according to his name badge—had arranged a snack tray on her small pull-down table.

Julie ate mindlessly. The food on her Egypt Air flight hadn't smelled very fresh, and she hadn't had time at Heathrow to do anything beyond head for this one at a dead run. As it was, they'd shut the doors right behind her. One of the other flight attendants, a middle-aged woman, had given her a disapproving look for being late.

She washed down crackers, cheese, and shrimp with bottled mineral water. Somewhat fortified, she replayed the last day-and-a-half. She and her team, University of Washington faculty and graduate students, had set up shop in the Nile Delta not far from Ismailia. Reports of bone fragments had drawn them, but Juliana hadn't expected much more than a dry hole. Archaeology was like that.

Chasing rainbows, as it were.

A few days into what she'd expected would be a one-week excursion, they'd unearthed the remains of a town. Even so, she'd held her excitement in check until preliminary tests yielded data dating the town back to two thousand B.C, placing it somewhere between the Middle and Old Kingdoms.

The university had flooded her project with money and people. She'd spent ten months living in a tent next to the Nile and wouldn't have left if it weren't for Sarah. Her twin was sick again. Never healthy, Sarah had gotten the short end of the stick while they were in utero and developed cystic fibrosis as a child.

That she'd lived this long was little shy of a miracle, but her time may have finally run out. Julie squeezed her eyes shut against a gush of hot tears. She'd asked about gene splicing, bone marrow transplants, anything to give her sister's lungs a new lease on life. She'd even offered to help with part of a lung for transplant surgery, but Sarah told her not to bother. The CF was systemic. New lungs would eventually become infected just like her current ones were.

The tears she'd tried to hold back dripped down her cheeks, and she swiped them with her napkin. Life was desperately unfair. Her sister had tried to finish medical school but lacked the stamina. Undaunted, she'd turned her sights to a nursing degree. She'd worked in clinics and hospitals until a couple of years back when her inhalers and treatments grew less and less effective.

Julie had considered moving Sarah into her home, but she

wasn't there enough. The compromise had been her parents, who'd redone a bedroom to accommodate oxygen and the array of equipment Sarah used each day. Julie checked in weekly, but she'd been so wrapped up in each pot shard and bone fragment they'd unearthed, she'd missed a week or two along the way.

Misery washed over her in waves as she huddled in her seat. She flipped her light off and hoped no one would bother her.

Come on, Sarah, she urged. *You're my twin. Hang on until I get there.*

Her parents hadn't wanted to bother her unnecessarily. By the time they'd patched through an emergency call, Sarah was on a ventilator and couldn't talk with anyone.

Julie pulled the blanket out of its plastic cover and wrapped it around herself. Exhaustion dragged her into blackness, and she must have passed out because the next thing she heard was a cheery voice advising they'd be landing at Sea-Tac in thirty minutes.

More food had materialized. She ate quickly, not tasting anything, and drank another bottle of water.

"I didn't want to bother you while you were sleeping, Dr. Wray." Richard loomed over her.

"Thanks. I really needed some rest."

"I figured. Don't take this wrong, but you look beat." He offered his million-watt smile again, the smile that probably lined his bed with hundreds of willing women.

"Yeah. Still am."

"I'd be happy to take you out to dinner once we land. You can tell me more about your anthropology project."

"It's archaeology," she corrected him automatically, not bothering to add it was a common misperception and that people frequently confused the two disciplines.

He shrugged. "See? I need guidance."

I'll just bet you do, honey.

She bit off the temptation to verbalize a tart rejoinder. "Sorry, but my parents are meeting me. We have to get to Overlake Hospital."

"Someone's ill?" He quirked a brow.

"Very. My sister."

"Well, I hope she feels better soon." Richard edged away. Discussions of illness probably made him uncomfortable. Death wasn't contagious, but people shied away from anything that smacked of mortality as if it brought bad luck to delve too deeply.

She'd devoted her life to assessing the remains of people's lives, what they'd left behind. Death was where she lived most of the time, but it didn't make losing Sarah any easier.

Come on. Buck up. She's not gone yet. I hope.

The plane swooped out of the sky and bounced twice as it connected with the runway. She flicked on her phone as soon as she could, scanning for the message that would kill hope.

It wasn't there. Lots of well wishes from her dig team and a terse one-liner from her mother saying they'd meet her at the gate. Julie stood as soon as she could and dragged her duffle from the overhead, slinging it across one shoulder. The door opened, and she bolted through it, walking fast.

Halfway to customs, a tall, spare uniformed officer, complete with a full weapons belt, caught up with her. "Dr. Juliana Wray?" His dark hair was cut short. Shrewd green eyes probably didn't miss a whole lot.

"Yes?"

"I'm here to expedite your way through customs. Passport, please."

She dug in a pocket and handed it over. "Did my dad send you?"

Instead of answering, he pasted a sticker in her passport, stamped it, and handed it back. "Come with me. A car is waiting." Turning, he marched about twenty feet to a gunmetal-colored door and tilted his chin to activate a retinal scanner. The locking mechanism whirred, and the door popped open.

Julie followed him, afraid to ask any more questions. Maybe he'd know about her sister. Maybe not, but she did not want to hear the words, "I'm so sorry, but she passed on..."

She latched her jaws together to hold emotion inside. She'd have her whole life to cry. Now wasn't the time to fall apart.

The officer stopped long enough for a second scanner to recognize him and pushed open a door leading outside. Gray murk typical of the Pacific Northwest surrounded her under skies spitting rain. She'd lost track of time after leaving Cairo, but it must be around noon since that was when her plane was slated to touch down.

Noon in mid-December looked pretty much like dawn and dusk. Gloomy. Dark. Short days that merged into long, damp nights. What a contrast to hot, dry Egypt.

"This way." The officer motioned. "We're headed for that limo."

A long, black car was parked about fifty feet from them. "It— It looks like a hearse," she choked out.

The officer shot her a surprised look. "It's a limousine, Dr. Wray."

And then her father was running toward her. A retired Marine general, he was tall and spry, despite being in his late sixties. Silver hair was shorn close, and his blue eyes—eyes just like hers and Sarah's—crinkled with pleasure at seeing her.

The officer stood tall and saluted. Chris Wray saluted back. "Thank you, Lieutenant. Dismissed."

Julie did a double take. Her escort was a Marine. How

could she have missed something so simple as the markings on his uniform?

Her father wrapped his arms around her. "Welcome home, princess."

Julie hugged him in return and reared back so she could look at him. "Sarah. Is she—?"

"She's still with us, honey. Come on into the car, and I'll let your mom fill you in. Here. Give me that duffle. Is that all you have?"

"Yeah, Dad." She handed it over and trotted to the car with him. Joy mixed with hope speared her. Sarah was alive. It was all that mattered.

The driver, also a Marine, took her duffle and held the back door for her and her father, who followed her inside.

"Juliana, sweetie." Her mother enveloped her in a hug, her familiar lilac scent washing over her. Ariel Wray kissed her forehead before letting go. Her black hair was shot with silver, and her brown eyes glowed with pleasure. "You were gone for a long time."

"Yes, I was. Tell me about Sarah."

Ariel nodded briskly. Five years younger than her husband, she'd been a Marine colonel and battle strategist until she retired after the last Iraq conflict.

The car lurched forward. Julie resisted the urge to pepper her mother with questions and waited for her to begin speaking.

Ariel drew her dark brows together. "Up until two days ago, I was certain I'd summoned you home for your sister's funeral." She tilted her chin up, nostrils flaring. Used to deployments and death, her mom was one of the toughest women Julie had ever known, and she wouldn't mince words or sugarcoat anything.

"Sarah was drowning in her own fluids. There wasn't much left to lose, so we trolled through the university's medical school for another pulmonologist, someone younger. It pissed our doctor off, but he couldn't stop us. In any event, we found a doctor who was willing to try something unproven—"

"A non-FDA-approved treatment," her father cut in.

"Yes, Chris. Sorry if I missed the exact nomenclature." Ariel blew out a noisy breath. "We gave our permission."

"And it seems to be working." Her father couldn't keep optimism out of his voice.

"Indeed, it does." Ariel chimed in. "She's off that damned ventilator. God but she hated it."

"If things continue as they have been, we'll get to bring her home in time for Christmas," Chris said.

All the pent-up emotion Julie had suppressed since her mother's call summoning her home hit her in the gut, and she bit back a sob.

"Aw, princess. It's okay." Her father gathered her close; she gave in and clung to him as she cried, great, choking sobs that made it tough to breathe.

Her mother patted her back and smoothed her tangled hair. "It's okay, Juliana. We'll keep her with us for a little bit longer. Oh, I didn't mention it, but you'll remember the miracle-working doctor."

"I will?" Julie lifted her head from the wet front of her father's jacket. "Who is he?"

"Brice McKinnon," her father answered, reminding her how her mom and dad tag teamed conversations.

The name slammed home, along with a slew of nasty memories. "Oh God," she moaned. "I mean, I'm glad he saved Sarah, but he is such a bastard. At least, he used to be."

"Be nice," her mother warned and handed her a bunch of tissues.

Juliana blew her nose. "Don't worry, Mom. I'll be the soul of nice."

"Dry your eyes," her dad advised, as always oblivious to things he didn't find worthy of attention. "We'll be at Overlake in about fifteen minutes."

Fifteen minutes.

She dabbed at her streaming eyes. Only a quarter hour before she'd come face to face with the two-timing slime ball who'd seduced both her and her sister. And ruined her life because she'd loved him.

CHAPTER 2

*B*rice McKinnon cruised through the doctor's lounge, hunting for a snack. He'd been awake the last thirty-six hours overseeing a relatively new intervention for late-stage cystic fibrosis, and weariness dragged at him. On a hunt for calories, he slogged down chicken, mashed potatoes swimming in congealing gravy, and a pile of canned green beans. Hospital food wasn't bad—so long as you didn't examine it too closely.

He washed the food down with a second cup of hot, black coffee. It had been sitting for a while and was incredibly bitter, but he needed a boost.

"Ha. What I really need is a drink," he muttered, but he'd pitch face down on the table if he had more than a few sips of anything alcoholic.

He balanced an elbow on the table and rested his chin in his hand. Whiskers poked into his fingers, reminding him he should drop by the physicians' locker room to shower and shave before Sarah Wray's parents returned, bringing Juliana with them.

Julie.

Breath rattled through his pursed lips. The one love of his life, she'd spurned him after finding out he'd had an affair with her sister. Except it hadn't been an affair. Not really. He'd spent one drunken night with Sarah, believing she was Juliana.

The women were identical twins. It had been dark, and he'd been pretty out of it. Brice winced. His excuses sounded just as lame fifteen years later as they'd been the day after it happened. Sarah could have exonerated him, but she'd remained silent, looking more like a wounded victim than the vixen who'd made him believe she was her sister.

He lifted his chin off his hand and raked it through his hair. He'd begged. He'd pleaded. Hell, he'd even groveled, but Julie had selectively cut him out of her life. Blocked his calls and emails, and run the other way if he was lucky enough to track her down.

After three months of hell, he'd pulled his life back together. He was failing his classes, and he'd be damned if he'd let a love affair gone bad ruin his chances of getting into medical school. Besides, if Julie had really loved him, she'd have at least listened before passing judgment.

There it was, staring him in the face. She hadn't loved him enough to try. He'd known it then, and it had haunted him through one failed marriage, and far too many flings where he knew better than to offer up his heart.

He counted how he'd spent the years since he'd last seen Julie. Two of them, he'd finished his undergrad degree. Four had been taken up with med school. Four more with a residency in internal medicine, followed by a two-year pulmonology fellowship. Brice grinned ruefully. Medicine took a long time, and he'd been eying another fellowship to fine-tune his skills with immune modulators.

They were what had pulled Sarah out of her tailspin. How long her remission would last was another question altogether. She'd recognized him, her eyes rounding into small moons, but the ventilator meant she couldn't talk. Nurses had removed it an hour ago, but he hadn't been in to see her since.

"Hey. Dr. McKinnon." One of the third-year internal medicine residents charged into the doctors' lounge and mock bowed. Her red hair was cut short. Her blue eyes glittered with enthusiasm. Her scrubs had a few blood streaks, and her white coat was missing.

He searched for her name and came up dry. "What's up?" he asked, sidestepping the lack of something to call her.

"The head nurse in ICU says you might want to stop by—"

Brice shot to his feet, adrenaline flooding his mouth with a bitter taste. "Damn. Why didn't Erika page me?"

"Sorry. Sorry." Dr. No Name waved a hand his way. "Not an emergency. Your patient is better. Vitals have totally stabilized. I told Erika I was headed this way, and I'd deliver the message."

His heart thudded against his ribcage, anxiety turning to anger. Before he said something he'd regret, he slammed out of the doctor's lounge.

The female resident charged after him and grabbed his arm. "Geez. I'm really sorry. I never imagined—"

Brice yanked his arm away. "That's the problem. You didn't think at all." He twirled and faced her. "I tried an experimental treatment on a dying woman. Do you have any idea what that means?"

She looked at the floor, her cocky expression subdued in the face of his tirade. "No. I'm sure I don't."

More words crowded the back of his throat. Words about how he'd gone out on a limb. Never mind Sarah had no chance at all without his intervention. He'd still have to live with it if what he did killed her even faster than her failing lungs. Because not much of it would come out coherently, he pushed past the resident still staring at the floor and bolted for the stairwell that would take him two floors down to where he could shower, shave, and don fresh scrubs.

He stood under water as hot as he could stand it. What was wrong with him? He'd been at the receiving end of tongue-lashings from older, wiser docs telling him how stupid and inadequate he was. And he'd sworn he'd never turn into one of the patronizing, self-righteous assholes who made him question his chosen vocation.

"Yup. And here I am. Just one more condescending jerk." At least he'd stopped before pounding the woman totally into the ground.

He shook water out of his eyes and flipped off the taps. He'd had the foresight to put a towel within reach, and he wrapped it around his waist before he shaved. He'd gotten so spun out because of who his patient was, not because of what he'd done to her.

He'd lost a lot of patients. If death bothered him, he'd have been better served going into ophthalmology or dermatology, where almost no one ever died. He sorted underwear and a clean lab coat blazoned with his name from his locker. That done, he plucked clean scrubs out of a stack the hospital laundry provided. He was mostly dressed and feeling surprisingly human again despite his lack of sleep, when the locker room door swung open.

"Brice. Good to see you. I heard about the woman in ICU. Nicely done." Dr. Lance Ammen, a cardiac surgeon, extended a hand.

Brice shook it. "Thanks. How are things in your neck of the woods?"

Lance shrugged. "Not bad. Lost one earlier today, but I was surprised when she made it through surgery. Her arteries were a mess."

Brice nodded. "We do what we can."

"We sure do, huh? I'm headed home. You?"

Brice thought about his home. A custom-built multistory structure on Lake Washington he rarely spent much time in. A live-in housekeeper kept it clean, but it never felt very homelike to him. Maybe he should get a dog... He immediately shelved the idea. The poor creature would never see him.

Lance shot him a peculiar look, and Brice rolled his eyes. "Sorry. No sleep the last two nights. I'm meeting with the ICU woman's family. Then it's home for me too."

"Good." Lance slapped his upper arm. "You look like hell."

"Should've seen me before I showered." With a jaunty wave, Brice jogged out of the locker room and glanced at a clock. He had time before the Wray parents were due to arrive. More to reassure himself than anything else, he headed toward the ICU with its banks of telemetry and uber-competent nursing crew.

He slapped his hand on a palm reader, and the door opened for him. Erika nodded briskly from her seat in the middle of an open-architecture ICU. He nodded back. Patient cubicles spread out from the central command station like spokes on a wagon wheel. It was an efficient arrangement. Fewer steps were needed to provide care than in older facilities where rooms lined both sides of a hall.

He donned a gown, mask, and gloves. Sliding the glass door aside, he let himself into Sarah Wray's space.

"Thank you." Her voice was harsh and raspy from her stint with the ventilator.

"You don't have to talk," he told her. "Must hurt like hell."

"Yeah. It does."

He scanned the instrumentation, satisfied with what he saw.

"Must look okay," she wheezed.

"Yes. Everything is within normal parameters." Brice retreated to doctor-speak and took in the tall, emaciated woman lying beneath the thin hospital blanket. Dark hair fanned across her pillow, and her blue eyes looked haggard. She had the same high cheekbones and full lips as her sister. Even in her wasted condition, she looked so much like Juliana, it still startled him.

"How long?" she asked, snagging his gaze with her own.

He understood what she wanted to know. Breaking protocol, he perched on the edge of the narrow bed and took her hand in his, taking care not to dislodge the IV. Her skin was so translucent, he could see veins and arteries beneath its surface.

"I honestly don't know, Sarah. You responded surprisingly well to the treatment, but I won't lie to you. It's possible the immune modulating chemicals will alter enough in your body, you'll have a few more years."

"How possible?" she croaked.

"I don't know," he repeated. "Your parents consented to an experimental treatment. Experimental means I don't have much data to determine if what we did will last." He took a measured breath. "What I can tell you is there are several drugs in this particular class. If the one we started with becomes less effective, there are others we can try."

"Like chemo?"

"Exactly like chemo."

Sarah tapped her chest with her other hand. "I'm a nurse."

Surprise ran through him. He known she'd had to drop out of med school, but not what she'd done afterward. "When you're stronger, you can tell me where you worked, what you did."

She nodded. He let go of her hand and stood. Before he turned to go, she waved a hand motioning him closer. He bent near, so she wouldn't have to work so hard to talk. "Whatever this is can wait," he reassured her.

Sarah shook her head. "No. Can't." She coughed, low and bubbly, but struggled to get more words out. "Julie. I'm sorry. I—" Another cough racked her.

"It was a long time ago," Brice kept his words low. "It's okay."

"Not okay. I should have fessed up." Her eyes sheened with tears.

"Hell, Sarah. We were young. None of us knew much of anything about what life would throw our way."

"You don't understand." She was panting with effort now.

"Sarah. Stop." He retreated to full MD mode to forestall further communication. "You're still very weak. I'll send one of the nurses in with a sedative."

"I wanted you too," she gasped out. "There. Said it. My cross to bear."

"It was a long time ago," he repeated. "Let it go, Sarah. Concentrate on getting stronger."

She nodded, not trying for further speech.

He turned and walked slowly out of her cubicle, deep in thought as he shucked his gloves and mask in the biohazard trash and his gown in the laundry bin. He finally understood what had transpired that long-ago night. Compassion for Sarah burned a track through him. Always the sick twin, she'd lived in Julie's shadow.

Erika bustled up, her navy-blue scrubs wrinkled as usual. A wiry dynamo with short gray hair and green eyes, she'd been a nurse for longer than Brice had been alive. "Hiya, Doc. She's doing great, huh?" Erika beamed at him.

"Pretty much a living miracle," he agreed. "She wore herself out trying to talk with me, though. Add five mgs of Valium to her IV."

Erika frowned. "But then she'll be asleep when her family gets here."

Brice smothered a grin. MDs who labored under the illusion they ran any of the hospital wards were dead wrong. Nurses like Erika were the true heroes. "Tell you what." He bent closer. "Take a look at her, and page me if you think she needs something."

"You got it, Dr. McKinnon." Erika pushed past him and into Sarah's tiny space.

Brice left the ICU and walked aimlessly to a nearby wing. Stopping near a window, he stared out into a gray, drizzling day. Sarah's words bounced around his head. "I wanted you too," she'd said, followed by it being her cross to bear.

Everything suddenly made a whole lot more sense. Sarah, the shadow twin, wasn't so shadowy after all. She had feelings and needs exactly like everyone else. How could he have been so stupid not to notice her pining after him?

Easy. All I had eyes for was Julie.

They'd all grown up in Twentynine Palms. Then it had been a truly small town in southern San Bernardino County. Sarah and Juliana's parents had been career military, holding positions at the Marine Corps Air Ground Combat Center. His father had been a Marine aviator, his mother a teacher at the base school.

Like lots of military brats, he'd kept to himself despite the Marine Corps providing more stability than many branches of the service. He'd been in first grade when they moved to the base at Twentynine Palms, and they'd still lived there when his father's plane was shot down over Afghanistan. He'd been sixteen then, and the Corps made it clear his mom could keep teaching as long as she wanted.

Susan McKinnon was a strong woman. She'd nursed her grief in private and made certain he'd always remember his father. Pictures of him were all over their modest quarters in base housing. His mom never remarried, never even dated as far as he could tell. She'd told him his father was the one love of her life and that she hoped he'd find his own soul mate someday.

Rain splattered the window he was still looking through, and he splayed one hand over the glass. He'd known Juliana and Sarah forever since they were in the same class at the base school, but something changed when he was a junior, and he'd viewed Juliana through different eyes.

It took courage—and a boot in the ass from him mom—but he'd finally asked her out. When she said yes, his world blazed into Technicolor, and he vowed he'd devote his life to making her happy. They'd dated through the rest of high school. Julie was attracted by the world-class archaeology department at University of Washington. When she applied for admission, Brice did too. In truth, he'd have followed her anywhere. His chosen career was medicine, but pre-med undergrad degrees were available from damn near every institution—

His pager vibrated. He tipped it up to see the message scrawled across its display and swallowed hard. The Wrays had arrived in the ICU. He hadn't seen Julie since the middle of their sophomore year of college when she'd told him he was a piece of crap and never to darken her door—or her life—again. Any hopes he'd held that she'd get over her pique vanished as days marched by, followed by weeks and then months where she rebuffed his attempts to talk.

He squared his shoulders. He'd get through this. She was probably married with a bunch of kids by now. He forced himself to move toward the ICU. It didn't matter if she was married. Or if she'd gained a hundred pounds. He'd always love her, but he'd be damned if he'd let any of that show.

Making a grab for his familiar MD persona, he quieted

his mind. He'd gotten through worse. Much worse. He'd survive the next half hour too.

Big words. He stopped outside the glassed-in ICU. General and Colonel Wray faced away from him, as did Julie. Dressed in crumpled buff-colored pants and a matching shirt, she still held herself like a queen. Erika handed the Wrays gowns, masks, gloves. Julie shrugged into her gown. Her black hair had been bunched into a rubber band, but it still hung halfway down her back. Maybe five feet ten, she was almost as thin as her sister.

For a fleeting moment, he hoped she wasn't ill, and then he got hold of himself. How she was—or wasn't—was none of his business. Hadn't been for years.

He slapped his palm on the reader and strode into the specialized ICU devoted to pulmonary care. His ICU—if you discounted Erika's claim to it. "Mr. and Mrs. Wray. Juliana. So nice to see you," he said in his best professional voice.

They turned almost as a unit, the elder Wrays both smiling. After a quick, furtive glance at his face, Juliana nodded once, sharply. "Thank you for saving Sarah. We appreciate your care."

"Welcome." He kept his smile in place, but it took effort—lots of effort.

Juliana was as heartbreakingly beautiful as she'd always been. The place in his heart—his soul—that had been empty since she dumped him seized all over again, forming a hard, painful knot.

"How is she, Doc?" Christopher Wray trained his forthright blue eyes on Brice and adjusted his mask.

"Probably a conversation we should have in a more private location," Brice replied.

Erika hurried over. "Shall I prepare the small conference room?"

"Thank you. That would be excellent," Brice told her. He

addressed his next words to General Wray. "Sarah is still quite weak. How about if you spend maybe five minutes with her? Talking is still hard, so do what you can to keep her quiet."

"We understand," Ariel Wray spoke up.

"When you're done, the nurse will bring you to me," Brice said and turned. He strode evenly out of the ICU. Whoever had said untended love dies was full of shit. The flame within him burned just as hot as it ever had. Juliana was the only woman for him. It was why his marriage foundered and died. Why none of his girlfriends turned into more than casual bed partners.

He ached for her, wanted to crush her against him and kiss her until the world dissolved around them in a flood of heat. His groin tightened, cock thickening against his belly. He dragged his lab coat over the damning evidence of his need.

Lost in lust and memories, he damn near ran right into Erika on her way out of the conference room. "You all right?" she asked, her finely honed nurse instincts apparently in full bloom.

"Fine. Just tired."

She patted his arm. "Go home and get some rest after your powwow with the family. I'll page you if anything happens that you need to know about."

"Thank you."

"It's what I'm here for."

Brice trudged into the conference room and fell into the chair at the head of the table. His chair. The doctor's chair. For the first time in a long time, it didn't give him the usual burst of confidence. At least sitting hid his unruly appendage from view, although it was subsiding.

Resisting an urge to bury his face in his hands, he waited for the Wrays to show up.

CHAPTER 3

*J*uliana stood in the ICU gazing through glass at her sister's sleeping form. She turned at the sound of Brice's voice. More than turned, it dragged her around until she faced him. The rich baritone notes kindled bone-deep longing in her, longing she believed she'd moved past long since.

Her gaze skirted his face and body. Same drop-dead gorgeous hunk with his curly blond hair and unusual hazel eyes, one greener than the other. He'd added muscle to his six feet two-inch frame, or maybe he'd simply filled out as he moved into adulthood. Regardless, his shoulders were wonderfully broad, his waist slender. She assumed his ass was the same. High, tight, well-muscled. Yearning burned a path through her, as bright as if only days had passed since they'd made love, not fifteen years.

Her nipples tightened into peaks, and her swollen labia slicked. Breath hitched in her throat. What the fucking hell? She never even thought about sex, but one glimpse of Brice was enough to remind her of her badly neglected body.

Aw crap. I've got to get hold of myself.

Because saying something seemed like the right thing to do, she ground out. "Thank you for saving Sarah. We appreciate your care."

"Welcome." His smile looked strained, but maybe he was tired.

It wasn't like she knew him anymore. Apparently, she'd never known him at all since she'd arrived home after a student dig to find him in bed with her sister. His stupid, lame, inane, shit-for-brains excuse was he'd thought Sarah was her, but that was impossible. Sure, they were twins, but no way could he mistake one for the other.

"How is she, Doc?" Her father's words broke into her churning thoughts as he trained his forthright gaze Brice's way.

"Probably a conversation we should have in a more private location," Brice replied.

A nurse offered to set up a conference room, and Brice cautioned them Sarah was still quite frail. Julie resisted a sharp comeback. Anyone with eyes could see how depleted her twin was.

"This way." The no-nonsense gray-haired nurse—Erika, from her badge—was back, duded up in mask, gown, and gloves. She opened a sliding glass door, and they filed in next to Sarah's bed.

Maybe because Julie was used to listening for it, she heard the gurgling of Sarah's lungs as she fought to breathe. "Can I touch her?" she asked the nurse, who hovered off to one side.

"Sure." Erika smiled encouragingly. "She's just worn out. She was trying to talk with the doctor, and it drained what little reserves she had."

Trying to talk with Brice, huh? Juliana thought sourly. Had her sister maintained some kind of relationship with him all these years? Behind her back? She hauled herself up short. What difference did it make? She'd made it crystal clear she was done with Brice. She couldn't very well cut her sister out of her life, but she could damn good and well eliminate Brice.

And she had.

Sarah's illness had closed a lot of doors. Most people reacted much like the overly enthusiastic flight attendant on her last plane. The moment they heard about a "life-threatening illness," they backed away. Pronto.

Despite setbacks, her sister had carved out a life for herself. They teased each other about being spinsters, and Sarah had always encouraged her to find someone special. They talked about lots of things, she and Sarah, but they never talked about Brice. Not after that morning she kicked him out of her apartment. Sarah had been apologetic, but she hadn't ever said she'd pretended to be Julie.

The mistaken identity explanation was so preposterous, Juliana didn't pursue it.

Over the years, she'd tried to find someone special. Maybe she hadn't tried all that hard, but she'd dated. Lots of guys. Some she even kind of liked, but not well enough to give them a piece of her heart. After the rocky breakup with Brice, she wasn't sure enough of her heart was left to offer much to anyone.

Graduate school had been a total grind, and she'd volunteered for every extra project that popped up. Being in the field kept her busy, and she liked it that way. After completing her Ph.D. dissertation on Native and Indigenous Peoples in the Guatemalan Highlands, she'd accepted a staff position at U.W. and quickly risen to tenured status.

"Ms. Wray?" Erika patted her arm. "It's okay. She's just sleeping."

"My daughter is a doctor," Ariel murmured.

"Fascinating." Erika's eyes lit with interest. "What kind?"

Here we go again.

Julie manufactured a smile. "Not medical. I'm an archaeologist."

"Even more intriguing." Erika lowered her voice. "Don't spread it around, but I get damn tired of the medical types."

The corners of Juliana's mouth twitched. She appreciated Erika's candor. Something about the no-nonsense older nurse was impossible not to like. Moving closer to the bed, she hunted for a stretch of skin that didn't have tubes or lines sticking out of it.

She stroked Sarah's upper arm, and her twin's eyes fluttered open. When she saw Julie, they flooded with tears. "Sister." Her voice was so rough, Julie wouldn't have recognized it.

Sarah held out her arms, and Juliana glanced at the nurse. Erika nodded. "Some things trump our protocols."

Sitting gingerly on the edge of Sarah's bed, Juliana gathered her into her arms, shocked by how thin she'd grown. The edges of her shoulder blades almost poked through her skin, and her upper arms looked like they belonged to a starving adult from sub-Saharan Africa. All knobs and sinew.

"I waited," Sarah rasped.

"Hush, sweetheart. Don't try to talk." Her throat thick with tears, Julie smoothed her sister's hair back from her forehead, and Sarah slumped against her, relaxed in her embrace.

"Just like when you were babies," her mother murmured, sounding suspiciously close to tears herself. Ariel never cried, or if she did, Julie had never seen it.

"That's right," her father broke in.

"What's right?" Juliana asked, still cradling Sarah against her.

"When we first brought you home from the hospital," her

mother said, "we put you in separate cribs like they told us to."

"But you cried and cried," her father added. "Endlessly."

"How would you know?" Ariel demanded. "You were deployed."

"Because you told me, sweetheart."

Juliana smiled. God, she loved her parents. What gems they were.

"Yes, well." Ariel cleared her throat. "The doctor said it was a bad idea, but I put both of you in the same crib—watching like a hawk, mind you."

"What happened?" Juliana was fascinated. She'd never heard this story.

"You cuddled up to each other just like you'd done inside me. And fell asleep." Ariel's words held a satisfied note. "I knew you were just missing each other. And I was right."

"You slept in the same crib until you were about a year old," her father chimed in. "By then, when we separated you, everything was all right."

Sarah had fallen asleep again, so Juliana laid her back against the pillows. "It was pretty close, wasn't it?"

Erika nodded, her expression solemn. "If it wasn't for Dr. McKinnon, you'd be sitting over her remains."

"We knew him when he was growing up," Ariel said.

"Really?" Erika's tone held interest. "What was he like?"

"A shy boy," her father replied. "Always very talented. Lost his father when he was maybe sixteen. Brave Marine. Decorated the hell out of him, but posthumously."

"His mother taught science and mathematics at the base school," Ariel noted. "She's still there."

"Thank you," Erika said.

"What for?" Julie asked.

The nurse shrugged. "Some of the docs are like open

books. I know most of what's to know about them. Not Dr. McKinnon, though. He showed up here three years ago, and no one knows much about him. Beyond his credentials, which are impressive as hell. Speaking of the good doctor, he's waiting for you. Follow me, and I'll show you where he is."

Julie leaned close. "I'll be back, sweetie. Thanks for hanging on."

Sarah nodded but didn't open her eyes. Maybe it was too much for her right now. Julie filed out of the ICU, bringing up the end of their little queue. They stopped long enough to toss their masks, gloves, and gowns. She flirted with making excuses and returning to sit with Sarah, but she wanted to hear Brice's assessment. Not that she was any judge of medical things, but Sarah appeared to have a long way to go before she was out of immediate danger.

Several corridors later, Erika pulled open a faux wood door and motioned them into a well-appointed room. An oblong table sat in the center, surrounded by chairs. The tang of coffee tickled her nostrils, and she caught the tail end of Erika saying "Help yourself. Coffee. Tea. Cocoa. Cups are in the credenza just below the hot water."

"Thank you." Her father shook Erika's hand, and the nurse left.

"Want anything?" Ariel asked as she walked to the electric kettle.

"Nothing for me," Juliana said.

"No thank you, Mrs. Wray," Brice said, followed by, "Sorry. Colonel Wray."

Her mom waved a dismissive hand Brice's way. "I'm retired. Plain old Ariel will do. Why, we were almost family at one point."

Julie avoided her mother's sharp glance.

"Did you attend medical school here?" Chris asked Brice.

"No. I graduated from here, just like your daughters, but

then I went to USF Medical School. From there I did an internal medicine residency at Harvard."

"Impressive," Chris said.

"Thank you. Post residency, I picked up a two-year fellowship in pulmonology at Johns Hopkins. I've been here for the past three years, for the most part. Just returned from the U.K. and Europe. They've done some intriguing things with immune modulation there. It's what gave me the confidence to try something new on Sarah."

"We're grateful for your expertise," Ariel murmured and finished brewing drinks for herself and Chris.

Brice waited until they were all seated. Juliana had taken a chair as far away from him as she could. It wasn't far enough. No amount of distance could quell the longing rioting through her, and she sent up a prayer of thanks no one could read her thoughts.

His mop of blond hair was the same, inviting her to sink her fingers within its lush curls. Beneath his lab coat, broad shoulders held a promise of graceful muscles. He'd always been a runner, and his lower body, what she'd seen of it in the ICU, was all long legs and slender hips. Desire surged until her belly clenched with wanting him, and she swallowed around dry places in her throat.

Clearly, she needed to get laid. Only problem was no other man had this effect on her, where she wanted to rip his clothes off and lick and suck every inch of him.

"I'm sure you're all tired," Brice began. "I know I am. We came within an angstrom of losing your daughter. She's still very depleted. I won't bother explaining CF to you. You've lived with it for a long time. The scarring in her lungs is extensive, but until recently, her pancreas was in relatively decent shape. It's hard to pinpoint why these things are stable for a long time but then deteriorate." He stopped to take a breath. "In any event, she developed digestive issues on top of her already severely compromised lung function. What I did was introduce an immune modulator. It seems to be working, and I'm cautiously optimistic. If it continues to work, and she grows strong enough, we'll try gene remodeling for a longer-lasting solution."

"Longer-lasting," Ariel echoed Brice, "but not permanent."

He nodded. "Not permanent. Nothing cures CF. Not yet, anyway. The thing with gene remodeling is it takes time. Immune modulators normally do too, but it was our best hope."

"We'll take what we can get," her father said.

"Any chance of having her home for Christmas like you told us earlier?" Hope underscored Ariel's question, as did her unspoken thought that this may well be the last Christmas Sarah would ever have.

Brice tugged a phone from his lab coat and clicked its display, probably bringing up a calendar. "Maybe. It's the sixteenth. I want her here for at least another five or six days." He looked from one to the other of them. "Any questions?"

Yeah. Why'd you sleep with my sister? The real reason.

Julie squared her shoulders to drive any and all thoughts of sex out of her head. "I have a question. CF is an autoimmune disorder, right?" At Brice's nod, she went on. "Autosomal recessive, not that I entirely understand what it means, but why don't I have it?"

"You are a carrier," her mother spoke up.

"Yes. I get that part, but Sarah and I are identical twins. Doesn't that mean we're exactly the same? Came from the same egg and sperm?"

"We thought you were identical," her father cut in. "You looked so much alike, we assumed you had to be. It was only after Sarah was diagnosed with CF we had genetic testing done."

"And found you two were dizygotic," Ariel finished her husband's thought.

Because she was watching Brice, Julie saw shock flutter across his face before he smoothed it of any reaction. As a doc, he had to be used to keeping his game face on.

"How come you never told us?" Julie demanded, followed by, "Never mind. We can have that conversation in the car."

She got to her feet, hating to walk away from Brice and wanting to put as much space as she could muster between them. Her unsettled emotions jabbed her. Maybe she just needed to sleep, get over jet lag, and wrap her mind around her sister still being alive.

She'd been certain Sarah wouldn't pull through this time.

"Want to add your cell to our list of family contacts for Sarah?" Brice asked in a perfectly neutral tone.

"Sure. I'll call the ICU after we leave." Her heart thrummed into overdrive, and she swept out of the conference room. Had his request been a backhanded way of him asking for her phone number? She ground to a halt outside the room, waiting for her folks. Even if that was what he was up to, it didn't matter. None of it did. He'd sealed his fate when he'd cheated on her.

Unfortunately, he'd sealed hers too. A loveless life stretched before her, sterile and devoid of anything except work. The prospect depressed her, but there wasn't a damn thing she could do to change it.

I have to figure out a way to stop loving him.

Yeah, right, she answered herself. *It's not as if I haven't tried.*

"There you are, honey," her father boomed.

"Want to come home with us?" Ariel asked.

Julie considered it. "I'll come over tomorrow. What I really need more than anything is to see my home again, take a long hot shower, and sleep off the jet lag."

"We'll drive you home," Chris announced.

Juliana shook her head. "You'll do no such thing. The traffic across the bridge is always bad. Besides, you need to stay on the east side of the lake. What if Sarah has a crisis? You'll be close enough to get back here fast."

"All right." Her father's tone brooked no space for disagreement—or further discussion. "Your mother and I will catch a cab home. I'll send the car and driver with you."

"You don't have to—" she began, feeling like she was about five years old.

"Case closed." Her father hooked a hand around her arm. "Come on. We'll walk out to the rotunda. The car will be waiting for you."

"Why didn't you ever tell Sarah and me we weren't identical?"

"Oh honey, what difference would it have made?" Her mother asked.

"You two were just so proud about being identical," her father cut in.

"We couldn't burst your bubble," Ariel murmured. "Although I have to admit I was relieved when the genetic testing came back. You girls were around eight at the time."

"Because it meant I didn't have cystic fibrosis?" Julie mumbled.

"Precisely," her mother said, followed by, "Come on, Juliana. It's not as if we kept something important from you. We made sure you knew you were a carrier. You know. In case you ever produce any grandchildren for us."

The barb was so pointed and so typical of Ariel's in-your-face communication style, Julie let it go. She'd given up longing for children. Good thing, since it appeared she'd never have any.

"You're getting ahead of the curve," she told her mother. "First, I need a husband."

"Not necessarily," Ariel replied. "With all those creative in vitro solutions popping up—"

"Not the time for this conversation," her father cut in, his tone brusque. Julie could have hugged him.

They made their way through the endless branching hallways typical of most modern hospitals until her father held the front door for her and her mother. The uniformed Marine driver from earlier hurried over and saluted.

"At ease, son," her father said, followed by, "Take my daughter to…" He rattled off her address north of the University District."

"What about you, sir?" the driver inquired.

"We'll take a taxi home."

The driver saluted again and sprinted to a line of Yellow Cabs, bending to talk with the cabbie.

"See you soon, darling." Her mother swooped in for a hug and a kiss.

"Yes. Good to have you home. Finally," Chris grumbled.

"You should talk," Ariel said to her husband and let go of Julie. "Your deployments lasted for months."

Juliana smothered a snort. "I love you guys."

"We love you too. Now get moving." Her mother and father trotted toward the waiting cab with its driver standing straight as a stick and holding the rear door open for them.

The driver opened the back door of the limo. Julie dove into its plush interior and considered stretching full length on the seat. Because she couldn't come up with a good reason not to, she lay down, tucking her hands beneath her head.

"I'll try not to, but I might fall asleep," she called to the driver.

"No worries, Dr. Wray. I'll wake you once I get you home."

Not for the first time, she kicked herself for not joining the military. The formality and courtesies appealed to her, but her mom and dad had earned every single one by service to their country.

Thinking about Brice or Sarah or her parents felt quite beyond her. They circled her mind like an out-of-control pinball game with sometimes one and sometimes the other popping up. As an experiment, she shut her eyes in hopes it would block everything out. The plunge into unconsciousness was almost instant.

CHAPTER 4

*B*rice stood to shake hands with Mr. and Mrs. Wray and usher them out. Julie had fled as if the dogs of Hell were after her. He retreated to the sanctity of the conference room once the door closed behind the Wrays. He never should have asked Julie for her cell number—even if he'd asked on behalf of the ICU. It was stupid. Her parents knew how to get hold of her, and she was a resourceful adult. More than capable of calling the unit on her own without his prodding.

He'd followed newspaper articles about her over the years and knew she'd become a world-renowned expert on ancient people and cultures. He was pleased for her and doubly pleased he hadn't seen a wedding ring. Not everyone wore them, but the absence meant she might not be married.

Beyond if she was married or not, how could her parents have treated her twin status so casually? Maybe if the girls hadn't still been dressing alike with identical haircuts through college, he'd never have made the mistake that ruined his life.

"Oh for God's sake," he muttered out loud to steady himself.

His life was scarcely *ruined*. Lonely, maybe. But he'd understood the consequences of picking a subspecialty on top of another subspecialty in medicine. He wasn't as old as some of his colleagues who'd received years' worth of high level training.

Except most of them had wives. Children. So long as he was on a tangent, he let his mind ramble. He'd been through thorough genetic testing back when he and Juliana were serious about a mutual future. He wasn't a carrier for the genetic anomaly responsible for cystic fibrosis, which meant he and Julie could, conceivably, be parents…

Brice slapped an open palm down hard on the polished wooden table. Pain traveled up his arm, but he welcomed it. Fantasizing about children with Juliana Wray was ridiculous. She'd barely been able to make eye contact with him from her vantage point across the room, and she'd left as soon as she could.

He paced to a window. Normally, he enjoyed the view. It looked east, and on clear days he sometimes caught a glimpse of the Cascade Mountain Range. Not today. The gray sludge was even thicker than it had been, limiting his vision to perhaps a hundred fifty feet.

He shut his eyes and rubbed them. He wasn't thinking straight, but how could he? He needed downtime. Sleep. When he rolled his shoulders back, the bones cracked, reminding him he hadn't gotten much exercise this week, either.

An idea formed. Before could talk himself out of it, he loped out of the conference room and took a back stairway. Pushing through the locker room door, he returned to the locker he'd left earlier and shucked his hospital garb in favor of sweats, running shoes, and a waterproof windbreaker. He'd jog home. It was just under five miles, and he'd be there is under an hour.

Pleased with himself, he checked out with the hospital operator and made sure his pager was firmly clipped to his jacket. He'd schooled himself never to miss an opportunity for productivity during medical school and residency. Time was precious during his training years, and he'd grown savvy at taking advantage of every second. He'd get a decent cardio workout, sleep for a few hours, and maybe jog back to the hospital. Failing that, he had a motorcycle sitting in his garage. Running also got him out from under the conundrum of whether he should drive or not in his current sleep-deprived condition.

He slipped out a side door and pulled his jacket hood over his head, settling into an easy pace. He loved running. He'd done track and field through high school and his undergrad years, missing the Olympic team by scant seconds. If he'd had wealthy parents, ones who could have hired class-act coaching, he'd have made it for sure.

But then, he'd have had to put med school on a back burner.

Brice inhaled deeply, letting the cold, dank maritime air sear his lungs. One of the best things about aerobic exertion was how well it reduced stress. Thoughts rumbled across his mind and out the other side, followed by more thoughts. None of them bothered him when his body hummed with an endorphin high.

Juliana. Damn she was prettier now than she'd been as a twenty-year-old. The roundness had left her face, revealing the classic sweep of wide cheekbones and a firm jaw. Not too firm. Still feminine. And her eyes. A deep, cerulean blue, they still drew him like a lodestone. He'd caught the swell of breasts and hips. A memory of suckling her high, tight breasts, of the nipples lengthening into peaks in his mouth, made breath hitch in his throat. His cock hardened, pushing against the front of his pants.

He shook his head and jogged in place, waiting for a light to change. It was their eyes that had tripped him up. Sarah and Julie had the exact same eyes, down to a sprinkling of golden flecks around their pupils. It was why he'd been certain Sarah was Julie. She'd been different in bed, but he'd been too drunk to absorb what those differences meant.

Reluctantly, he replayed that evening, searching for clues after Sarah's confession about wanting him for herself. He'd arrived at the girls' apartment around ten. The quarter had just ended, and he'd been out celebrating with a bunch of guys from the track team. Sarah/Julie had looked surprised to see him, but she'd motioned him inside and offered him still more booze.

The lights had been low, and she'd settled on the floor, patting the spot next to her. He'd asked where Sarah was since the shadow twin rarely left home during the evening. Sarah/Julie had murmured something noncommittal, but reassured him she wasn't worried about her twin.

She'd wrapped an arm around him and leaned close…

And he'd been lost, just like he always was when Julie kissed him. Sex was new in those days. They'd only just graduated from necking to the real deal. Maybe if he'd been more familiar with Julie's body—and less drunk—Sarah wouldn't have pulled off her charade.

They'd fallen asleep on the floor, wrapped in blankets. Sometime before dawn, lights flashed on, followed by an outraged shout, and then Juliana—the real Juliana—was dragging his half-clothed body out of her sister's arms and screaming at both of them.

Sarah had shrugged and headed for the apartment's single bedroom, closing the door with a sharp bang and leaving him to face a livid Juliana. The harder he'd tried, the worse things got until he'd finally dressed as fast as he could and fled.

That had been that. She'd apparently made peace with Sarah, but had less than zero interest in even listening to his apologies. At first, he'd been frantic, then angry, and finally bitter. As he ran through Bellevue, headed toward Kirkland, he realized he still blamed her for not believing in him enough to listen to his side of what happened.

Maybe Sarah lied. She'd said it was her cross to bear. If she'd told her sister he'd been a willing participant with full knowledge of who she was, he didn't blame Julie for cutting him out of her life.

The hot squeal of brakes on wet asphalt dragged him out of his trip backward in time. He ground to a halt and stared in horror as an enormous pickup plowed into a subcompact, driving it into two more vehicles. The sounds of glass shattering and metal crunching and bending against itself battered his ears.

He fished his cell out of his pocket and dialed the hospital, giving his location and requesting at least one ambulance, maybe two. The operator assured him she'd call 911 to alert the cops. He put the phone away, anxious to wade in and start doing what he did best. Triage and saving lives. He loved emergency rooms and the excitement of something new at every turn, but he'd opted for a corner of medicine where he could get to know his patients on more than a cursory level.

Vehicles were still spinning and pounding into each other like bumper cars. Brice started forward, but jammed his hands into his pockets, waiting. He couldn't do a damned thing if he got himself killed because the accident unfolding in front of him wasn't done yet.

Outraged shrieks and groans joined the telltale *thunks* of cars hitting one another. He scanned the scene with practiced eyes. The subcompact the pickup had plowed into was in the worst shape, its side door and hood crumpled into the passenger compartment. No one else seemed to have sustained serious injuries since they were piling out of their vehicles in droves.

If the squashed small car had airbags, he hoped they'd deployed. The area was safe enough. He couldn't wait any longer.

Brice ran a gauntlet, weaving through stopped traffic, until he reached the crumpled subcompact. No airbags. The driver slumped against the shattered window, blood running down her face. He tugged on the driver's door, not expecting it to open.

Sirens blared, brakes screeched, and two cops pushed through the growing crowd, barking orders.

Brice barely looked up. "Help me get her out of there," he called.

"Who are you?" one of the officers demanded.

"Yeah," the other one grunted. "Which one of these vehicles is yours?"

Brice straightened, not used to explaining himself. "None of them. I was on foot. I'm a doctor. I already called Overlake. Ambulances are on their way." He took a measured breath. "I need access to that woman." He pointed at the car. The smell of gasoline was growing. Between dripping fuel and hot engines, he hoped nothing blew up.

The first cop tried the passenger door, but it was just as stuck as the other one. "I don't like this," he muttered.

Brice didn't, either. A thin wail came from deep inside the subcompact. At first, he wasn't certain he'd heard anything, but the cries escalated. "There's a baby in the backseat," he told the cops.

"Yeah. I heard it too." The second cop's rough demeanor softened.

"Stand aside." Cop number one was back with a pry bar. He jimmied it beneath the trunk and the car's body and bent his weight into it.

The baby was crying in earnest now. Loud, hiccupy sobs that boded well. If it was badly hurt, it wouldn't be crying like that.

"Give me a hand," the cop with the pry bar told the other officer.

Between the two of them grunting and swearing, the trunk finally popped loose. Brice tried to see inside, but the officers' burly bodies blocked his line of sight. Something gray and fuzzy whizzed out of the trunk, landing on the wet pavement. It took a moment before Brice figured out it had to be the panel separating the trunk from the backseat.

"Here we go. He was in a car seat." Cop number two backed out of the trunk, cradling a screaming toddler in his arms.

Brice took the child. Far from a pediatrician, he ran hands and eyes over the screaming baby boy. Maybe two years old, he didn't appear hurt. The whine of klaxon sirens announced Overlake's ambulances were closing on them.

"Doc." Cop number one was back.

"Give me the boy." Cop number two held out his arms, and Brice handed him over.

"I'm afraid to move the driver," cop number one said, but I got the passenger door open for you.

Brice ran around the car and slid onto a front seat littered with glass fragments. The woman sagged against her seat belt. He hunted for a pulse, relieved when he found a faint flutter around her carotid. Moving accident victims without a backboard was risky. He could make a spinal cord injury so much worse, she'd end up in a wheelchair.

"Dr. McKinnon. We're here." One of Overlake's EMTs hovered in the car's doorway.

"Backboard and cervical collar," he barked and glanced over his shoulder to see Juan Carlos.

"We figured as much," Juan said in his softly accented voice and gave Brice a stethoscope.

"Thanks." He was partway through an assessment when two more EMTs showed up.

Working as a team, they transitioned the still unconscious woman to a backboard for transport. By then, he'd determined she had at least two broken ribs, a collapsed lung, and a broken fibula. Maybe a concussion.

"Nice work." The first cop was back.

"Good thing you were here," the second cop said.

Brice shrugged. "She'll make it. None of her injuries were life-threatening." He straightened in time to see the ambulance's rear lights disappearing. While he'd been working on the driver, the cops had cleared one lane in each direction, and traffic was moving again.

"Where were you headed before all this happened?" Cop number one asked.

"Home. I had a tough case. Haven't slept much since Monday night."

Cop number two whistled long and low. "Sheesh. And here I thought we had it rough with our shift work. Want a lift?"

Brice thought about it. "Yeah. Home's still about two miles. I'm in Kirkland."

"I'll take him," cop number one said.

"Good plan. By the time you're back, the wreckers will have arrived," the second cop agreed.

Brice trudged to the waiting cop car. He was wet to his

skin and starting to shiver. At least the car was warm inside. The cop got behind the wheel, and Brice gave him his address.

"The baby?" he asked, chagrined he'd all but forgotten about the squalling toddler.

"It left with the first ambulance," the cop said. "That happened after you were inside the car with Mrs. Davidson."

"Good you found out who she is," Brice mumbled. The adrenaline spurt was fading, and he stumbled over the words.

"This it?" The cop pointed to the driveway leading to Brice's house.

"Yeah. Thanks. I'll get out here. There are electric gates. No need for you to bother with the code."

"You sure? You look trashed."

Brice managed what he hoped was a reassuring smile. "Yes. I'm sure. It's only another hundred feet to my front door." Without waiting for the cop to lodge more arguments, he let himself out of the car and walked up his long driveway. When he got to the wrought iron gates, he punched in the code and walked through once they opened.

Lights blazed all over the house, and he pushed irritation aside. His housekeeper was a gem, but she squandered electricity like it was free.

The front door flew open; Lupe Garcia barreled out. Her kindly face was seamed with concern, and long, gray hair billowed around her. She'd stuck with the flowing skirts and colorful tunics typical of Central America, and her brown eyes brimmed with compassion.

"There you are, Doctor. Come inside. Hospital called. Said you helped with a car crash. I ran you a hot bath…"

Brice tuned out her soft flow of words. He'd met Lupe when he was on a six-week rotation in Honduras years ago. They'd struck up a friendship, bolstered by email and snail mail. Two years ago, he'd helped her and her daughter come to the U.S. The daughter and her husband and family lived north of Seattle, but Lupe had insisted he needed a housekeeper—and a cook.

He hadn't argued too hard because he recognized truth in her observation.

He stumbled up the brick stairs leading into his house. Buying the place had been a splurge, but the market had tanked, and prices were attractive.

"What you want first?" Lupe asked. "Food or bath?"

"Bath."

She nodded approvingly. "Then maybe you sleep. After that, we talk food."

He made his way through the foyer and up winding stairs straight out of *Gone With the Wind*. Lupe remained below, offering him privacy.

As he stripped out of his wet clothes, leaving them in a heap on the bathroom's green-veined marble floor, he took stock of everything.

He was grateful he'd been able to help the accident victims. Equally grateful they hadn't been so badly injured, he'd worry about whether they survived. A sideline benefit was he hadn't thought about Juliana.

Until now.

Nothing to think about. Not really. She wrote me off a long time ago.

He'd utilize his professional demeanor—hide behind it and keep it in place until she headed back to Egypt. Or wherever that damn dig was. After that, he'd go back to normal, whatever normal was. Deep inside, something rebelled. He didn't want "normal," he wanted Juliana. Ached for her. Yearned for her. If she got on a plane before he had a chance to lay his heart at her feet—or she heard him out and left anyway—it would be the second saddest day of his life.

The first had been when she'd found him in Sarah's arms.

He sank into the steaming water, letting it soak into the knots his muscles had turned into. Exhaustion washed over him in waves, and he barely remembered stepping out of the tub, drying off, and staggering into bed.

45

Juliana cursed as she bent over the engine compartment of her Toyota 4Runner. Why the hell wouldn't it start? She'd gotten decent rest, maybe fifteen hours' sleep since the Marine driver had dropped her off. It was time to get back to Overlake. Would she have to swallow her pride and call a cab?

She wiggled cables, aiming for methodical as she scanned the Toyota's under-the-hood components. When she got to the battery, understanding—and memory—slapped her across the face. She'd unhooked the negative battery terminal before leaving for Egypt, so the few things that ran all the time wouldn't drain the vehicle down to bedrock.

She plopped the negative cable back in place and hunted for a wrench to tighten it. Back in the cab, she hit the ignition switch and felt vindicated when the car purred to life. Spending a chunk of her life at dig sites in primitive locations had given her a decent mechanical skillset.

Yeah. No one to call but me when something breaks.

Letting the Toyota warm up, she shut the hood and went back inside to gather her bag and laptop. She'd probably have downtime at the hospital and could get some work done. Check in with her team. See how the dig was progressing.

Guilt pricked her. She was here for Sarah. Not to lose herself in the latest bits excavated from the dig. Her gaze played over her small, neat cottage. A Cape Cod style, it had a wide veranda extending along the front and one side. One story, it had been built in the 1930s when families had more modest expectations about their homes.

A generous living room took up one side of the front of the house. The other half housed a combination kitchen and dining area. In the back were two bedrooms, one of which she'd converted to an office, and a bathroom with an old-fashioned clawfoot tub. She'd added a shower for convenience, but it was about the only modification she'd made. The place had scuffed hardwood floors and bay windows. The overall effect was homey, and she'd fallen in love with the cottage the moment she laid eyes on it ten years before. Even though she could have moved to something larger and fancier, she'd never wanted to.

Her sister owned an even older bungalow about a mile away. Her parents had rented it out after Sarah became too ill to live on her own. One of Sarah's nursing friends with either one or two kids had been delighted by the arrangement. Affordable rentals within spitting distance of the University District were hard to come by.

Julie hustled out the door before her father called wanting to know if she was all right. So far, her phone had been quiet this morning. She backed the car out and set it in park, so she could shut the garage. Maybe one of these days, she'd spring for an automatic door opener.

"Or not." Her words made her smile. She'd never been one for modern conveniences. Most of them required repairs eventually. Better to make do with the tried and true.

She backed the SUV onto her quiet street and headed

toward the northernmost of two bridges spanning Lake Washington. Traffic, an almost twenty-four-hour phenomenon around Seattle, snarled to a standstill as she waited for an opportunity to merge onto the freeway. The sun had been poking through when she got up, but it had retreated, leaving nothing but gunmetal-colored clouds floating overhead.

"At least it's not raining," she mumbled and searched for a news station to listen to.

Ninety minutes later, she pulled into one of Overlake's visitor parking lots. Because she lived and worked west of Lake Washington, she didn't fully appreciate how hideous the bridge traffic had grown. Julie took a few deep breaths to steady herself. She was out of practice, had lost her competitive edge during the months she'd barely driven at all in Egypt. Today's journey had given her more than a few, "Aw crap, he's going to hit me," moments.

She pushed her door open and grabbed her shoulder and computer bags off the passenger seat. Overlake Hospital loomed above and around her. It was an enormous, sprawling facility, and she was on the other side from where she'd been last night.

Julie strode toward the nearest place she saw a green entrance sign. Once inside, she studied a map complete with a "You are Here" arrow. When moments ticked past, she understood she was dragging her feet.

Why wasn't she scurrying to her sister's bedside as fast as she could? Was it because now that Sarah's death wasn't imminent, Julie had feelings to sort through?

She and Sarah had put that awkward, horrible night behind them. At least, on the surface. Sarah had sort of apologized and chalked it off to Brice's overactive libido and too much wine. Juliana needed to believe her because, if she didn't, the only other option was jettisoning her twin and hating her forever.

She'd be damned if she'd do that. Sarah's health had been far more robust, but even then Julie suspected her sister probably wouldn't make thirty. She resituated the strap from her computer so it didn't cut into her shoulder as deeply. Treatments for cystic fibrosis had improved over the years of her sister's illness. So much so, she'd lived longer than any of them anticipated.

Insight rocked Julie, and she moved back through the door, needing fresh air. She'd buried the hatchet with Sarah because she'd figured her sister would be dead soon. How could she live with herself if she let something as minor as a sexual fling stand between her and her twin? She clenched her jaws so hard, she was surprised her teeth didn't crack.

"Oh yeah," she muttered, talking out loud to steady herself. "I hated her for what she did. It wasn't minor. She slept with the man I loved—and ruined everything."

No. I let it ruin everything.

Julie winced. She'd refused to hear Brice out. Afraid if she did, she'd be forced to choose him over her sister. Her terminally ill sister, who was still alive fifteen years later. She quickened her pace. Maybe she shouldn't have been so Draconian, but she'd only been twenty. At twenty she knew less than nothing except her heart was broken.

She ducked into a covered alcove lined with benches. Ashtrays suggested this was one of the sheltered outdoor smoking areas. She didn't smoke, but she sat anyway, stacked her bag and computer case on her lap and wound her fingers together on top of them.

Her knuckles turned white from the pressure, but she had to get hold of herself. Christ! She needed therapy. Should have gone years ago. Julie felt small and petty and mean-spirited, but she'd been waiting for Sarah to die for years. As if her death would be fitting punishment for stealing Brice.

"What's wrong with me?" She untangled her fingers and buried her face in her hands. "Sarah dying won't bring Brice back. All it will do is leave me with a piss pot of guilt for not loving her enough."

Looking back on the incident through thirty-five-year-old eyes, she understood a whole lot more than she did when it happened. Sarah had a hell of a time attracting men once they found out about her CF. Even sleeping with them wasn't enough incentive for them to stick around. She must have been envious of Julie and Brice, wanted some of their love for herself...

She and her twin had gone their separate ways as soon as they graduated, Julie starting graduate school and Sarah med school. It had been a relief to not be roommates anymore, to not have to pretend she wasn't hurt and angry. They'd still gotten together for dinner and movies and idle girl-chat from time to time. Sarah always seemed glad to see her, and Julie had risen to the occasion. After the first few years, she didn't have to fake it as much.

The door next to the smoking area swooshed open, and a nurse slid through. She tugged a cigarette and matches out of a pocket and lit it, inhaling deeply. Blonde hair going gray was tucked under a surgical cap. "Horrible habit." She offered a sheepish smile. "I'm down to maybe four a day, but I can't get below it."

Juliana nodded, grateful to have something else to focus on. "You'll get there. Be patient with yourself."

"Did you ever smoke?"

Julie shook her head. "No, but it has to be like any other addiction."

Her phone rang, and she dug for it and glanced at the caller ID. Her father. She was surprised he'd waited this long.

She tapped the display and held the phone to her ear. "Hi, Dad."

"Hey, princess. Where are you?"

"I'm here. Give me a few minutes and I'll be right there."

"Excellent. I told your mother you had to be close. Meet you in Sarah's room."

The connection clicked off before she said goodbye, but her father rarely bothered with any extra words.

The nurse narrowed blue-green eyes her way. "You're not a smoker, but you're sitting here and not inside with whoever's waiting for you. Everything all right?"

Juliana started to reassure the nurse all was well, but the words refused to come. What emerged was, "No. I'm not okay, and I don't think I ever will be again." Before the nurse could dig further, Julie bolted to her feet and fled into the hospital, hooking her bags over one shoulder as she went.

Being honest with a stranger was a start. Being honest with herself—finally—was a relief except it left her with a whole lot of crap she had no idea how to handle. She couldn't confide in her parents. She had no close friends, only lots of acquaintances and bunches of associates in her field. When the rubber met the road, she didn't know a single soul she was willing to bare her secrets to. Not secrets like these that made her look like a petty, vindictive bitch.

What kind of sick, sad loser held a grudge against a dying woman?

She hurried to a bank of elevators and found her way to the ICU. A different nurse presided today, a young, African American with a no-nonsense demeanor. She handed Julie the requisite mask, gloves, and gown and told her she had to leave her personal items outside Sarah's cubicle.

Her parents were already inside, standing next to Sarah's bed. Julie inhaled sharply and tossed her shoulders back. She pasted a smile on her face and hoped to hell no one looked at her too closely.

The nurse slid the door back, and Julie walked through. "Hi there, sunshine," she quipped. "Sorry I'm late. Jet lag's a real bitch."

Her mother and father turned as a unit. "Happy you're here." Chris's eyes crinkled at the corners, so she assumed he had to be smiling beneath his mask.

"You look better than you did last night," her mother announced.

"Thanks." Julie didn't bother adding she didn't see how she could possibly look like anything other than a fallen angel with a tarnished soul.

She edged closer, so she could see her sister. Sarah nodded. "Hi, Sis. Sorry to be such a drag." Her voice was much clearer than it had been yesterday afternoon. So was her breathing.

Julie caught her hand and held on tight. "You are not a drag. I'm happy you're pulling through this last crisis."

An odd look fluttered across Sarah's gaunt features. "I suppose I am too," she said.

"Why, honey. Of course, you're delighted you're getting stronger." Ariel grasped her daughter's other hand.

"Yes, Mom. Of course, you're right." The pinched look left Sarah's face, replaced by a faint smile. "How's your house?" she asked Julie. "Still in one piece?"

"More or less. A couple of dead rats and a battle with the furnace, but nothing I couldn't manage." She neglected to mention she'd given up and used electric space heaters last night.

They chatted for maybe ten more minutes before the nurse tapped on the glass and motioned for them to wrap things up.

"We'll be back as soon as they'll let us," Ariel said.

"Yes," Chris seconded. "That nice nurse said we could have one more visit around suppertime."

Sarah's eyes were closing as they left her bedside.

"Sorry to interrupt"—the nurse trained liquid dark eyes on them—"but Sarah needs sleep more than almost anything right now. She's not fighting for every breath, so rest will help her heal."

Julie removed her mask and gloves and gown and followed her folks out of the ICU.

"We thought we'd grab something in the cafeteria," her father said.

"Feel like joining us?" Ariel cocked her head to one side.

Julie thought about it, but her stomach was twisted into a knot and making small talk with her parents, who'd see through to her inner turmoil quick enough, wasn't a good idea.

She waggled her computer their way. "I ate before I left home," she told them brightly. "Brought work with me. I'll be in that lounge at the far end of the hall."

"Sure we can't bring you something?" her father persisted.

"No, Dad," she called over one shoulder. "I'm good for now."

She waited for her parents to charge after her and insist she join them, but they didn't. Chris and Ariel Wray had always been a closed system. So long as they had each other, anyone else just got in the way. They'd altered their parameters to accommodate their growing twins, but Julie had known from childhood her parents only needed each other.

It wasn't that they didn't love her and Sarah. They did, but they'd found something special in each other. Something that didn't come along every day. She wanted what her parents had, but she may as well wish for the moon delivered on a platter.

She smothered a disgusted snort. No one found love hiding out in a tent at dig sites or barricaded into their office at the university. She hadn't even gone on a date in maybe three years. Or it might be four. She'd lost count. If there was a way to appear enticing to men, she'd stopped trying a long time ago, and the thought of picking up that banner now made her tired.

Because she wanted to look convincing, she made her way to the lounge and set up her laptop in one corner along with a 4G hotspot. At least she could sort through her emails. They had to be piling up.

Julie booted up and stared at the Microsoft logo flaring across her screen. She was still staring as her desktop came into view. Instead of her various apps and programs, all she saw was Brice and Sarah.

Today was her day for insights into both herself and her twin. Sarah was tired of living. She'd almost been brave enough to admit it today but hadn't quite made it. Julie tried to put herself in her sister's shoes. Teetering on the edge of death—forever—had to take quite a toll. Maybe Sarah was disappointed she was still here because it meant she had to put on a brave, pretend face and keep going when it was the last thing she felt like doing.

Julie blew out a tight breath. She'd try to find a private moment with her sister. Tell her however she was feeling was okay. Julie wouldn't try to humor her or talk her out of it. Depending on how that went, she might have a heart to heart about that night with Brice. Clear the air after all these years.

She closed her teeth over her lower lip. Not a good idea. Sarah wasn't strong enough. Julie wanted to ease her own conscience, but she should have done that a long time ago.

Clicking apps, she brought up Word and wrote

Psychology is a crappy, non-scientific discipline that never helped anyone.

The words made her smile—and lightened her mood—but she still wondered if she should hunt down a therapist. She had to talk to somebody. If she went another fifteen years with all this hate and misery and anger bottled up inside, she'd be beyond salvage.

"Hell, maybe I already am," she muttered and clicked the mail icon determined to get something useful accomplished.

$\mathcal{B}$rice was on his way to the pediatrics wing to look in on the small Davidson boy when his cell vibrated. He pulled it to eye level, surprised and pleased to see his mother's number. Ducking into a side hall, he tapped accept and said, "Hello, Mom. What a lovely treat."

Susan McKinnon's smooth alto voice shook with laughter. "You always were a charmer, my boy. How are you? Is this a good time to talk?"

"I'm good." Brice lied through his teeth, but Susan was too far away to nail him with her penetrating dark eyes. "And now is as good a time as any."

"I know this is sudden, but how would you feel about some company over Christmas? We'd arrive on either the twenty-fourth or twenty-fifth and stay for a few days."

"We?" Brice was confused. "Um sure, Mom. Always happy to see you." He waited for her to clarify what she'd meant by the plural pronoun.

"Great. Thanks, son. Now for the *we* part. I didn't mention this because I was waiting to see how it developed, but I met someone."

"That's wonderful." Brice grinned into the phone. "I'm happy for you."

"Wait. I'm not done."

"I'll try to refrain from interrupting." He leaned against the wall, still holding the phone close to his ear. Whatever his mother had to say, he wanted to make sure not to miss any of it.

"Around this time last year, a new boy entered my tenth-grade math class. His father had just transferred in as one of our base surgeons. The boy had some troubles. His mother died from cancer just before they moved, and he was angry, alienated." Susan paused long enough to blow out an audible breath.

"I understood exactly how he felt because of how we lost your father. Anyway, we grew close, the boy and me. One day, he invited me home to meet his father. I'm still not sure quite how it happened, but we'll be getting married in the spring." Her words were lined with joy.

"Oh, Mom. I'm truly happy for you, and I'd love to meet your fiancé. And his son. What are their names?"

Susan laughed. "I was so excited to tell you—and a little bit scared too—I guess I left that out. My boyfriend's name is Trevor Wilder, and his son is Rob. Trev is two years younger than me," his mother went on, "but I'm thinking it's not important."

"No. It's not. Hell, if the age difference were reversed, you wouldn't give it a second thought. Wasn't Dad like four years older than you?"

"Five."

"Plan on staying with me," Brice said. "I have a huge, mostly empty house and a wonderful housekeeper. I've told you about Lupe. She'll be delighted to have guests to fuss over."

"If you're sure it's not any trouble…"

"Wouldn't have it any other way. I'll even try to get a day or two off from work. We can catch a ferry out to the islands."

"Thanks, Brice. You'll really like Rob. He reminds me a lot of you at that age."

"I'm sure I'll like them both. See you soon, Mom."

"Looking forward to it." She ended their connection

Brice stared at his phone, dumbstruck and absorbing the impossible. His mother. With a new husband. And a new son.

"Good for her," he mumbled. His mother was a stellar woman. She deserved to be happy.

What about me?

The question was rhetorical. He deserved to be happy too. Everyone did, but he had a hard time coming to terms with being happy in a world that didn't include Juliana.

Mom figured out how to find joy without Dad. If she could do it, maybe there's hope for me.

He stood and headed for Peds once again. He'd promised he'd stop by. The toddler was asking for him. Brice buzzed himself into the children's ward and stopped by the charge nurse's desk to glance at the wall chart delineating who was in which bed.

A nurse hurried over from one of the patient rooms. "Dr. McKinnon." She smiled, warm and genuine. "What you did for that family last night, well, it went above and beyond. Timmy's been asking for you every time he wakes up."

"Is he all right?" Brice lowered his voice.

"Oh my, yes. More than all right. Problem is, his mother will be with us for a few more days. No one's at home to take care of him."

Brice frowned. "Did Social Services troll for grandparents? Aunts? Uncles?"

"I'm sure they did, Doctor." The nurse pursed her mouth into a thin line. Maybe in her late forties, deep brown hair fell to chin level, and her brown eyes held a worried cast. "We can keep Timmy for maybe forty-eight more hours, but after that, he'll end up in temporary foster care."

An idea pricked Brice, but it was so preposterous, he buried it. "Where is this little boy who wants to see me?"

"Right this way, Doctor."

The nurse set a quick pace for the far end of the ward and pointed to an open door. Brice walked inside. A nurse's aide stood from where she'd been reading Timmy a story.

He jumped up from where he'd been sitting cross-legged in his crib and screeched. "Doctor. Doctor. You came."

"I told you he would, honey." The nurse's aide smiled indulgently. "I'll just leave the two of you alone for a bit. Make sure you let one of us know when you leave, Doc."

"Of course." Brice smiled back and trotted to Timmy's crib.

The little boy stretched out his arms, and Brice couldn't resist. He lifted him out of the crib and held him close. "You're going to be okay," he said. "Your mom too."

"Momma hurt bad. Worse than me."

"Yes, but she'll be home with you in no time."

Timmy wrapped his chubby little arms around Brice's neck, hanging on tight. "I want stay with you until Momma's home. Can I? Can I?"

Brice didn't know what to say. He'd been thinking the same thing, but the logistics were daunting. Social Services would have to assess his home and approve it as a placement. Those things took time, and a major holiday was looming. The boy's mother would have to agree...

What am I thinking? I'm never home.

But Lupe is, and children love her.

My mother's coming too.

Susan adored children. When she and his dad couldn't have any more of their own, she'd thrown herself into teaching. Her students might graduate, but they never forgot Mrs. McKinnon. She was flooded with cards every single holiday.

Brice untangled Timmy's arms and looked into the boy's small, anxious face. The child's blond hair hung in untidy ringlets, and his blue eyes were caked with dried tears. "It's not as easy as you might think," he said, "but I will try my hardest to make it happen. So long as it's okay with your mom."

"It will be," Timmy said with all the assurance a two-year-old could muster.

"Want to go for a ride?" Brice asked.

"Sure. Where?"

"Just around the hospital. Maybe we could look in on your mother." Brice was going out on a limb. For all he knew, Mrs. Davidson was in surgery, but they'd find out quick enough.

"Yes. Mommy. Go now."

"Do you need anything before we leave? Water or a fresh diaper?"

Timmy squirmed in his arms. "No. Hurry."

Brice grinned. He'd created a monster, but Timmy was adorable. He carried the little boy out of his room and stopped by the nurses' station. "I'm kidnapping your patient for a while. Do we know where his mom is?"

The nurse who'd greeted him smiled back. "Sure do. One floor up, bed six."

"Kidnap!" Timmy repeated, giggling. "Want go kidnap."

"Back soon," Brice said and walked out of the pediatric unit with Timmy in his arms.

"Mommy first."

"That's the plan, my man." Brice shouldered into a stairwell and started up a set of risers, wondering what had become of Timmy's father. It wasn't the kind of question to ask a two-year-old, though. Especially one who'd just survived a traumatic accident.

"Your hospital," Timmy crowed.

Brice laughed. "In my dreams. I only work here." He activated the palm reader, and the door to the Med-Surg floor opened.

"What's that?" Timmy asked.

"You're on top of everything, aren't you?" Brice avoided launching into an explanation of the palm reader and started along the corridor to the unit housing less-serious patients.

The boy offered him a big smile. It touched a spot Brice thought he'd buried beneath layers of denial. He'd assumed children would be part of his life, but if he didn't get going locating a mother for them, fatherhood would pass him by. Lupe offered oblique comments on occasion. She'd watched him play with her grandkids. With the wisdom inherent to older women, she'd sensed his longing and the empty places he slathered over with busyness.

He was plenty busy, and he made certain not to leave himself too much unstructured time. To cut the direction his thoughts were heading before he got too honest with himself, he said, "Your mom is close. Just on the other side of those big doors."

Brice entered a code and the doors slid open. Eventually, the hospital would have either palm or retinal scanners guarding every access point, but they were expensive. Insurance reimbursement had done nothing but go down. The whole topic of payment was such a snarl, he was glad he didn't have to deal with it. Not directly, anyway.

He made for the nurses' station to check in and let them know he was bringing Timmy to see his mother. The nurse sitting behind a computer monitor glanced up and broke into a smile. "Dr. McKinnon. What brings you to Easy

Street?" Dark hair framed her face, and her café au lait skin was dotted with freckles.

Brice nodded and returned her smile. He'd forgotten the nurses' nickname for the ward housing non-critical patients. "Do you suppose it would be all right for young Mr. Davidson here to see his mom?"

"More than all right. She's been worried about him. We've all reassured her he's in far better shape than she is, but nothing like the real deal to convince her. Room six." The nurse shot to her feet and led the way.

"Mrs. Davidson," she called. "You have a visitor."

Brice rounded the doorway, hoping the woman from last night wouldn't look so horrible, she'd scare the crap out of her two-year-old.

"Momma. Momma." Timmy wriggled furiously, clearly wanting to get down and run to his mother's bed.

"It's okay. We're almost there," Brice told him, unwilling to let go. Millicent Davidson was still hooked up to enough equipment, her boy could unwittingly do some damage.

"Timmy. Honey." Millicent held out her arms. "It's okay, Doctor. Just one quick hug."

Brice turned to Timmy. "See your mom's one arm? Be careful not to touch it." He set the boy down next to his mother.

Timmy extended one small hand and stroked his mother's other arm. "You hurt?"

"Not that hurt, honey. We'll be home in no time."

The little boy's face crumpled, and he laid his head on his mother's stomach, crying softly. She stroked his hair, crooning to him.

"I'm sorry," Brice said. "Maybe this wasn't such a good idea, but I thought—"

"He's relieved," Millicent broke in. "So am I. When that truck plowed into me last night, I was sure I was dead." She narrowed her eyes. "You must be the doctor they said saved me."

Brice felt his face heat. "I didn't save you, but I was there. I'm going to have a chat with the nurse, and then I'll be back to collect your boy."

Millicent trained dark eyes on his face. "Timmy's not injured. They'll want to discharge him really soon, huh?"

"Yes, and you and I will talk about that after I've had that chat with the unit nurse." He aimed his best reassuring smile at the Davidson clan and backtracked to the nurses' station.

"What a nice thing for you to do," the nurse murmured. "Bringing her boy to see her."

He pulled a chair close, so he could keep his voice low. "How long before she'll be ready to go?"

The nurse frowned and clicked a few keys, staring at her monitor. "She's Dr. Wilson's patient. His estimate is four days."

Brice knew Patrick Wilson well. He was a competent, caring physician who didn't give a damn what insurance companies were willing to pay for. He provided the care he felt his patients required.

"It's a problem, huh?" the nurse whispered. "No way we can keep her son that long."

"Let me talk with Mrs. Davidson," Brice said. "Feel like taking Timmy for an ice cream?"

"Sure. Let me call one of the other nurses to watch the fort, and I'll be right there."

Brice walked back to room six. Timmy was perched on the edge of the bed holding tight to his mother's other hand, the one not sporting an IV catheter. The two were deep in conversation.

"Can I ask a favor, Timmy?"

The child's blond head shot up. "Sure."

"I'd like some time alone with your mom. Miss Em will take you for ice cream while your mother and I are talking."

Emily poked her head around the doorframe. "We have vanilla, chocolate, or strawberry—"

"Want stay with Mommy." Timmy edged closer to her.

"It's okay, sweetie." Millicent smiled, sweet but firm. "Go with Miss Em. Maybe you could bring some ice cream back for me?"

"You want some?" Timmy's eyes lit with enthusiasm. "What kind?"

"Vanilla."

Emily scooped Timmy into her arms. "Ooph. You weight more than you look like, child."

Brice waited until they'd cleared the room before dragging a chair close to the bed. "Is there anyone who can watch Timmy until you get out of here?"

Millicent shook her head. "No one close. My sister's in the Army in Guam. My folks are dead."

"Timmy's father?" Brice hoped it wasn't too sore a topic.

Millicent rolled her blue eyes. "He's a priest. I used to work at St. Ignatius Monastery as a cook."

"Does he know about Timmy?"

She shook her head. "Father John is a good man. He'd have done the right thing and left the priesthood. I didn't want him to have to make that choice."

"Maybe a girlfriend could stand in for a couple of days?" Brice wasn't sure what to say about Father John, so he searched further.

"I'm just not sure." A vertical line formed between her eyebrows. "What will that mean for Timmy? Strangers taking him in? What if they don't treat him right?"

She struggled to sit up, and Brice activated the electronics to raise the head of her bed. "Social Services has a comprehensive screening process—" he began.

"No. I'll have them discharge me. I'll figure things out at home. How bad could it be?"

Brice leveled his gaze at her. "You have broken ribs. They punctured one of your lungs. Thank goodness you didn't have a concussion, but you do have a hairline fracture in your right lower leg, so you'll be on crutches for a while."

A corner of her mouth twisted downward. "You're telling me not to leave early."

He nodded. "That I am." He sucked in a breath. Here it was. He'd either offer or not. "Look. Mrs. Davidson. I can explore keeping Timmy with me for a couple of days. I have a live-in housekeeper, a competent older woman from Honduras. Lupe is wonderful, and she'd—"

"You'd do that for us?" Millicent clutched for his hand. "You don't have to."

"I may not be able to," he said. "I don't want to give you false hope. But I will get hold of our Social Services Department. Because it's for such a short time—and they know me—they may waive some of their requirements."

"Thank you, Doctor. Even if it doesn't work out, thank you so much for trying. It means a lot."

Brice tugged his hand out of hers and patted it. "They'll be back soon with the ice cream, but I'd like you to consider something."

"Anything." She tracked his movement with her gaze as he stood.

"The priest has a right to know about his son. Has a right to get to know him if he wants to. I understand you thought you were doing the proper thing, making a noble choice, but if he's as good a man as you say, he deserves to know."

"Do you really think so?"

"I do. If I had a boy like Timmy, I'd want to be part of his life." Brice's throat thickened, and he swallowed around a tight place.

"Here we are." Emily's voice preceded her, and she swept into the room with Timmy in her arms. His face was streaked with chocolate.

"We bring ice cream," he announced.

Emily dropped a small dish on Millicent's tray. "Indeed we did."

"I'll take him." Brice transferred Timmy to his arms and stopped by the sink to wet a towel and clean the worst of the smears off his face. "Time to go," he said to the boy. "The nurses downstairs are getting lonely."

"Kiss Momma first."

Brice trotted to the bed and bent so Timmy could kiss his mother's cheek. "See you soon, tiger," Millicent said. Transferring her attention to Brice, she added, "Thanks for everything, Doctor."

"I'll be in touch." Emotion was still far too near the surface for him to be comfortable saying much more.

He strode out of the unit and was on his way down the corridor listening to Timmy talk about Miss Em and ice cream and Momma. A startled gasp broke into the boy's monologue. When Brice sought its source, he saw Juliana, her mouth hanging open, standing stock-still a few feet away.

For once, he didn't mute his delight at seeing her. "Julie. Meet one of my young patients." He started toward her, but she turned and fled.

Brice stared after her. So did Timmy. "Who she?" he demanded.

"An old friend," Brice answered, as puzzle pieces clicked into place. Julie hadn't heard him when he'd identified Timmy as a patient because she wasn't listening. She wasn't listening because she must have assumed the boy was his.

"She okay?" Timmy lurched forward, straining against Brice's hold on him, clearly wanting to follow her.

"I'm sure she is. Let's get you back down to your room." He ruffled Timmy's hair and set a quick pace for the stairs.

"Thanks for Mommy."

Brice tightened his hold on the squirming toddler. "Take good care of her once you're both home. All right?"

"I will," he said solemnly. "Very good. Promise"

Brice waited until after Timmy was reunited with the Peds nurses before allowing himself to think about Juliana. The more he reflected on her reaction, the angrier he became. This was one time she'd hear him out, by God. They weren't twenty any more, and rejecting a two-year-old whose only crime was being in Brice's arms wasn't a thing he was willing to overlook.

He curled his lips into a tight line. He might not have been strong enough to stand up for himself after the episode with Sarah, but Juliana had to get over being a highhanded bitch. Taking her down a peg couldn't happen fast enough to suit him.

CHAPTER 7

*J*uliana had been on her way to the ICU when Brice walked from a side hallway carrying a small boy who was a dead ringer for him. Shock punched her in the guts. He was married. Or at least he'd hooked up with someone for long enough to produce a child.

Why had she assumed he'd spent fifteen years pining for her, waiting for her. Jesus, she was both naïve and stupid. Just because she'd tabled her love life for eternity was no reason to think he would have done the same.

He said something to her, was hurrying over to her, probably to introduce his son. Feeling like a loser and a fool, she turned on her heel and ran. What kind of adult ran away from a child?

A restroom door flashed past; she ducked inside and locked herself into a stall. Tears gushed down her cheeks, and she stuffed a fist into her mouth, biting hard to keep the low, keening moan filling her chest from emerging.

The toilet lid was closed, and she slumped onto it. She didn't like herself very much. She'd behaved very badly. No excuse for it. Planting her feet on the floor, she emerged from the stall and walked to a sink. Flipping on the taps, she sluiced cold water through her fingers and onto her face.

She had to apologize. Immediately. Aw crap. What if he'd gone home? Even if the hospital had something like a take your kid to work day, it wouldn't extend to anyone as young as the boy. Sadness tugged the corners of her heart. What a beauty the boy was. Cuddly and cherubic.

Her mother had been nagging about grandchildren for years. Julie had blown her off, but the hard truth was pretty soon it would be too late. Women had kids after forty, but the odds of birth defects skyrocketed, and she was a carrier for CF.

"Stop. Just stop." She splayed a wet hand across the mirror and then grabbed a paper towel to wipe it clean. "This isn't about me or my hurt feelings. If Brice finally found a woman who loves him, I should be glad for him, not a sour, prune-faced spinster."

Fortified, she dried her hands and face and marched from the bathroom. If Brice was still in the hospital, she'd find him and say she was sorry. Maybe the best place to start would be the ICU.

"Juliana. Stop right there." Brice's voice sounded from behind her.

She twirled to face him, not ready, not yet. "Look." She raised her hands, palms outward. "I don't know what got into me. I'm sorry. Your son is beautiful—"

"He is not my son," Brice ground out. She knew him sell enough to sense the fury pounding through him. "He's a patient. I happened to be there last night when he and his mother were in a horrible accident."

"N-not your son?" she stammered. "But he looks so much like you."

"So do a hundred other fair-haired little boys," he

countered. "Now that we have that straight, I have work to do." He pushed past her, moving full-steam ahead.

She wanted to call him, tell him to wait, but what right did she have? None. He wasn't hers anymore. Maybe he never had been. Emotions buffeted her from a hundred different directions. At least she'd apologized, but she didn't feel like she'd done enough.

"Wait!" She ran after Brice.

"What?" He glanced over one shoulder, not even turning around.

"Where is the little boy?"

"Why?"

Julie stood taller. "I want him to know I wasn't running away from him."

A corner of Brice's mouth twisted downward. "And how are you going to phrase things so a two-year-old understands it wasn't him but leftover baggage from you and me?"

"Easy," Juliana shot back, anger displacing her earlier angst. "I'll tell him my sister is sick, and I'm worried about her."

"Nice of you," he sneered. "Slightly more compassionate than the woman I remember, but the answer is no."

Before she could come up with an argument, he was gone.

"Damn him." She curled her hands into fists until her nails cut into her palm.

Her phone rang, and she fished it from a pocket. "Hi, Dad. I was just on my way back upstairs."

"Good, honey. Sarah's been asking for you."

"Be right there." Julie tapped the end call button. What could Sarah possible want? She'd been planning a heart-to-heart with her twin, but now wasn't a very good time. Not when she felt ashamed and humiliated by her reaction to the child in Brice's arms.

Brice had dismissed her like yesterday's trash, and she didn't blame him. He'd always had a streak where he stood up for those who couldn't stand up for themselves. It was one of the things she'd loved about him. His altruism and his principles.

Shaking her head, she trudged toward the elevator that would bring her up one floor to the ICU. What on earth could Sarah want? Maybe to tell her to go back to the dig. Julie had told her enough about it for her to recognize what an important find it was. A few papers with first authorship would be enough to set Juliana up for life. She'd be able to write her own ticket. Teach anywhere she wanted and have major research institutions underwrite her next digs with the full court press of photographers and enough underlings to fill a small town.

The names of her cult heroes marched through her mind. Men and women she'd idolized from girlhood. Louis Leaky. John Lloyd Stephens. Gertrude Bell. Jesse Fewkes. Kathleen Kenyon. Jane Goodall.

It was easier than thinking about Brice dressing her down, never mind she'd deserved everything he'd dished out and more. She was lucky he hadn't ordered her out of the hospital. If it weren't for Sarah, he might have.

If it weren't for Sarah, I wouldn't be here.

She reached the glassed-in ICU and pressed the buzzer for entrance. Erika let her in and handed her a mask, gloves, and a gown. "Everything all right?" she asked.

"Yeah. Fine." Julie's voice was muffled by her mask.

Erika hooked a hand beneath her arm and moved her mouth close to Julie's ear. "I'm plainspoken, Dr. Wray. Always have been. You do not look like everything is fine, but no matter what else is wrong in your life, you will put on a pleasant face when you see your sister. She's far from out of the woods, and she does not need to worry about you—or your parents—but they're always upbeat from what I've seen."

"Got it." Julie glanced pointedly at the nurse.

"Good. I've been at this for longer than you've been alive. It's the smallest things that sometimes mean life—or death."

A chill slid down Juliana spine, and she turned toward Erika, no longer angry. "Sarah's tired, isn't she? I picked that up earlier."

"How would you feel," Erika countered, "if you'd been sick your whole life? Not just sick, but wondering if this bout of pneumonia will be the one that does you in. Or this particular round of pancreatitis, although that hasn't bothered Sarah much until recently."

"I'd wonder if it was worth it," Julie murmured.

"So does she." Erika skewered her with eyes that had seen a whole lot. "The only thing keeping women like her alive is hope. When it sinks in that this is all there's ever likely to be, hope dies. After that..."

"What can I do?"

"Listen to her. Don't preach. Don't judge."

Julie nodded solemnly. "I'd already come to that conclusion. Before, I've always tried to humor her along."

Erika patted her arm. "It's never easy," she said. "For the patient or their loved ones. You'll be here after she isn't. What you do now will make that possible to bear—or not."

Juliana winced. She'd always known Sarah would die, but hearing it out loud held a finality that drove a stake through her heart.

"Lecture's over," Erika said. "Thanks for hearing me out. Oftentimes, folk cut me off long before where we got to."

"I can see why."

Erika offered a sad little nod but was done talking.

Julie walked to Sarah's enclosure. Her parents stood on opposite sides of the bed, chatting with their daughter. After taking a deep breath, she walked inside.

Sarah nodded her way. "Thanks for coming, Sis."

"You don't have to thank me."

"We'll see you outside, honey," Ariel said.

"Yes, Sarah wants some twin time with you." Chris inclined his head and left the room with his wife.

Julie perched on the edge of Sarah's narrow bed. "Holler if my sitting here causes you discomfort."

"It's okay." Sarah stretched out a thin hand, the skin over her fingers pale and translucent.

Julie laced her fingers with hers. "What's so important?"

"Lots of things. But, mostly, I can't pretend anymore. I'm dying. No matter what rabbit Brice pulls out of a hat, I'm still dying. I feel myself slipping into a shadow world. I've been there lots of times before, but this time it feels different. Soothing. Not threatening like it once did." She inhaled shakily. "Not sure why, but I'm not scared to let go anymore."

Julie bit back words. She wanted to urge Sarah to fight harder, not to let go, but this wasn't her battle. "Go on, sweetie. I'm listening."

Sarah nodded, her eyes clear, her gaze direct. "You'll leave for Egypt. Not right away, but in a couple of weeks. The next time you come back, I probably won't be here."

Tears threatened, but Julie blinked them away. "It's all right, Sis. I didn't truly understand until a little bit ago because I never put myself in your place, but I do now."

"Really? You're not going to—"

"No. I'm not. I love you, Sarah. No conditions. No requirements. Even if it means I have to let you go."

Sarah's blue eyes glistened with tears. "Thank you. There's one more thing."

Julie didn't trust herself to speak, but she held eye contact.

"Brice told you the truth. I didn't plan it, but when he showed up that night and mistook me for you, well, things got out of hand." Her grip on Juliana's hand tightened. "I only meant to kiss him, but"—she looked away—"it won't make sense, but I wanted what you had. Someone to love me. A life filled with possibility and light and love and children and a future."

Sarah was panting. Her words had cost her, or maybe it was the emotion behind them.

Julie waited for her sister's breathing to even out. "Why didn't you ever tell me?"

"I was ashamed. I had no idea you'd never forgive him, and by the time I figured it out, so much water had flowed under the bridge, I wasn't willing to face your anger." She smiled crookedly. "You always had a legendary temper."

"Still do, but I'm better at keeping it under lock and key. It's okay, Sarah. Truly it is. I forgive you. It I hadn't been such a stiff-necked, self-righteous bitch, I'd have listened to Brice."

Sarah's eyes fluttered shut. "Thank you for hearing me out. It was my last piece of unfinished business. I was scared I'd die and never get a chance to come clean."

Something about the words *unfinished business* grabbed Julie by the throat. "Promise me."

"Maybe." Sarah opened her eyes.

Julie licked dry, chapped lips and picked her words carefully. "Give this new treatment a chance. I looked it up, and it might buy you a few more years. Death is pretty damned permanent. Don't hurry it along unless you believe you've truly run out of options."

"Very politically correct and spoken like my sister. I'll take it under advisement." Her eyes closed again, and moments later she was snoring softly.

Julie stayed for a few more minutes before letting herself out of the room. After divesting herself of the mask, gloves, and gown that protected Sarah from infection, she walked into the corridor feeling at loose ends.

Brice had told the truth.

She'd been wrong not to believe him, but too much time had passed. He didn't love her anymore. Hell, she probably didn't know the man he'd grown into well enough to love him, either. Love took being together. Sharing your lives and hopes and dreams. It was way more than the instant attraction he engendered when she looked at him. If she expected to find true love, she needed to look elsewhere, but the point was she needed to look period. Love wasn't going to drop out of the sky and find her.

Feeling surprisingly steady, and at peace with her sister for the first time since that night in their apartment, she walked out of the hospital. She and Sarah had done a great job pretending. Hell, they both deserved Oscars for stellar performances, but their bond had cracked that night. Badly. They'd shored things up, talked around the fissure, pretended it didn't exist.

Except it had.

Until now.

She should hunt down her parents, but she needed to be by herself. Sarah didn't require her presence, and she had to figure out who the hell she was beyond the title archaeologist. She'd shut the door on the parts that made her human when she kicked Brice out of her life. Whether she could resurrect any feelings beyond anger and resignation remained to be seen.

CHAPTER 8

*B*rice exited Skype and pushed his laptop off to one side of his cluttered desk. Journal articles, papers, charts, and graphs were inches deep in places. His hospital office was tucked into a corner between the doctors' lounge and the Med-Surg unit. He'd declared it off limits to the cleaning crew after a critical journal article disappeared a few months back. He'd replaced it easily enough, but he'd wasted hours hunting for it before breaking down and looking it up online.

Most of the limited floorspace was taken up by an antique mahogany desk. The rest contained shelves heavy with resource texts he'd been collecting since medical school. Everything was digital these days, but he'd begun his training studying material on paper. He still mapped out equations to determine dosage and other critical issues by hand, not fully trusting the many programs that had popped up to get it right.

The MacBook dinged again, the Skype icon pulsing.

He clicked accept and smiled at his colleague, a Scotsman working at the Paris Institute. They'd just hung up, but a key point must have slipped Angus's mind. Usually, he was more organized.

"Forget something?" Brice asked.

Angus MacDuff's brusque demeanor slipped briefly. He almost smiled back before he cleared his throat. "Aye, that I did." He spoke with a deep, melodic brogue. "You'll recall I worked with your patient, Ms. Wray. Years back, when she was in medical school, I was a freshly minted professor."

Brice angled his head to one side. "You may have told me, but I didn't remember. Why is it relevant?"

The other doctor shrugged. "Perhaps it's not. I met her before the strain of managing her class load proved too much along with her illness." He took a measured breath. "You are going to introduce gene remodeling, are you not?"

"As soon as her labs fall closer to normal parameters. Your ideas were sound, and I'd be a liar if I said I wasn't excited to see how this pans out."

"What if I feel the same way?" Angus raised one dark brow. Coal-black hair fell across his brown eyes; he brushed it aside. He was dressed in scrubs and a white lab coat, the only garb Brice had ever seen him in. "We're in uncharted waters, colleague. I want to be there when we push off."

Brice stared at his associate. "You'd come across the Atlantic to wait on the outcome of a few procedures?"

"Aye, that I would. I haven't had a holiday in years, and Christmas is soon. What better time to—?"

Brice laughed, cutting off Angus's words. "Sorry. Didn't mean to interrupt. Seems to be my season to entertain. If you don't mind sharing my home with my mom and her new boyfriend and soon to be stepson, you're welcome to stay with me. There may be a two-year-old as well—he's the son of an accident victim I bailed out—but he should have left before Christmas."

"You always were kindhearted." Angus cast a speculative

glance across Skype's airwaves. "Let me guess. The parents were injured more severely than the boy, and he needs a place to stay."

"Close enough." Brice didn't mention the operative term would be parent, singular.

"I swear, my man, you really should move across the Atlantic. We have excellent resources to address such circumstances."

"So do we. You practiced in the States, so you're aware of them. This is a rather special case. I'm not in the habit of providing temporary housing for kids."

"Touché!" Angus did smile that time. "Back to the topic of staying with you. Are you sure? It sounds crowded. I can book a hotel if you'd be so kind as to recommend something close to the hospital."

"Won't be crowded at all. It's a big house, and it's usually just me and my housekeeper."

"Brilliant. I'll be close at hand and receive news of Ms. Wray's progress the moment you do. It's settled, then." Angus reached for his display.

"Hang on," Brice said. "I've known you a long time. What aren't you saying? Did you leave something out about how you anticipate gene splicing will unfold in her case? Is that why you want to be front and center? In case something you've omitted goes awry?"

"Just tell Ms. Wray I look forward to renewing our acquaintance." Angus disconnected.

Brice stared at the monitor. Renewing their acquaintance? Had Angus been interested in Sarah? It wasn't the type of thing he could ask his patient, but he'd watch carefully while he delivered the news of Angus's impending visit.

He raked both hands through his hair. It was past time to call it a day. He'd had a decent conversation with Social

Services, and things were looking good for Timmy, pending the outcome of a home visit tomorrow.

He slapped a palm across his forehead and picked up his phone to call Lupe and tell her. She answered on the first ring. "Doctor. Will you be home for dinner tonight?"

"Yes. I will." He sketched out the Social Service visit slated for ten tomorrow morning.

"Wonderful, wonderful. A child here." She switched to Spanish, sounding as excited as he'd known she would be.

"While I'm delivering news, my mother will be visiting."

A burst of Spanish obliterated his next words, so he waited for Lupe to calm down before adding, "Mom finally met someone. He's coming too, along with his teenaged son."

"You make me very happy. I love having people to take care of," Lupe gushed, practically crowing her delight.

"See you in maybe an hour," he said and disconnected. He could add Angus to the guest list after he got home. What was one more?

He did an abbreviated version of rounds, hitting the ICU last. Sarah was sitting up eating Jell-O and crackers. He donned a gown and slipped into her cubicle, casting a practiced eye over her from head to toe. "You're looking much better. Labs are improving too."

She offered him a shy smile. "For someone who'd come to terms with meeting her maker, I'm feeling surprisingly decent." She narrowed her eyes. "I told Julie."

"Told her what?" Brice felt confused. The last few days had been far too full for him to puzzle through her meaning.

Sarah set her spoon on the tray. "About your telling the truth that night. That I'd led you to believe I was her."

He made a grab for his M.D. demeanor, the one he hid behind when the going got rocky. "She never knew?"

Sarah shook her head and looked away. "The more time

that went by, the harder it was to revisit. After a few months, I stopped trying."

His heart skipped a few beats, but he said, "It's like I told you yesterday. None of it matters anymore. That was a long time ago. All of us have moved on."

Sarah dragged her blue eyes—eyes the same shade as Juliana's—back to his face. "She never found anyone else. All she has is her work."

He almost said, *kind of like me*, before he stopped himself. Just because he'd known Sarah from childhood, it wasn't appropriate to bring the personal into their conversation. To cover his discomfiture, he said, "An old friend of yours will be here soon."

"Wasn't aware I had too many of them," she muttered. "Who?"

"Angus MacDuff."

The joy that suffused her too-thin face was genuine. "But how? Why?"

Brice nodded, relieved to have redirected their communication to safer ground. "He's a colleague of mine. I worked with him at Johns Hopkins, and then he went to the Paris Institute for some advanced work.

"He's from Edinburgh," she murmured. "He was one of my professors in medical school."

"He said as much." Brice smiled encouragement, wanting to hear more.

"You never fleshed out why he's coming to see me." Her tone was tentative, as if his answer meant a lot to her.

"He and I pioneered the use of immune modulators in cystic fibrosis. As you know, the treatment you received is still highly experimental as is following it up with gene remodeling, which is the next step. Dr. MacDuff is delighted you've responded so well, and he wants to be here when we—"

"So it's about the CF. Not about me." Her voice took on a dull, dead note.

Brice watched her, making an effort to read between the lines. "I've treated other patients, and he's never made a point of being present. He told me he knew you personally, and it sounded as if he respected—"

"I'm tired," she spoke over him.

The words hung between them, as clear a dismissal as if she'd told him to get lost. He murmured, "Try to get a decent night's sleep, Sarah. I'll be back tomorrow."

He left her room, nodded to the charge nurse who told him to have a pleasant evening, and divested himself of mask, gloves, and gown before leaving the ICU. He checked out with the hospital operator and was halfway to the garage when her comment about Julie sank in. It never occurred to him Sarah hadn't cleared the decks with her twin.

When she'd admitted she wanted him too, he'd figured she was squaring things with him, not that she'd never admitted her deception to Juliana.

Hope flickered, flared, and then crashed. This had all the underpinnings of a Shakespearean tragedy, complete with miscommunications, misunderstandings, and a dying heroine. Except Sarah wouldn't die. Not this time, anyway. If his intervention worked, it might buy her another decade of a decent quality of life. One where she wasn't tied to machines and drugs.

He reached garage level and walked to his shiny black BMW roadster. One of his few splurges, he'd brought it back from his last jaunt to Europe. Well, he'd had it transported by ship, but he'd taken time off to fly to Halifax and drive his baby back across the country.

Pretty pathetic, when you cut to the chase. He had a fancy house and a fancy car and a pile of fancy degrees lining an ego wall. What a sterile haul for a guy closer to forty than thirty. He glanced at the time and nosed the car into Bellevue's ever-present traffic. Lupe would cluck over him as she pulled supper out of the oven, where she'd kept it warm. She didn't believe in microwaves, said they ruined the food.

From a nutritional perspective, she was absolutely correct.

He wiped his mind clear of everything but the route home. He'd driven it so often, he could do it in his sleep. A wry chuckle bubbled out. He'd done it damn near half-asleep more times than he was willing to admit. One of the aspects of medicine no one talked about was zombieville. The ability to project the appearance of alertness when most of your cerebral cortex had checked out.

Because it was easier than thinking about Juliana, he considered Angus—and Sarah. There'd been something between them. He was nearly certain of it, judging from Sarah's reaction. Had she chased Angus away because of her illness? Or had he been the one to call it quits? Not many people were willing to sign on, knowing their partner would experience progressively more severe bouts of debilitating illness. As a pulmonologist, Angus would understand more than most about the trajectory of Sarah's disease.

Brice trolled through his memory. Angus had been married, but it was years ago, and it hadn't lasted long. He'd never mentioned anyone since, and Brice had wondered from time to time if he weren't gay and coming to terms with it. He wrapped his fingers more tightly around the leather steering wheel, curious what would happen. He had a feeling he'd find out soon enough. Regardless, it would be a plus to have Angus working side by side with him as they moved Sarah's treatment to the next level.

As if on cue, his phone bleeped, telling him a text had come through. He didn't bother pulling over to read it. He'd be home in less than five minutes. If the hospital needed him, they'd page, not text. So whatever was waiting on his screen wasn't urgent.

He turned onto his street and then up his driveway, stopping to punch in the gate code. The lights of his oversized house came into view, and he jammed on the brake.

Lights, but not only the normal ones. Someone—probably Lupe and her son-in-law, had strung Christmas lights. It looked like thousands of them, but it was probably only a few hundred. They twinkled white, red, green, and blue, lending the house a fairyland appearance.

For the first time since he'd let a slick-talking real estate agent prod him into what had turned out to be an excellent investment, the place felt like home, not simply a dwelling where he hung his hat. He switched his right foot back to the accelerator and pulled into the circular driveway.

Lupe stood framed in light spilling through the double front doors, but she didn't hurry to his car like she usually did. Brice killed the engine, pushed the door open, and jumped out, for once leaving his phone, computer and briefcase in the passenger seat.

"It's beautiful," he yelled across the space separating him from Lupe.

She did walk toward him then, her seamed face spread in a broad smile. "You like it?"

"I love it."

Her smile expanded another notch. "Wait until you see the tree."

"Tree? There's a tree?"

She nodded enthusiastically. "Si. Fifteen feet tall."

He pictured his double story living room, and figured it must be epic. "How'd you do all this between morning and now?"

She looked away. "My family came over. They say house

looks not much like Christmas. I tell them, it looks same as last year, but they say it no good and leave. When they come back, truck is full." Lupe spread her arms wide. "We finish around three."

"It's wonderful, but you must let me pay you back. Decorations are expensive."

"No." She shook her head until gray hair danced around her face. "My family's gift to you. You bring us to United States." Her dark eyes glistened with unshed tears. "We can never repay you for your kindness. Your heart."

His own eyes stung. Before his emotions got the better of him, he said, "I want to see the tree. I haven't had one since I left home."

Lupe turned and trotted toward the still-open door. "*Tu madre*," she said over one shoulder. "She will love it too?"

"Oh my, yes. My mom is nothing if not a sucker for Christmas."

Text message long forgotten, Brice ran through the doorway after his housekeeper. He'd meant to get a tree last year. And the year before that, but something always intervened, and then Christmas was over. Pine scent filled his nostrils before he reached the great room. Along with the rich, piquant smell came memories of him and his mom and dad sitting next to their tree on Christmas Eve.

Happy. Laughing. Opening gifts. Loving each other as only families can.

He reached Lupe. She stood facing the tree, gazing at it, and he hugged her. "*Gracias. Muchas gracias.*"

She trained wise, old eyes on him but didn't say a word.

CHAPTER 9

Juliana thought long and hard before texting Brice. She owed him an obscenely overdue apology. Even if it was yesterday's news, she didn't see how she could move her life forward until she said what she should have fifteen years ago. She constructed—and erased—at least ten texts before she settled on:

I am very sorry for not believing you about Sarah. I should have. No excuses. I'm not offering any. I was wrong. I'm hoping you can forgive me, so I have a prayer of forgiving myself. Julie

She looked at her screen for moments that stretched into a quarter hour, figured she couldn't do any better, and punched send. Her first efforts had mentioned Sarah, almost blaming her, but she'd deep-sixed those texts. Sarah had been wrong, but not as culpable as herself for not believing in the man she loved.

How could she have been so stupid? So shallow? So self-absorbed she'd discounted their years together, chucking them all out? Good with the bad in one fell swoop. Not that there'd been much bad. Only that lone incident. Julie winced.

She'd sacrificed their love on the barren shores of her hurt feelings because the only other option was hating her twin forever.

Bull crap. I could have forgiven them both and moved on.

If I hadn't been so young and righteous.

And stupid. Yeah. That too.

She was edging into melodrama, so she stopped staring at her blank screen. A scant few minutes had elapsed since she'd sent the text. What had she expected? Instant results? Not after this long.

Putting the phone aside, she hooked her seat belt and prepared to leave Overlake's sprawling parking lot. Her phone dinged, and her heart jumped into her throat, making it hard to breathe. She snatched up the phone and saw a text from her mother.

Disappointment it wasn't from Brice threatened to annihilate her as she read her mother's message.

Where are you? Feel like dinner?

Julie most assuredly did not feel like dinner. Not with her parents. Not at all. Her stomach was jittery, and she was worried introducing anything into it would make her puke. She texted back.

Can I beg off for tonight? Still getting over jet lag, and feel like I might be coming down with something.

She winced. Lying wasn't part of her makeup, but nor could she put on her game face for even as long as it would take to sit through dinner. Her parents would figure out something was wrong quickly enough, and like hunting dogs who'd scented prey, they wouldn't quit digging until she told them.

Her text tone beeped again.

Sure, honey. Let us know if you need anything. See you at Overlake around ten tomorrow.

This time the message was from her father. Juliana rolled

her mental eyes. Her parents even tag-teamed texting.

Thanks. Sorry to miss visiting with you.

NP. We love you, sweetie. Signing off for now. Dad.

She switched the phone to airplane mode, done with communicating with the outside world for now. Brice had had plenty of time to get back to her. Surely, he'd seen her message, and he wasn't going to respond.

I don't know that.

Maybe he's in emergency surgery or something.

Tapping the ignition, she started for home. It wasn't as if he owed her anything, but she'd hoped for at least an acknowledgement.

"Why?" she muttered. "What's in it for him? Besides, what the hell is he going to say? Thanks for coming to your senses. Finally."

She closed her teeth over her lower lip hard enough to draw blood. The world was so damned instant these days. She'd been stupid to send that text at all. Back in the days of snail mail, or even email, she'd have put more thought into a communication this important.

What the hell was wrong with her? She hadn't thought about Brice in years, well not much, anyway. She'd done a most excellent job of burying herself in her work. Archaeology was like that. It had so many nooks and crannies, she'd been able to fill twenty-hour days, pass out, and do it all over again. Her single-minded dedication was how she'd risen through the ranks of academe so quickly.

"Yeah. Youngest full professor in the history of U.W.'s archaeology department." Back to talking out loud to fill the hollow places in her heart, her voice echoed through the empty car.

She edged through solid lanes of traffic, intent on the 45th street exit. Finally, at the last possible moment, before her only other choice was running up onto a center divider, some humanitarian made room for her. She slid the 4Runner neatly into the few feet of real estate and focused on positioning herself to make a right turn at the traffic light.

The nonstop flow of vehicles didn't bother her most of the time. For one thing, she rarely left the University District unless she was out of the country. For another, she rode her bike or set out on foot for local destinations—like campus, for example.

Her mother had left the Marines five or six years ago. Since Ariel needed projects, she'd thrown herself into locating a home for them. A spot they could relocate once her husband retired. The elder Wrays had been determined to settle in the Pacific Northwest. Both daughters were there, and they wanted to be close. No one had come out and mentioned Sarah's precarious health, but it was definitely a driving factor.

Julie executed a series of turns and stopped at a grocery store near her home. Her cupboards were bare, as was her refrigerator. Just because she wasn't hungry now didn't mean she wouldn't be later—or tomorrow morning. She cast a glance at her phone. The airplane mode indicator mocked her, but she resisted an urge to bring the device back online. She lived for months with limited Internet at dig sites. No reason she couldn't mimic that pattern here.

In truth, she got a hell of a lot more accomplished without the constant dings, tweets, and squawks signaling emails, texts, news, and other incoming garbage, most of it meaningless. Exiting the car, she trotted across the parking lot and grabbed a cart. The little market that used to be a quiet spot had been discovered, and it took her almost an hour between selecting items and making it through one of three overloaded checkout lines.

Back at her car, she offloaded her bags and started for home. It was only a few blocks away, and she reached the cottage quickly. Another half hour, and everything was inside and put away. Because she had time, and an abundance of nervous energy, she pulled the trap door to the crawl space open and climbed down a short ladder to where she could take a closer look at her malfunctioning furnace.

The project sucked her in. It was one of the sideline benefits of her training. She enjoyed problems and liked winning. After several trips back up the ladder to locate a lantern, her tools, and the furnace manual, she had enough to interpret the error code. Luckily, she didn't require parts. The oil burner was old and cantankerous. The few times she'd hired workmen, they'd always shaken their heads and told her what she really needed was a more modern unit.

After clearing a valve and two lines, she hit the igniter, Triumph swelled through her when the burner burst into life, and she fist pumped the air. Gathering everything she'd used, she carted her tools and the manual up the ladder, taking care to put everything away. She hated wasted time, and hunting for something because she'd been too lazy to return it to its proper place would have annoyed the crap out of her. She'd read the riot act to many graduate students for not taking care of their implements.

Her hands were coated with oily film; one nail had broken. She shrugged at the collateral damage. She had heat. It mattered more than her fingernails. Julie stood over the utility sink in her small laundry room and scrubbed her hands with mechanic's soap enjoying its citrusy smell. Her stomach growled, and she smiled. Diverting her attention had worked. She was hungry. She'd have one of the salad kits she'd purchased, take a bath, and go to bed.

And she wouldn't look at her phone until tomorrow. Her parents could call her on the landline if they needed to reach her. Sitting over toast and an Asian chopped salad, she took in her homey kitchen with its knotty alder cabinets. Nothing like squatting over a cookfire in a third world country to pound home how lucky she was.

Her phone blatted, the sound intrusive and shocking. How long had it been since anyone actually called her on the landline? Long enough, she'd considered disconnecting it. Only reason it was still active was sloth on her part—that and not being around enough to think about it.

Julie lunged for the phone, fully expecting one of her parents. "Hello?"

"Dr. Wray." The connection was scratchy and the other person's voice so garbled she couldn't place it. One thing was certain, though, it wasn't one of her parents.

"Yes," she replied. "Who is this?"

"Katie. Sorry about how bad this connection is. I didn't want to go all the way into Cairo."

Juliana pictured Katie Johnson, a fourth-year graduate student nearly done with her dissertation. Tall and muscular with long blonde hair and blue eyes, she looked like the Swedes who'd been her ancestors. Julie would miss Katie, but the young woman was a rising star in the archaeology world.

"What's up?" Julie dragged the phone back to her spot at the table where she'd left her meal.

"When are you coming back?"

"Maybe a couple of weeks. Looks like my sister will pull through, but I want to spend more time with her in case I'm wrong."

"Not soon enough. You'll—" The rest of Katie's words dissolved in a fizz of static.

"Hold up. I didn't catch that."

"Didn't figure you did. Let me make a few adjustments. Is this better?"

"A little. How about if you email me?"

"Can't. Don't want a paper trail. Kicked it around with Tom and Eve. We decided I had to call you."

Julie's eyes widened. Whatever this was, it wasn't sounding good. "Go on."

"Orestes. Dr. Conom. He claims to have uncovered another layer, but it's the same one we found. He's claiming credit. Called *NG*. They're sending a photog."

Julie tightened her grip on the phone until her hand cramped. *National Geographic* and photographers, huh? Academic theft was common. It was why people like her hunkered over their finds like feral cats.

More static crackled against her ear. "Have to come back. Now. First plane," Katie insisted.

"I— I'm not sure I can."

"You said your sister was out of the woods. Can't you fly back here, fix things, and then return to Seattle?" Katie pleaded.

Juliana got it. Katie's dissertation research was tied up in this dig. If Dr. Conom, an unscrupulous Greek, claimed it for his own, she'd be cut out of the action—probably in favor of one of his students.

"I'll talk with the department head tomorrow." Julie tried to sound reassuring, but she didn't hold much hope. The odds of him even being in town this time of year were slim.

"Do something. Please. I've got to go before Conom catches me." The ever-present hiss morphed into silence. Katie had disconnected.

Julie stared at the remains of her meal. Her appetite had once again fled, but she forced herself to finish everything. She'd lost a lot of weight in Egypt and grown far too thin.

As she ate, she catalogued the history of the dig. She, Katie, and two other graduate students, Tom and Eve, had comprised the original team. Once they'd struck pay dirt, they'd been joined by Dr. Conom and three of his grad students. Between them, they'd hired a phalanx of local workers to speed things along.

She didn't know Orestes Conom well. He'd joined the department three or four years ago, fresh from a university in Athens. She'd voted against hiring him, viewing his dissertation research as sloppy, but she'd been in the minority. Young, strikingly good looking—if you liked the dark, slick type—he'd proceeded to make a play for every woman who crossed his path.

Including her.

Juliana turned him down flat, but a blonde departmental secretary ended up marrying him, falling for his line of Lothario crap. All he'd wanted was a fast and easy path to citizenship. Once he'd secured it, he dropped the secretary by the side of the road, breaking her heart and those of her two teenaged children who'd assumed he'd be their daddy.

Rage thickened her throat, but it wouldn't help digest her meal, so she left the table and her house, walking fast to blow off tension. The thought of hopping back on a plane wasn't very appealing, but losing almost a year of work to a corrupt con artist wasn't, either.

The university had an ethics committee. She could file a written complaint, but school was closed and wouldn't reopen until after January first. Depending how much of an in Oretes had with *National Geographic*—

"That's it. I'll get hold of them." She had connections there from earlier digs where her finds had made archaeologic history. Julie wasn't under any illusions—if *NG* did a big, splashy spread, the university would close ranks around Oretes. No one would care if he'd stolen her work or that he'd argued against digging deeper, labeling it a waste of time and resources. As senior researcher at the dig site, she'd insisted, and once they'd unearthed the next level, he'd been as excited as all the rest of them.

As a courtesy, she'd have to start with her boss, Dr. Smithwick. Like most people in his position, he hated being blindsided by anything that might besmirch the respectability of his department. Feeling more settled, she switched direction and set a brisk pace toward home.

Not much she could accomplish tonight, but she'd clean up the kitchen and go to bed. At least she'd stopped perseverating about Brice. Even though she tried to frame her non-Brice orientation as another victory, she couldn't do it.

Some mistakes cut deep, and the one she'd made with him had left gouges in her heart. She had to let things go. Had to let him go. Confusion reigned. Hadn't she shut the door on him fifteen years ago?

When the answer came, she didn't care much for it. Despite her bold thoughts about not knowing him anymore, she'd never stopped loving him. Not really. Too little and too late, she'd finally apologized—for all the good it would do either of them.

I have to move on.

She let herself back inside her house thanking all the gods in the universe she'd never shared this place with Brice. She did need to move on. The question of the hour was how the hell she'd manage it. If hard work and success could have accomplished it, she'd have sealed over her memories years back.

A good first step would be not being such a wimp she couldn't look at her phone. Resolute, she picked it up and worked her way to settings where she took it off airplane mode. A text from her mother popped into view.

Hi, dear. Hope you're getting good rest. And food. You're too thin. I just got an email from Susan McKinnon. You'll remember her. She was one of your high school teachers. She's driving up here for Xmas with Brice. We'll all have dinner at least one night. Probably Xmas Eve. It will be great to see her again.

Juliana groaned and put the phone down. No matter what

plans she made, Brice would play a peripheral part in her life, and she'd damn well better get used to it.

CHAPTER 10

*B*rice woke refreshed and looking forward to having guests in his home. He'd thrown a housewarming party right after he bought the place, but between conferences, patients, and teaching at the medical school, he'd found one excuse after another to avoid anything that smacked of a social life. After a while, it became a habit, and invitations to other people's homes had dried up as well. Many of the conferences had been in Europe, the U.K. or Asia, which hadn't helped matters. A two- or three-day conference could eat up ten days counting jet lag at both ends.

Jet lag.

Juliana.

He focused on getting out of the house to push his thoughts elsewhere, but they remained stubbornly focused on her. Jesus. She looked anorexic. She'd never had an eating disorder when they were together, but those things sometimes didn't surface until a woman was in her mid-twenties or even later.

He winced at how desperately clinical he sounded. Did he

still know how to be a human being? Or had he been a doctor so long, it colored everything, snuck into every nuanced thought and created the professional buffer that had turned into his comfort zone?

Afraid he wouldn't like the result, he didn't even try to come up with an answer.

He hunted for his phone and remembered he'd been so delighted by the Christmas decorations, he'd left everything in the car. Maybe it was why he'd slept so well. He'd relegated the work demons to the driveway, leaving them to their own devices. Even better, maybe it boded well for him that he'd made it through eleven hours without making an emergency trip to the BMW to collect his phone, computer, and briefcase.

Smiling sheepishly, he clipped his pager to his belt and hurried downstairs. The smells of coffee and toast mingled with the heady smell of the tree.

Lupe thrust a thermos and paper bag into his hands. "Never too late to eat," she announced with conviction.

"Thanks." He took the items. "Call me if there are any issues with the Social Services people."

"No worry. All will be fine. When little boy arrive?"

Brice thought about it. "Tonight or tomorrow."

"You bring?" She raised one eyebrow.

He shook his head. "The social worker will transport Timmy."

"I make cookies this morning. Brownies too."

Brice tossed his head back and laughed. "He can't live on sugar."

Lupe placed her hands on her hips, elbows akimbo. "I sneak food in between."

Brice hoped things would work out. To avoid voicing his usual spate of cautions, he said, "See you tonight," and then added, "On the houseguest front, there will be one more. A doc I know."

Lupe angled her head to one side, her smile infectious. "Invite more. Still five empty bedrooms. Six, if count guesthouse."

"But that's yours," he protested.

She shrugged, clearly willing to share her space if it came to it. "You invite all you want, Doc."

He patted her arm, grateful for the burst of benevolence that had pushed him to bring her and her family to the States. In one of her many, newsy letters, she'd confided fears the latest bout of civil unrest would mean her son-in-law would be conscripted. It was enough to galvanize Brice into action. Lupe and her family had been more than kind to him. He'd stayed with them as a student and during a Doctors Without Borders assignment, hoping to improve his Spanish and do some good at the same time. Over those few weeks, they'd shown him every kindness and shared everything. When he'd expressed concerns he was leaving them short, they'd waved him to silence.

He'd only planned to finesse her and her family's transition to the States. It never occurred to him she'd take a stand about working for him. Or that he'd accede to her request.

"You're a good woman, Lupe. Thanks for taking care of me."

She winked broadly. "I substitute. Until you locate wife."

He grinned at her. "Better watch those promises. The wife part isn't looking likely."

"Go. I have baking."

With a cheery wave, he strode to his car. He was almost to the hospital before he remembered the text from the previous night. The one he hadn't looked at. He waited until he'd pulled into the parking slot with his name above it—one of the few perks working for Overlake. Once he'd gotten out and slung the straps for his computer and briefcase over a shoulder, he picked up the phone and glanced at the screen.

The message was so unbelievable, he stood rooted in place and read it twice more.

I am very sorry for not believing you about Sarah. I should have. No excuses. I'm not offering any. I was wrong. I'm hoping you can forgive me, so I have a prayer of forgiving myself. Julie

How had she gotten his number? He jammed his jaws together. Of all the reactions to a message he'd hoped and prayed for, why the hell had he zeroed in on the least important aspect? And the easiest one to figure out. He'd never changed his cell number. It was the same as it had been during the years they'd been together.

He locked the BMW and trudged into the hospital. She'd texted him last night. By now, knowing her, she'd rebuilt whatever chink in her armor had allowed her to reach out to him.

What if he'd seen the message last night?

It wasn't as if he would have dropped everything and raced into her arms. Not after all this time. He might still love her—maybe, he wasn't sure—but he didn't trust her. He re-read the message. At least she wasn't blaming her sister. Maybe it meant she'd grown up.

He ground his teeth until they ached. Of course she'd "grown up." She ran archaeological digs in the world's hellholes. She hadn't come as far as she had by shifting blame off onto others.

He pushed through the door into the locker room, deep in thought. Someone had taped a note to his locker. Couldn't be about any of his patients. He doublechecked the pager clipped to his belt, but its screen remained empty. So what the hell was the note about? No one wrote anything down anymore—except him.

Guilt stabbed him. Not only had he neglected his phone, he hadn't logged on once last night, which meant no email, either. No journal articles. No news. Not being plugged in had felt good, as if he'd played hooky and had eked out a few hours to himself. Hours when he wasn't Brice McKinnon, M.D., but just plain old Brice.

He inhaled raggedly. He was being stupid. He'd worked like a dog to get where he was. For a moment there, he'd sounded downright ungrateful. He pulled the note off his locker. Unfolded it and read:

Sorry to bother you, Doc, but your friend said it was urgent, and you didn't answer my emails.

Brice let his gaze track to the bottom. The message was from one of the hospital's many phone operators. If this was urgent, why hadn't she paged him? He returned to her message.

Dr. MacDuff will be arriving tonight around ten via military transport. His plane is landing at Fort Lewis, and he was hoping for a ride. Leave a message for him on Skype. Include your address and if he will need to hire a taxi.

Brice spun the dials to open his locker and changed from street clothes to his hospital garb of scrubs and a lab coat. One thing was obvious. Angus had already put the wheels in motion for this trip before telling Brice about it. Their conversation had been pro forma at best.

What if he'd told him not to come?

He smothered a snort. The Scottish doc would have said he was being ridiculous—and come anyway. This revolved around Sarah. Maybe Angus had an epiphany. If Sarah chased him away, he was going to try again. Or if he'd been the one with cold feet, perhaps he'd found a way around them.

Regardless, Angus must have been sitting in an airport while they Skyped. Or been damned close. He'd been a helicopter pilot for the RAF. Convenient he could still access military flights. Brice had no idea if U.S. vets had the same perks, but he bet the elder Wrays would know. He'd have to ask them when he saw them later today.

His thoughts returned to Juliana. He'd see her later today too. What the hell would he say? He tried out—and discarded —at least ten possibilities. They all sounded stiff, formal. Nothing like he was feeling inside, which was soft and messy and vulnerable.

~

JULIANA PERCHED on the edge of a chair in Dr. Smithwick's waiting room. She'd tried his office by phone and email and received the same message. He was out for the Christmas holiday, returning January seventh. January seventh was almost three weeks away. By then Orestes would have done the photoshoot with *National Geographic*.

She'd taken a chance and called Dr. Smithwick's home. His housekeeper had hunted him down. Juliana blundered through effusive apologies, but said it was really important she talk with him.

After several attempts to pry "whatever was so bloody urgent" out of her, he'd grudgingly agreed to meet her in his office at ten thirty sharp. The intimation being if she was one minute late, he wouldn't wait for her.

Juliana had been early by a good quarter hour. Dr. Smithwick was ancient. Worse, he was one of the old breed of academics. The ones who barely tolerated their female colleagues, probably because he remembered a day when their ranks had been close to a hundred percent men.

He strode through the door. Tall and angular, with a full head of silvery hair and shrewd dark eyes, he wore his usual cashmere sweater and dark slacks. He must have fifty cashmere sweaters in a variety of dull, dark shades including gray, brown, and black. In her mind, she'd often compared his bones and angles with Ichabod Crane, figuring he was as fair a shot at a lookalike as she was likely to find.

"Right on time, Ms. Wray," he barked in his staunch, upper-crust British accent. Thirty years in America hadn't put a dent in that accent, which made her suspect he cultivated it on purpose.

"Right on time," she agreed jauntily, not bothering to comment on his purposeful snub of neglecting to address her as doctor. He'd never have done that if she were a man.

Juliana got to her feet and waited for him to fumble with his keys to unlock his inner sanctum. She might not care for him, but she adored his office with its book-lined shelves and glass artifact displays. It smelled of leather and antiquities.

He finally got the door open and waved her through first, ever the gentleman. When she got closer, she caught a whiff of stale whiskey. Rumors had fluttered about for a long time he might have a drinking problem, but he'd retire eventually, and the university was famous for turning a blind eye to something as benign as famous professors who drank more than they should.

Not for the first time, she vowed to take up drinking. It might improve her temper, the legendary one Sarah alluded to.

With a grunt and a sigh, Dr. Smithwick settled into his massive, leather desk chair. It creaked, although he scarcely weighed enough to stress it. He splayed his hands across his desk. "What's this all about, Ms. Wray?"

Juliana shut the door and stood in front of him, unsure if she should sit.

"Oh for the love of God, take a chair, Ms. Wray. Don't stand over me like you're on the verge of a fainting fit."

Anger surged, skirting the surface, so she tried for black

humor. "Not much danger of that, sir. I might puke on you, but I'd never faint."

He drew his patrician features into a distasteful moue. "Now we have that small tidbit out of the way, please elucidate me as to why you've disturbed my holiday."

She'd spent the walk over here deciding how to proceed. Being wimpy and counting on Smithwick to do the right thing would be the wrong approach. Working on the hypothesis it was better to ask forgiveness than permission, she launched into the speech she'd prepared and then mostly memorized.

"I apologize for asking you to come to your office. I'd never have done it if this wasn't important. I sent all my field notes in to the department secretary. Please feel free to check with her or read my notes as verification for what I'm about to tell you."

She eyed Dr. Smithwick, grateful he wasn't rolling his eyes or falling asleep or motioning her to hurry things up.

"Nine weeks ago, on October 27th, we extended our excavation. I believed I'd unearthed sufficient evidence to allocate the necessary resources to go deeper. My colleague disagreed, but I outranked him—"

"I know all this, Ms. Wray," he interrupted. "Did you call me in here to rehash the past?"

"No, sir, but background is how we understand the present. It's one of the underpinnings of our field."

"Spare me." His words were dry.

"I'll be brief."

"Please." He spun one hand in tired circles.

"As you know, the lower layer proved a treasure trove. We're still working it, but Dr. Conom is claiming the find is his. It's not. It's mine."

"And you know this how?"

"I received a call from one of my graduate students worried about her dissertation project."

"Not what I meant, Ms. Wray. Why is it more yours than his? He's been working side by side with you in the field for months."

Juliana sat back, mouth hanging open. "Because if it were up to him, we'd never have opened the lower layer. If it were up to him, the field team would be home now."

Smithwick shrugged. "You have your creds, Ms. Wray. Let Orestes have a crack at some of his own."

Her temper snapped, and she surged to her feet. "Not if he hasn't earned them, and it's Dr. Wray."

Smithwick trained rheumy dark eyes on her. "Give it a rest, Ms. Wray. Oh, sorry. Dr. Wray. This conversation is over."

"No," she retorted. "It's not. I've spoken with my own contacts at *National Geographic*, staking my right to the lower layer finds. If there are journal articles about this, I will have first authorship. Katherine Johnson will have second. Orestes is welcome to third if he'd like, even though I'm not sure I want my name associated with his on anything." She stood taller. "I've filed a report with the university ethics committee, complete with copies of my field notes for verification of my claim."

"You wouldn't do such a thing," he sputtered.

"I would, and I have." Juliana narrowed her eyes. "I wanted to tell you personally. So you'd have all the information before you decide which horse you want to bet on, *Mr.* Smithwick."

Before she told him he was an old sexist pig, she turned and stormed out of his office. He couldn't fire her. She had tenure, but he could make her life damned miserable. He also wouldn't pull the plug on a successful field expedition, no matter how much she'd pissed him off. If he did, the wealthy patrons who funded archaeology projects would jump down his throat. Grateful she'd walked to this meeting, she settled into a fast jog as she headed home.

She'd be late to meet her folks at Overlake, but she'd already texted them, told them she had something critical and work-related to take care of. Fury still bubbled, and she curled her hands into fists. Despite affirmative action and the addition of boatloads of female staff and grad students, academe's hallowed halls were still pathetically biased against women.

She hoped she'd lived long enough to see the tides shift.

The only good thing about her standoff with Smithwick was it had driven Brice to a back burner. So what if he hadn't texted her back? She had bigger problems than an old love affair gone bad. She needed to get a message to Katie, something to reassure her.

What was the best way to accomplish it?

Far from dumb, Orestes would probably be monitoring all incoming and outgoing communications. No way around it. She'd have to go in through the front door. She'd call and ask for Katie and tell her the problem was handled. Let Orestes stew in his own juices figuring out what she meant by it.

"Geez. Never realized what a vindictive bitch I am," she muttered and ran faster. If everything went well, she'd be at the hospital before one.

CHAPTER 11

*B*rice shouldered out of the operating room. He'd been called in by oncology to assist with a highly complicated lung cancer surgery. The patient had waited far too long before bringing his condition to anyone's attention. Understandable in today's insurance market. This particular patient hadn't had any and wasn't willing to compromise his family's finances with an expensive medical intervention.

His wife had brought him to the ER shortly after midnight, gasping for breath because his lungs had filled with fluid.

Brice shucked his surgical paraphernalia. Some days he hated the U.S. medical system where the very rich and very poor had coverage and large percentages in between languished. He and the oncologist had bought today's patient time, not much, but enough to get his affairs in order.

Enough for his wife and children to say goodbye.

Brice slammed a fist into the wall. Not so hard as to injure himself, but it had a centering effect. He used back corridors to get to the locker room where he showered and dressed. He still had time to pick up Angus. Not an overabundance, but enough.

He scrolled through texts, zeroing in on one from Lupe. Social Services would be delivering Timmy tomorrow morning before noon. Brice smiled softly. Not that he'd see much of the boy with his schedule, but at least Timmy would have a safe, protected environment until Millicent was well enough to be released. He texted back a thumbs up icon. Lupe sent him a picture of cookies.

What had gotten short shrift today was his rounds. He hadn't seen any of his patients, but he'd checked with nursing, and they were all progressing. Sarah was doing so well, Erika had practically crowed.

For some reason, the charge nurse had taken a shine to the Wray girl—and her family. Brice drew himself up short as he shrugged into a sports shirt, slacks, and loafers. Sarah was hardly a girl, and it was disrespectful to characterize her as one. He grabbed his jacket, transferred his pager from his lab coat to his belt, and got ready to leave. The only thing left was stopping by his office for his briefcase, laptop, and phone.

He climbed the stairs—a joke in the exercise department, but slightly better than nothing—and came out in a hallway off limits to visitors. It was his normal route to his office since it cut down on the possibility of anyone waylaying him. Ducking inside, he collected what he needed and left by the main hallway, selecting the most direct route to the garage.

"Brice, hold up."

He froze. He'd know Julie's voice anywhere. The breathy contralto that promised passion and never failed to deliver.

"I looked for you all day, the afternoon part of it, anyway." Catching up with him, she wrapped her long fingers around his upper arm.

Heat from her hand seeped through his jacket and shirt as

if they weren't there, and a shock traveled up his spine. Her touching him brought everything roaring back. Heat. Need. Memories of intense conversations where they'd solved all the world's problems and then gone out for pizza and beer. In those days, he'd have done anything for her. Followed her to the ends of the earth—beyond, if necessary.

He wanted her touch, craved it, longed to crush her in his arms and slash his mouth over hers. Dangerous ground. Treacherous territory. He tugged out of her grasp to lessen the temptation. While he was at it, he shifted the position of the jacket he'd tossed over one arm, so it covered the suddenly tented out front of his trousers.

"Sorry. I was in surgery. I got called in."

She nodded. "Erika told us." She scanned his face. "Your patient made it, huh?"

Uncomfortable beneath her frank stare, he looked away. "I can't discuss patients with you or anyone else."

"Maybe not, but I can still read your expressions. I can't explain it, but you'd look different if your patient died." Without waiting for him to reply, she forged ahead. "I'm sorry about texting you. It was bold of me and uncalled for. I am sorry, though, and I wanted to make certain you knew. I won't bother you anymore, but"—her forthright inspection shifted to floor level—"you were the best thing that ever happened to me. I blew it, and I blew it big-time. I hope you find someone wonderful. You deserve to be happy."

Before he could come up with anything to say, she turned and fled.

Longing beat a path through him. He wanted to go after her, tell her she deserved every happiness too, but if he did, he'd be late picking up Angus because he wouldn't stop with just talking. Once he kissed her and felt her enticing body pressed against his, he'd be lost.

His heart hammered against his ribs. His breath came

fast, and his cock strained, hard as it ever got. The place she'd touched his arm still throbbed from her touch, and her scent clung to him. He inhaled hungrily, swept away by memories of how they'd been together.

Breath rattled out of him. Angus could call a cab. Brice ran a few feet in the direction Julie had gone, but stopped. Now wasn't the time. Putting his own needs second was so ingrained, he felt disgusted with himself.

If not now, then when? an inner voice argued.

He didn't articulate a reply because it was "probably never." Their time had come and gone. That boat had left port years before. He might still want her, but it took more than sexual attraction to build a lasting partnership.

He moved slowly toward his car. He was a coward when it came to women. No two ways about it. After Julie's abrupt dismissal, he'd searched for a woman who'd be a sure thing, someone who'd never hurt him no matter what. No such creature existed. The ones who had no spirit, no backbone, also held zero appeal.

He edged close enough to the car for it to recognize he had its clicker in a pocket. Pulling the door open, he got in, doing his damnedest not to think about anything. Not the poor son of a bitch with stage-four small-cell lung cancer. Not Juliana with her sparkling, challenging blue eyes and acres of dark hair.

Never mind the long legs she used to wrap around him and the purring sound she made when she wanted him. His body ached for her, alight with desire. He told it to stand down.

Traffic moved along at fifty miles per hour, so it took him a while to reach the Army post located south of Tacoma. The gate guard was expecting him and waved him through with a smile.

What the hell? Maybe Angus had been something slightly

more important than one more RAF chopper pilot. He'd have to ask him, except the military was even more closemouthed about their exploits than doctors.

He followed the instructions the gate guard provided and pulled the BMW into a convenient parking place adjacent to the airstrip. He'd been told to remain near his car, that Angus would come to him. It was a mild evening for so late in the year. He got out and raised his arms over his shoulders, rotating tight muscles in his back and neck.

The roar of a jet shook the ground, sounding closer than close. Brice looked up in time to spot its sleek form hurtling from the sky. He didn't see it land because of solid fencing between where he stood and the runway. The plane had looked more like a business-class jet than a military transport, but maybe the Army flew them too. Or the Air Force.

About ten minutes later, Angus ambled toward him, a camouflage duffle slung over one shoulder and a black leather bag dangling from his left hand. Tall and rangy, all bones and angles, he stood about an inch taller than Brice's six feet two, but probably weighed thirty pounds less. Black hair fell straight as a stick to his collarbones. A beak of a nose sat over thin lips, a square chin, and a mouthful of very white, very straight teeth.

"Hey there, mate," Angus called. "Damned decent of you to come for me."

Brice clapped him on the back and hit the remote to open the car's trunk. Angus whistled and dropped his gear inside. "I remember this. You bought it and had it shipped home, right?"

"Yup. You should remember. You were there." He pulled the passenger door open and gestured Angus inside.

The Scot fell through the door and scrambled for the seat

belt. "Great to see you. Apologies in advance if I fade out. How far to your place?"

"Depends on traffic. Might be two hours."

"I'd offer to drive, but I'd be a road hazard what with righthand drive hardwired into my brain."

"Yeah. It's always taken me a while to make the transition when I'm on your side of the Atlantic. Not so much the steering wheel being on the wrong side, but everything else is reversed too."

"My point exactly. Except it's yours that's on the 'wrong side.'"

Brice waited until they'd cleared the gate and were heading north on the interstate before starting with the easy questions. "How come the military offers you rides in their planes?"

"I'm in the RAF reserves."

"Not buying it." Brice shook his head. "I know dozens of folks in the reserves, and they fly commercial. The U.K. is smaller, but so's their fleet, plus that looked a whole lot like a business-class jet."

"Good eyes. It's why you're a world-class physician."

Brice snorted. "Spare me. Fancy words won't get you off the hook. Why do you merit perks usually reserved for generals?"

Angus angled his body until he almost faced Brice. "The plane was one of the long-range Gulfstreams. The RAF owns a few of them. They're handy because they can transit the poles and most of the globe without refueling."

"Still doesn't explain why you hitched a ride on it."

"Some questions can't be answered. Not directly. Let's just say I've been helping for years with a type of biological warfare. Some of my experiments have been brilliantly successful, and every once in a while I call in my chips."

It was as perfect an in as he was likely to get. Brice

jumped on it. "Why exactly were you wanting to call in chips? What's unique about our treatment for Sarah Wray? I can name at least ten other patients where we've done the same thing. Double that if we count the ones at the Paris Institute."

Rather than answering, Angus inserted a question of his own. "Did you tell Sarah I was on my way?"

"I did."

"And?" Angus cocked his head to one side watching Brice intently.

"And nothing. She wanted to know why."

"How did you answer her?" Something sharp as glass sat just beneath his question.

"I couldn't since I didn't know. I mentioned you and I had pioneered her treatment, though. Once I said that, she told me she was tired and shooed me out of her room."

"She would." Angus spoke softly, almost to himself. "She'll think I'm here to view her as a fascinating guinea pig, one whose experimental parameters are worthy of attention."

"Cut the crap," Brice said. "What happened between you two?"

Angus was quiet so long, Brice figured he wasn't going to answer, but the Scot started talking out of the blue. "'Tis a verra old story," he began, his brogue thick as clotted cream. "I was her microbiology professor in med school. She was fascinated by the wee critters, as was I. We fell in love with our heads bent over binocular scopes.

"We had two problems. One was dating students was forbidden, but we worked around it by keeping our relationship secret. The other was her illness. She hit a bad patch around the end of her second year of med school. So bad she opted to drop out."

"Opted to?" Brice cut in.

"Had to, really. She'd missed so much, she would have had

to redo the entire second semester. You understand how CF drags at you. She had no energy. The thought of waiting half a year to redo the semester was too much for her." He took a deep, noisy breath. "She jettisoned me along with school."

"I'd put most of that together," Brice said. "Except I wasn't certain who'd dumped whom. Why are you here now?" He nosed the car off the primary interstate onto the freeway leading to Seattle's East Side.

"I'm here to tell her I love her. That I don't care she didn't finish med school. Hell, I don't give a crap if she never works again. I have no idea what her mortality timetable looks like, but if she'll allow me to be part of however much life she has left, it would make me a very happy man."

Brice framed his next question carefully. "Does it mean you'd be willing to move back to the States?"

"If I have to. Why?"

"Her parents are here. So's her twin sister." Brice stopped there. He'd never confided in anyone about Juliana, and he wasn't ready to start with Angus.

"Look, mate. I can live anywhere. So can you, and you know it."

"True enough. We certainly can. Thanks for trusting me. I wish you all the best," Brice said and meant it. "When I first consulted with you on Sarah's case, she'd moved out of immediate danger, but you do know she almost died?"

"Of course I know. How could I not? I'm thorough. I review every case I consult on. Where I was remiss was not disclosing I'd had a personal relationship with her."

Brice dove in headfirst because Angus needed to know how ambivalent Sarah was about being alive. "I'm not certain she was pleased when she found herself back in the land of the living."

"I ken how that works too. You don't have a corner on doctoring the dying, mate." Raw pain roughened his brogue.

"Never claimed to. On a more upbeat note, that two-year-old we talked about will show up tomorrow. Such an interesting story behind the boy. His mother had an affair with a priest—"

"As in a genuine, cassock-wearing padre?" Angus cut in.

"Aye, the same." Brice copied Angus's thick brogue, and the other man broke into laughter.

"Have a care there, laddie. Another attempt like that, and Scotland will bar her doors to you forever."

"A man can dream. Och, to never be faced with haggis again. Or blood pudding."

Angus socked him softly in the arm.

"Oomph. Even your knuckles have angles."

"Thanks for having me on such short notice."

"Thanks for being my friend," Brice replied. "You know how it is."

"Aye, that I do. A piss pot of acquaintances and even more colleagues, but no one you trust enough to bare your soul to."

"You nailed it. Hey, your prediction about fading never happened. Another quarter hour and we'll be home."

"Pithy conversation has a way of keeping one awake."

"Oh, so now it's my fault?" Brice joked.

"Nay, mate. I turned over a whole lot of ways to tell you about Sarah. You saved me the trouble. Be sure and wake me in plenty of time for coffee and a run before we go to work."

"I would absolutely love a running buddy. You're on. I'll wake you at five."

"It can't be light that early."

"It's not. I have headlamps."

"Aye, torches will be just the thing." Angus's words slurred with weariness.

"Another mile. Hang on. We're nearly there. You'll love Lupe."

"You got married?" Shock ratcheted through Angus's words, and he sounded way more awake.

"Oh hell no. She's my housekeeper. Motherly. She'll fuss and cluck over you."

"Brilliant. She can cluck me up to bed."

Brice turned into his drive and activated the electronic gates. They crested the hill, and his house came into view.

"Holy mother of God," Angus gasped. "You live here? It's big enough for fifty."

"Maybe twenty," Brice corrected him and brought the car to a stop. "Come on in. You're too tired to appreciate it tonight, but Lupe and her family decorated the place for Christmas." He pushed his door open and got out of the car. Angus mirrored his actions.

As if on cue, the front door flew open, and Lupe ran lightly down the steps. "You must be doctor friend. Hungry? I make whatever you want. Maybe drink? Wine? Whiskey?"

Angus laughed. "Lupe, I love you already. A nightcap would be appreciated."

"What kind?"

"Single malt Scotch. What else?" He tilted his chin until Brice could almost picture him with bagpipes and a kilt.

"I bring it to your room." Lupe bobbed her head and turned back for the house.

Angus shouldered his duffle, grabbed his bag, and followed her up the brick stairs with Brice bringing up the rear.

Angus had given him a lot to think about. Grist for the proverbial mill. Juliana wasn't the only Wray woman to chase a man away. Granted, her motives were quite different, but the net result had been the same. The words from her text felt as if they'd been stenciled on his soul.

I'm hoping you can forgive me, so I have a prayer of forgiving myself.

Next time they had a private moment, he'd tell her all was forgiven. It was the least he could do. He might still be angry, and he certainly didn't trust her, but those weren't sufficient reasons to withhold forgiveness.

Christ! I sound like a sanctimonious piece of shit.

He waited while Lupe herded Angus to the room she'd made up for him and bid his friend good night.

"Same to you," Angus replied. "Can't wait to get my teeth into that five a.m. run."

"It'll be cold."

"Not as cold as Scotland," Angus countered.

Brice laughed. "Not as damp, either."

"Few places are." Angus laughed. "We Scots are a hardy breed. If we weren't, we'd have died out eons ago."

CHAPTER 12

"Katie. You have to quit worrying about this." If Juliana could have reached through cyberspace and shaken her graduate student, she would have.

"Isn't there some way you could come back here? Not for very long. Just a day or two."

"I'm pretty sure it won't be necessary," she replied, thinking there was no such thing as a "quick trip" to the Nile Delta's hinterlands.

"But you said you walked out on Smithwick. Who knows what the hell he'll do?"

"I walked out on him because the only other option was bashing my fist dead center into his sexist face. I really do need to get moving. I've been late getting to the hospital the past couple of days."

"I understand. Truly, I do. Sorry to be so needy, but walk me through why you're so confident things will work out."

Julie blew out a tight breath. "Because Smithwick's first loyalty is to the university. His next is to the archaeology department. Our find is big. Possibly world changing, once we've moved those bones and artifacts out of the field and can study them properly. Smithwick may be a pompous ass, but he's not going to compromise such a monumental discovery by cuing the world in on how much infighting—and outright theft—mars the hallowed halls."

"Yeah. You're probably right. Thanks, Dr. Wray. I'll try not to bother you again."

"It's not a bother. If something else happens that I need to know about, by all means get hold of me pronto."

Katie signed off. Julie stared at her phone through a count of ten. She hoped she was right about her boss, but men like him were old school. It hadn't yet sunk in that women had rights. Never mind being worthy of those rights because they'd earned them by being more competent—and much harder workers—than their male counterparts.

She threw everything she might need into her car and pulled out of her driveway. Her parents had insisted on sharing a meal with her whenever she got to the hospital. They were clear they didn't care if it was breakfast or lunch or dinner or some hybrid meal that fell between traditional food consumption times.

Julie closed her teeth over her lower lip. They were worried about her, food her mother's panacea for everything. If she dug a little deeper, the one they were truly alarmed about was Sarah. It didn't feel safe to focus on her, so Julie received the brunt of their attention.

Something had definitely changed during Sarah's last cystic fibrosis flareup. Juliana's best guess was she'd come face to face with her mortality and fully embraced death since it meant she didn't have to fight any longer. Though she'd grown visibly stronger each day—even her skin wasn't quite as transparent—she hadn't glommed onto the proof she wouldn't die tomorrow with her usual blend of relief and enthusiasm.

Julie drove on autopilot, her thoughts busy as she viewed

her twin from an entirely different angle. Before, Julie had signed on with Team Parent and begged, cajoled, and cheerlead. Whatever it took to get Sarah past the crisis *du jour*. One huge problem was they'd been doing that for themselves, not for Sarah. None of them could stand the thought of losing her, so they had the doctors pull out all the stops to keep her alive.

It's what families do.

No. It's what first-world families with adequate resources do, she argued.

She'd lived in enough third world countries to embrace and appreciate death for the blessing it was. For a brief time, she'd dated another M.D. He'd joked that this was America where death had become optional.

It wasn't far from the truth.

One thing was certain. She was done playing her usual role. What she'd said to her sister was the party line she'd stick with. She loved her and would support whatever Sarah decided. It wasn't as if she hadn't made the round trip to hell more times than Julie could count. Watching her sister fight for every breath while her scarred lungs seized, drowning in thick mucus, had given her a new interpretation of the term courage.

A quick glance outside told her she'd reach Overlake in about ten minutes. For once, traffic was at least moving on the northern Lake Washington bridge. She thought about calling Smithwick, but it would be the wrong thing to do. By now, he'd made up his mind. Assuming he'd told Orestes to back off, she didn't want to appear to gloat.

What she could do was get hold of her contact at *National Geographic*. Mike Willis sat near the top of the heap of antiquities photographers. If the field trip to her dig site was still on, he'd tell her.

And then maybe she'd have to fly back to Egypt, after all.

She guided the car into a slot, grabbed her computer and bag, and trotted smartly into the hospital. Over the days she'd been visiting Sarah, she'd figured out the most expeditious routes from Point A to Point B. It was around eleven, so maybe she and her folks could have lunch at the "normal" time. It would please them. Their military backgrounds meant they liked "normal" and "regular."

She caught a nurse's eye, and they buzzed her into the ICU. Sarah was alone and smiled when she saw her. Julie held up a hand to indicate she'd be there in a flash and hurriedly donned the requisite gloves, gown, and mask. She'd be delighted when they transferred her sister to a less germ-free environment.

"Hiya!" She moved into Sarah's glassed-in enclosure.

"Hi, yourself."

"Where are the folks?"

"They called. Dad had some conference thingie come up. Someone wants to pick his brain about Iraq or Afghanistan." She rolled her eyes. "He lives for stuff like that."

"He does indeed." Julie perched on the foot of the bed facing her twin. "You really are looking a whole lot better."

Sarah's smile faded, replaced by a serious expression. "I know, huh? Beyond that, I feel better than I have in the last two or three years. I'd been heading downhill for a longtime, but I was in full denial."

"Why?"

"Because if I admitted how sick I was, I…" She coughed and tried again. "Okay. No more secrets. Last time I got this sick, I promised myself I wouldn't go through it again. That I'd…take care of things before I sank into purgatory for like the fortieth time."

Julie nodded and selected her words carefully. "I'm not questioning your decision or your right to choose the where and how of your death, but what was it about your last bout that made you decide it wasn't worth it anymore?"

Sarah angled her head to one side. "You really do want to know, don't you?"

"Yes. I do."

Sarah pushed her dark hair out of her face. "It wasn't just one thing, but a whole lot of little ones. Cumulative, I guess." She extended the fingers of one hand, counting on them. "One. I wasn't well enough to keep working. Two. I was tired of the pitying glances people angled my way when they thought I wasn't looking."

Sarah hesitated. "And that includes from you and the folks."

"I'm sorry."

"Don't be. It means you care, but, like most of us when we're confronted with something we can't control and don't understand very well, we establish a safe distance."

Julie started to protest she hadn't done that, or if she had, she hadn't meant it that way, but she kept the words inside. Instead, she said, "Go on."

"Not so much more. I can't have kids. Not with all the drugs I have to take. I've never had a man interested enough to get past the specter of my impending death." She shrugged. "You'd think with all those movies like *Love Story* out there, I'd have found someone."

Julie's eyes stung with tears, but she blinked them away. This wasn't about her. Careful of the tubes and wires, she gathered Sarah into her arms. "I've always loved you."

"Not true." Sarah's voice was muffled. "You hated me over Brice, but it's okay because I hated myself." She pushed out of Julie's arms. "You have no idea how good it felt to finally clear my conscience on that one."

"You could have told me anytime."

"No. I wasn't brave enough. I've had you and Mom and

Dad. And a few friends from nursing school. That's it. My social circle was too limited to risk alienating anyone."

"I understand. More than you think I do, and you're right about my temper. I told my department head off just yesterday."

"You didn't." Sarah's eyes widened.

"Oh yeah. I did. It felt damned good, and it's one of the plusses of having tenure. The old creep can't fire me. He could if I burned crosses in lawns or committed criminal offenses, but telling him off will never make the penal code hit parade."

A look that was part shock, part terror, and part sheer joy washed over Sarah's face. She was facing the rest of the ICU; Julie's back was to it. "What?" she asked and turned in time to see Brice and another smocked man—presumably another M.D.—on their way to Sarah's enclosure.

Sarah had turned on her side. "Tell them I'm tired," she begged and placed a hand over the side of her face.

Them? Must mean Sarah knew the other man. "Who is he?" Julie asked.

"Doesn't matter," Sarah moaned. "Make them go away. Sisterly solidarity and all that."

Uncertain, Juliana got to her feet. She'd just turned, intent on trying to honor her sister's wishes, when Brice and the other man walked into the enclosure. Brice nodded her way. He might have been smiling, but it was impossible to tell under his mask.

"May I introduce the other Wray sister," he said. "Angus, this is Juliana. Juliana, meet Dr. Angus MacDuff."

Automatically, she extended a gloved hand his way. "Nice to meet you, Doctor."

"The pleasure is mine," he replied in a thick, Scottish brogue. "Sarah told me she had a twin."

Aha! Sarah does know him.

Brice motioned to her. "Let's take a walk, Julie. Give them some time alone."

A stifled moan rose from Sarah. It galvanized Julie into action. "Uh, she says she's too tired for visitors. Maybe you could come back later?"

Angus, who'd been focused on Sarah's prone form, turned to face Julie. His dark eyes blazed with determination. "I traveled all the way from Paris. I most certainly am not about to come back later."

Moving to the bed with coiled precision and grace, he dropped a hand on Sarah's arm. "I'm afraid it won't be quite so simple to give me the slip this time, my dear. I've had a lot of years to think about you. Nay, about us."

"Come on," Brice urged. Sliding the door to Sarah's cubicle open, he motioned Juliana through. When she hesitated, he added, "Angus won't hurt her. Please."

Reluctantly, Julie left her sister's side. "Who the hell is he?" she asked Brice once the door to her sister's room had slid shut.

He removed his mask, gloves, and gown. "Get rid of all that stuff and come outside the unit with me, where we can talk privately."

Mystified, she complied. Once they were walking down a corridor, she sputtered, "How is it you know something about Sarah that I don't?"

He turned an infuriating grin her way. It had the same boyish quality that had stolen her heart as a sixteen-year-old. "Is that the worst part?" he inquired archly. "Me knowing something you don't?"

She ducked down a relatively deserted side corridor, and he followed her. "This should be private enough," she said. "Now spill."

"He was one of her professors in medical school. They had an affair." Brice took a measured breath. "Do you remember the bad time she had at the end of her second year of med school?"

"Of course I do. Question is how do you know about it? You and I had split up something like four years before."

His cheeks developed a rosy hue, but he held her gaze. "Because I kept tabs on both of you. Your parents and my mom stayed in touch, so I'd hear news from time to time."

"Mmph. Would have been nice if they'd told me," she muttered.

"Kind of like they were consorting with the enemy?"

Julie shook her head. "No. They never knew about us. Not much, anyway."

"Keep telling yourself that, sister. My mom knew, which meant your parents did too."

Heat rose from the open neck of her T-shirt to the top of her head, but she couldn't go there. Not with him. She'd confront her humiliation in private. "Sarah. What about Sarah and this Dr. MacDuff?"

Brice shrugged. They were lovers but kept it on the Q.T. since he was her professor. After she nearly died, she told him to go away, to find a woman who could give him children and a full life."

Julie swallowed hard. Tears were close to the surface— again. All the ones she hadn't shed for her sister during the years she'd put on a brave face.

Brice was eying her as intently as he probably viewed specimens beneath his microscope. "Juliana?"

"I'm all right. Go on." Her words didn't match her expression or her body language, but Brice didn't point it out. The air between them vibrated with her longing to throw herself into his arms, but she'd lost the right to do that when she refused to listen to him.

"Angus did move on. Tried to, anyway. He married once that I know of, but it didn't last long. He and I have known one another professionally for over a decade, but we only began working together about five years ago."

"What does that have to do with my sister?"

"Patience never was one of your long suits," he observed.

"Touché." She spun one hand in a come along motion, still fighting an inane desire to throw her arms around him and hang on.

"Angus phoned—well, actually it was Skype, but that's splitting hairs—quite recently. Told me he was on his way stateside, and he'd be working with me on the next phase of Sarah's treatment. At the time, I had no idea they had history, but when I picked him up from the airport last night, I asked a lot of questions. We've shared plenty of patients, and he never felt the need to be present for any of them."

"Which means you just found out about him and Sarah too?" Julie arched a brow.

"Yup. It's exactly what that means."

"What did he tell you—about Sarah?" Julie pressed for more details.

"That he'd always loved her, and he was going to take his best shot at convincing her to become his wife."

Julie slumped against a nearby wall, too overcome to speak. When she located her voice again, she said, "But that's wonderful. Aside from it being incredibly romantic, it might be just the thing to rekindle her interest in living."

Compassion flared in the depths of Brice's hazel eyes. "Maybe. Don't get your hopes up, though."

"Why not? She's better. Even I can see that, and she admitted she feels more energetic than she has in years. Having Angus here now is brilliant. Just the added element to—"

He dropped a heavy hand on her shoulder. "Juliana. You cannot live her life. Stop trying." Before she had a chance to fire off a snappy rejoinder, he added, "Oh yes, in line with your text, I forgive you. 'Tis the season and all, plus I suppose I forgave you a long time ago, but you weren't around for me to tell you."

Her mouth fell open, and she fought for words. Before she came up with anything profound—or anything at all—he spun and started down the side hallway.

"Wait," she croaked.

"Nothing to wait for." He stopped long enough to turn back toward her. "Forgiving you does not mean I don't think what you did was a slap in the face to all the time we had in as a couple. It was, and I don't trust you as far as I can see you."

He did go then, leaving her fighting a combination of fury, resignation, and the sad, slow realization she still loved him. If she'd had doubts about the last, they evaporated, blown away like so much pixie dust.

Maybe she should pack up and go back to the dig site. A place people had to work to find her. The more she thought about the idea, the more appeal it held. Sarah was out of the woods. Her parents had everything they needed in each other.

Something Brice said nagged. Her parents. They'd known about her and him, which meant they also knew about Sarah. How many other secrets were they sitting on? She bit back a snort. This was what happened when both your parents had backgrounds in military intelligence, and everything was on a "need to know" basis.

Maybe thinking about them alerted her mother's parental radar because her phone dinged with its text tone.

The ICU nurse said you're here somewhere. Meet us in the cafeteria, honey.

Julie re-read the text. Nowhere to hide. Not the ICU with Sarah and the Scottish doctor. Certainly not her car. Besides, she hated lying. At her age, she shouldn't even be considering it. Blowing out a ragged breath, she texted back.

See you in five minutes.

Her mom replied with a smiley face.

She set off at a brisk walk and pushed through a nearby door. Surely five minutes' worth of fresh air would clear her jumbled thoughts enough to make her decent company through a one-hour meal.

She hoped.

If fifteen years away from Brice hadn't been enough to purge him from her heart, soul, and mind, what chance did five minutes have of doing anything?

CHAPTER 13

*B*rice had to remove himself from Juliana's side. If he'd stayed, they'd have ended up in each other's arms. He'd recognized the softness in her eyes, the emotion that turned them liquid with longing, and he wasn't strong enough to resist her. He made a beeline for the locker room. It was one place she couldn't follow him, and he needed to think.

His body hummed with needing her. Touching her shoulder had kindled vivid memories of them straining together, pushing closer and closer to release as they made love. They'd both been virgins, and they'd figured things out as they went. The feel of her nipples, hard as marbles and pressed against his chest, was as intense as if they'd just gotten up from tangled sheets. If he closed his eyes, he could feel the heat of her vault closing around him as he sank into her.

His balls ached. His cock was rigid with desire. The locker room was empty, and he ducked into a stall, unzipping before he even had the door locked. Feeling furtive, guilty as hell, he wrapped his fingers around his burning erection and fantasized making love with her. A handful of strokes was all it took before his cock shuddered in his hand, semen jetting from it into a wad of bathroom tissue.

Feeling like an idiot, he stuffed his still-erect cock back into his pants and willed his breathing to return to normal. Not much he could do about his face, which had to be flushed from his orgasm. He waited for a few moments before exiting the stall. Luck was with him, and the locker room was still empty.

He stood in front of his open locker, considering his options for the remainder of the day. He wasn't on call; another pulmonologist was, which meant he could work on damn near anything.

Or nothing. I almost never take any time for myself.

The more he thought about heading home for a few hours, the better he liked the idea. For one thing, it lessened his odds of running into Juliana. She still read him well, and he needed to carve out a more centered place before he faced her again. He would need to stop by and see his patients before he left for the day, though. Millicent Davidson as well, to reassure her everything would be fine.

He fished his phone from a pocket and texted Lupe.

Did Timmy arrive?

Her response was almost immediate and consisted of a string of smiling faces and hearts.

Brice texted back.

Tell him I'll be home around the middle of the afternoon. He and I can go to the park.

Another smiling face followed by:

He eat and nap. Ready for you when you get here.

Brice smiled at the display. Lupe was a godsend. The perfect combination of mother and friend.

Julie's face rose before him, so real it made his heart ache. Lupe was wonderful, but what he longed for was a wife, children of his own. Before he got lost in his earlier funk, he shut his locker and headed off to do rounds. Yesterday's surgery patient wasn't really "his," but he checked on him anyway. He was doing as well as could be expected. Everyone else on his patient roster was moving toward discharge.

He started walking toward the ICU and Sarah's bed but hesitated, not wanting to disturb her and Angus. After moments of indecision ticked past, he decided to stop anyway. She was his patient, and he needed to let Angus know he was leaving early.

If Juliana was there, which she probably wasn't for the same reasons he'd had second and third thoughts about horning in on Sarah and Angus's reunion, he'd smile pleasantly and go on his way. He still needed to see Millicent, but it wouldn't take long.

After that, Timmy would be waiting. Brice liked the idea of sharing the park with its pond and ducks and pigeons with the boy. They could play on the swings and slide. He curved his fingers and dragged them through his curly mop. He needed a haircut, but it was fairly low priority.

Ready as he'd ever be, he pushed into the ICU. Relief weakened his knees after a quick scan verified Juliana wasn't there. She'd been at the top of his worry list. Not disturbing Angus had been only an excuse. He grabbed a gown, gloves, and a mask and let himself into Sarah's cubicle.

Angus sat at the midpoint of the bed, cradling one of Sarah's hands between his. He twisted his neck and glanced at Brice. "Cheers, mate."

"Cheers back at both of you." Brice looked from one to the other, trolling for cues. Both Sarah and Angus appeared happy, relaxed. Surely, it meant their discussion had gone well.

"If you're here for daily rounds," Sarah said brightly, "I've already got a highly competent M.D., so feel free to check me off today's list."

Brice came closer and punched Angus lightly in the shoulder. "We need to get you added to our staff roster, so you'll have hospital privileges. A badge, door codes, the whole nine yards."

"Aye. Already thought of that. I'll stop by admin when I leave here."

It was a decent lead-in, so Brice jumped on it. "I have one more patient to see and then I'm going home for the day. That little boy we talked about arrived, and I'd like to spend some time with him."

"What little boy?" Sarah glued her gaze on him, eyes so like Julie's they always gave him pause.

Angus saved Brice the trouble of picking his way through the minefield of patient confidentiality by saying, "The wee lad and his mum were in an auto accident. Brice happened to be there. Both will be fine, but the mum needed a few more days in hospital."

Sarah tilted her head to one side, eyes turning mellow just like her sister's. "Awww. You volunteered to take care of the child, you old softie."

Brice nodded. "'Fraid so. Angus, how will you get back to my house tonight?"

"Don't wait dinner on me. I'll have someone in admin find me a taxi when I'm ready to leave."

"It's okay," Sarah spoke up. "You can have dinner with Brice. I'm not going anywhere."

Angus turned to face her. "I already ordered something special just for the two of us. You may even get candlelight." Bending close, he kissed both her cheeks. "Until you get out of here, I'm spending as much time with you as I can. Once they spring you, I'm not leaving your side."

The smile that illuminated Sarah's gaunt face was so

radiant, Brice felt he was intruding on a private moment. "See you whenever you get home, Angus. Sarah, I'll stop by tomorrow."

"Bye, mate. See you soon." Angus waved.

Brice grinned—their joy was so infectious, it was hard not to—and left Sarah's enclosure. Lost in thought, he almost ran into Erika.

She hooked an arm through his and dragged him off to one side. "I have no idea how you pulled it off," she whispered, "but Dr. MacDuff is perfect. Sarah's dragged all four limbs back into the land of the living. Heart and soul too. I have to admit I was plenty worried about her. So worried, I talked with the twin, but she already knew."

"Yes, Juliana's always been pretty quick on the uptake where Sarah's concerned. I didn't pull anything off," he added, keeping his voice low. "They've known one another for years. If this is anyone's coup, it's Angus's."

"Whatever. I'm just delighted this story will have a happy ending. For now. So many of ours don't."

Brice understood all too well. "Thanks for caring."

She shrugged, looking uncomfortable. "It's what I do. I've considered getting out, doing something easier after all my years in the trenches, but something draws me back. There's passion in medicine. We save lives."

He gave the nurse a quick hug. "That we do, Erika. More you than me, most of the time."

"But you do all the splashy stuff." She tilted her head back to look at him.

"And you make sure that splashy stuff doesn't go south. It's a match made in heaven. I'm off to see the Davidson woman. If you need anything, page me."

Erika cast an appraising glance his way. "I heard you'll have the boy for a while. Whole hospital knows by now. You're a good man, Doc." She looked like she wanted to say more, but instead she turned and walked to her desk, settling in front of her screen.

Brice discarded his mask, gloves, and gown and headed for Med-Surg. The charge nurse, a youngish redhead he didn't know, nodded pleasantly after coming close enough to take a look at his ID tag. "I'll be in room six," he told her.

"Millie already has a visitor," she informed him, "but the more the merrier."

Curious, Brice traversed the corridor and listened before knocking. A man with a U.K. accent, Irish not Scottish, was laughing and chatting with Millicent Davidson.

Was it the mysterious Father John? If so, Millicent had done more than pay lip service to his suggestion. Brice knocked and strode into the room. Millie looked ever so much better, not from a bruising perspective, but her eyes were alight with happiness, and she'd graduated to no longer needing an IV.

"Dr. McKinnon, I'd like you to meet Father John."

Brice extended a hand; the priest got to his feet and shook it. He wore dark slacks and a tweed jacket tossed over a dark shirt, but a clerical collar circled his neck. "Sure and 'tis a right pleasure," the priest said, following it with, "'Tis on account of you, I know I have a son."

"Timmy is the reason I stopped by today." Brice shifted his focus to Millicent. "He made it to my house fine. My housekeeper is doting on him, and I'm on my way home to take him to the park."

"Thank you so much for everything." She smiled warmly. "My doctor says I should be able to go home day after tomorrow. Of course, I don't have a car anymore, but—"

"I'll see Timmy home safe," Father John broke in. "And I'll help you file an insurance claim too. Once we see what they'll give you for your car, we'll go shopping and get you another."

"Maybe." Millicent shrugged. "Mine wasn't worth much."

"Don't you worry. I already told you the Church will help as needed."

He turned toward Brice. "You certainly don't have to, but I'd take it as a great kindness if I could make an appointment to stop by and meet my…" He hesitated and stood taller. "My son. Sorry. 'Twill take a wee bit of time to get used to the idea."

Brice glanced at Millicent. "Okay with you?"

"More than okay."

Father John drew his brows together. "Millie was trying to protect me, and I love her for it. She's truly one of Our Father's blessed creatures. I won't have to leave the priesthood, but I will gladly shoulder my fatherly responsibilities toward my son. I expect 'twill take a wee bit of time before he accepts me, but I have infinite patience. The Church will help with the expenses of raising him as well."

Brice frowned, not sure if he should ask but wanting to know. "Did something change? I was fairly certain the Church took a dim view of such things."

"Sure and they do." The priest nodded. "Problem was so many of us were celibate but not precisely chaste, the Pope issued an edict addressing this specific issue. 'Tis about the children's needs. mind you, not about me."

"Timmy will love you," Millicent said. "He's asked about his father so many times. Right now, he's easy enough to put off, but that won't last through too many more years."

"Won't be an issue any longer." The priest faced Brice. "When would be convenient for a first visit with my son?"

Brice started to say anytime, but what he didn't know about raising young children was legion. "What do you think?" he asked Millicent. "You know your boy better than anyone."

She screwed her face into a mask of concentration. Clearly, this was important, and she wanted to maximize the chances of it going well. She cast a worried glance at the priest. "Don't take this wrong, but—"

"Millie," he broke in. "Sorry for interrupting, but I want what's best for young Timmy too. I'm just as clueless as the good doctor here about the care and feeding of toddlers."

Brice bit back a smile. The priest had seen through Brice's reason for punting the question into Millie's court.

"All right. I'll just say this right out." Millicent pushed the button to raise her bed to a more upright position. "Today was a big day for Timmy. He left the hospital—and being close to me. He's in a new place with a woman he only just met. I'm sure she's wonderful"—this time Millicent's doe-like gaze settled on Brice—"but she's still new."

"Would you rather wait until you and he are home?" Father John asked.

"It's only a couple of days," Brice tossed in, thinking perhaps having Millicent present would be best.

"It's what I was about to suggest," she murmured.

"How about this?" Father John looked hopeful. "I'll come by and pick you up when the hospital discharges you. Then we'll swing by Dr. McKinnon's and get Timmy, and then I can drive both of you home. If things go well, I'll bide a bit, make sure you're comfortable and can get around enough to manage."

"You don't have to—" she began.

"I know. I want to."

"In that case, I accept."

"I'm going to get going," Brice said. "I'll call you early this evening and put Timmy on the phone. You can tell one another good night."

"Thank you again, Doctor."

"No thanks needed. Happy to do it." He transferred his attention to the priest. "Nice to meet you, Father."

"Even nicer to meet you. I have no way to repay you for the kindness you've done, but good deeds have a way of repaying the doer tenfold."

"Sounds suspiciously biblical."

"Almost everything is when you cut away the fat. I take it you're not a religious man."

Brice bit back a stock response. The priest deserved more than a cursory answer. "I wouldn't say I'm not religious, but I've never followed any of the organized religions." He took a breath and blew it out. "No one could sit with a dying patient and not appreciate the numinous aspect of passing from this life to whatever comes next."

"Aye. Birth and death are both miracles. I understand you right enough, and I'd love to talk more, but I won't hold you here nattering philosophy with me. Millie and I have a lot to catch up on."

Brice smiled and left them. He nodded to the charge nurse and headed for his locker to change into street clothes. Some of his cronies lived in scrubs. But the hospital had a laundry, and he preferred them to take care of his scrubs and lab coats. It had never felt fair to bring blood-stained clothing home for Lupe to wash.

As he covered the distance to his BMW, anxious to get home, he whistled a tune his mother used to sing. So far today, two long-lost couples had found their way back to one another. Was the energy of the Christmas season whipping Cupid into a frenzy?

He laughed, but it held a bitter edge. Cupid was Valentine's Day, not Christmas. And if the pudgy little elf was passing out connubial bliss, how come he'd avoided Brice?

"What exactly is it I want?" he asked the confines of his

car, not expecting an answer but needing to hear the question out loud.

The few miles between the hospital and his home would flash by quickly enough, and he wanted to be totally present for Timmy, not lost in what-ifs about Juliana.

Was it too late for them?

He suspected the answer was yes. Fifteen years was a really long time. Far too long to just pick up where they'd left off. Hell, they'd been kids. Wet behind the ears. Neither of them knew much of anything about living, except it wasn't how they'd have characterized themselves at the time.

The hubris of youth was legendary. They'd thought they knew everything, had the world by the balls. Lessons like compassion and humility would happen far in the future.

He pulled the car over a couple of blocks from home, determined to come to a more settled place. Either he sat with Juliana and they talked this out, or he let it go forever.

No middle ground. He hadn't exactly not thought about her in years, but she hadn't haunted him like she was now. Could he go back to before Sarah's illness had brought Julie front and center in his life?

Not just can I? Do I want to?

He shut his eyes. This wasn't a place for lists of pros and cons. He'd nursed an empty spot ever since Juliana kicked him out of her life. He'd spackled it over and made it shiny, glossy even, but a hole remained beneath his repair work. One which would apparently never heal enough to let him love someone else. If it was going to, he'd have gotten past this long since.

He opened his eyes and put the car back into drive. Maybe it was being surrounded by lovebirds making second-time-around relationships work, but he'd find a time and sit with Julie, see if they could unearth common ground. He'd come clean, tell her he'd never stopped loving her and see where it led.

She might spurn him a second time, but at least he would have gone down fighting. Before, she hadn't even been willing to talk with him. This time, he had a feeling she'd hear him out. What would happen after that was anyone's guess.

Relieved to have picked a path, he pulled into his driveway anxious to get to know Timmy Davidson better. For once it wasn't raining, which meant they'd have a grand time in the park. He and his father had spent time playing in parks just like the one near his home. As he'd grown older, they'd graduated to shooting hoops, fishing, hunting, and jogging together. A career Marine aviator, his dad could have been a poster boy for physical fitness.

As he got out of his car and strode briskly toward the front steps, he vowed to do his damnedest to patch things up with Juliana. He wanted her by his side forever, wanted to see their children grow up…

The door flew open before he got to it, and Timmy raced toward him. "You're here," he crowed.

"I am," Brice agreed. "Ready for the park?"

Lupe crowded close behind the boy, chattering away in Spanish.

"Park. Park," Timmy echoed and turned to Lupe winding a hand into her skirts. "Picnic."

Brice raised his eyebrows, and Lupe laughed. "I make snacks and drinks. I get and put in car."

"Great!" Brice picked Timmy up. "Looks like we won't starve. Ready to roll, little man?"

"I am." Timmy tilted his chin at a jaunty angle, and Brice carried him to the car intent on strapping him into the passenger seat.

"Wait!" Lupe dragged a child safety seat onto the porch. "Need this."

Brice set Timmy down. "Wait right here."

The boy's eyes widened as he took in the sleek car. He ran his fingertips over the shiny paint. While he was absorbed, Brice fetched the car seat. Lupe followed him, a wicker picnic basket dangling from one hand. He was examining the safety seat to determine how to hook the seat belt through it when Lupe pushed between him and the open car door.

"Let me, Doc. Seat go in back."

"Lucky you're here," he said. "Otherwise I'd have been forced to resort to You Tube."

"We both lucky," she said and straightened. "All ready. Watch." Scooping up the boy, she placed him in the seat and showed Brice how the straps clicked into place.

"Home in a couple hours," he told her.

"Where other doctor?" she asked.

"At the hospital. Don't worry about dinner for him."

Lupe kissed Timmy and shut the back door. "Have wonderful time," she said and walked back into the house.

Brice got in and started the car. Timmy made *vroom-vroom* noises from the backseat. "Louder," he urged. "You're helping, and the car likes it."

CHAPTER 14

*J*uliana and her parents had moved to one of the sheltered smoking alcoves beneath an overhang. Her father pulled out the pipe he allowed himself on special occasions and tamped tobacco into it.

"So happy for Sarah," her mother was saying. She'd voiced some iteration of the words at least a dozen times.

"We were quite emphatic she was making a mistake when she told him to go away," Chris broke in, also repeating himself.

"How come you never told me?" Julie asked.

Ariel skewered her with a maternal glare. "You wouldn't have liked us sharing private items from your life with your sister, would you?"

"Uh, no. I guess not."

"We've waited a long time for you girls to settle down," her father said.

"No kidding," Ariel muttered. "First, we waited for you to finish school."

"Yes, and after that, we waited while you made tenure younger and faster than anyone on record," her father cut in.

"When was that?" her mother piped up. "Half a dozen years ago?"

"Stop." Julie held up one hand, palm facing out. "I don't tell you two how to live your lives."

"Of course not," Chris said, logic dripping from his words. "We're your parents."

"Which means we have carte blanche to offer unwanted advice." Ariel turned a toothy grin her way.

"Did Brice tell you his mother will be here for Christmas?" Chris's question was like grinding salt in the open wound her heart had turned into.

"No reason for him to tell me," she mumbled, "but Mother did."

"Yup, in a text. Well, we're excited to see her again," Ariel said.

"Even better, she finally met someone," Chris tossed out. "A Marine doctor with a teenaged son."

"Susan is more excited than I've heard her in years," Ariel trilled. "She lost Brice's dad almost twenty years ago."

"We're happy for her," Chris chimed in.

"She says the boy reminds her a lot of Brice at that age." Ariel's smile widened.

"What happened to his mother?" Julie asked, wondering if a divorced Marine was a good marital prospect. The service either made or broke marriages, without much middle ground.

"It's very sad," Ariel replied.

"Yes. She died from cancer a few months before her widowed husband and son were transferred to the base where Sue teaches." Chris got his two cents' worth in.

A light went off in Julie's mind, its flare bright enough to sear her corneas if it had been real. "Explains why the boy reminds her of Brice. They both lost a parent."

"Exactly." Her father clapped her on the back. "Anyway,

she and her fiancé and soon-to-be stepson will be staying with Brice. Ariel and I will be spending Christmas Eve with them, and we're hoping you'll join us."

"We'd love to have Sarah there too. Angus says he's certain she'll be out of the hospital by then, but she'll still be regaining her strength," Ariel added.

"You do know Dr. MacDuff is bunking with Brice?" Her father quirked a silver brow her way.

"Which means it's a logical place for Sarah once she's discharged," Ariel went on.

Julie's stomach twisted into a knot of tension. It was tough to stay put, but her father's hand was still resting on her shoulder. Heavy. Determined. It made fleeing out of the question, which was probably why he'd put it there in the first place.

"I should go back to Egypt," she mumbled.

"On Christmas?" Censure ran beneath her father's question.

"Not just Christmas, but the first one you'll have spent with your family in forever." Ariel ladled parental guilt into the equation.

Julie shut her eyes to buy herself time to think. Her folks hadn't ganged up on her since she was in high school, but apparently all bets were off. She blinked a few times and looked from one of them to the other. Love shone from their eyes. They wanted the best for her, and from their perspective "the best" included a husband and children. Not a lonely life camped in a tent at dig sites.

With his unfailing daddy radar, Chris tightened his grip on her shoulder. "I gave a big chunk of my soul to the Marines. Your mother did too, but we always had each other for balance. We'd pull one another back when we got in too deep. So deep, we might not have had an easy time living in a world where the Marines weren't everything."

"You saw it growing up." Her mother apparently couldn't remain silent any longer. "All those failed Marine marriages where one or both partners couldn't compete with the siren call of danger and adventure."

"I haven't forgotten," Julie answered. "In truth, it was the first thing that popped into my mind when you said Susan's new love was in the service and raising a boy by himself. I assumed he'd gotten divorced and wondered if he'd make her a good husband."

"Do you remember Brice's father?" Chris asked.

"Not very well," she admitted.

"He was a stellar human being," Chris said. "He loved his family, flying, and the Marines in that order. And he never, never got his priorities mixed up."

"It was such a sad day when we received news of his death," Ariel murmured. "I stayed strong for Susan, but it took all my years in the military not to break down at his funeral."

Chris caught Julie's gaze and held it. "You'll be at Brice's on Christmas Eve?"

"Please? For Susan. She'll be delighted to see you again. You were always one of her favorite pupils. She told me over and over she wasn't surprised by how far you've risen." Ariel joined the stare-down.

"It might be uncomfortable." Julie swallowed hard. "Brice isn't overly fond of me, and I don't blame him."

"Have you tried sitting down? Talking with him?" Chris asked, adding, "We know what happened. It's another of those things we never brought up. For obvious reasons."

"Yes, but we kept hoping the two of you would find your way back to each other," her mother said.

Julie shook her head. "The time for me to have done that was fifteen years ago."

"Those types of discussions don't have a season." Her mother offered an encouraging smile.

"Tell him you're sorry," Chris urged.

"I just did that."

"And?" Ariel leaned toward her.

"He said he'd forgiven me a long time ago, but that what I did wasn't justified, and he doesn't trust me."

"Perfect!" Ariel clapped her hands together.

Julie shook her shoulder out from under her father's iron grip. "Huh? How the hell is that perfect? I don't get it."

"He's being honest about how he feels," her mother replied.

"Yes, and if he didn't care about you, he'd have simply said he's forgiven you and it's all water under the bridge. If he's still viewing you in terms of your trustworthiness quotient, he hasn't given up—or moved on. Trust me on that. I'm a man, and we know these things."

Hope swept through her, but she pushed it to a distant place, one where it wouldn't get in the way. "Brice aside, there's another problem. I really may have to return to Egypt."

"Eventually, sure," Ariel said. "But why in the next handspan of days?"

"The other professor on site is claiming my find as his."

Chris drew his brows into a thick, concerned line. "Can't you square it away after the first of the year?"

"Normally, yes. One of my grad students got hold of me, frantic. Her dissertation research hinges on this dig site. The other professor, Orestes Conom, had already called in *National Geographic* to send a photographer to document 'his' monumental find. When Katie, my student, protested, he told her she'd have to come up with another dissertation topic because one of his students would be taking this one."

"You have connections at *National Geographic*," her mother spoke up.

Julie twisted her mouth into a crooked grin. "You two are how I learned to stand up for myself and fight back. I do indeed have *NG* connections, and I've already talked with them. Further, I rousted the head of the archaeology department to alert him we had problems."

Her father made a sour face. "That stuffy old Brit. Smithwick, wasn't it?"

"The same. He's a sexist ass who blew me off. Said I'd earned my chops and to stand aside so Orestes could do the same. He didn't seem to get it that Orestes hadn't earned the right to stake a claim to any of the dig, let along the lower level." She sucked in a tight breath. "I told Smithwick I'd already spoken with *National Geographic* and filed a complaint with the university ethics committee."

"That's my girl." Chris's eyes shone with approval.

"We'll see," Julie retorted. "I haven't heard from anyone recently. Not my grad student, and not Smithwick. But if the shit hits the fan, I will have to catch the first plane I can—actually a series of them—to return to the dig site. Orestes is a bully, but he's afraid of me. Only reason he's doing this is because I'm not there."

"You let me know," her father said. "I can put you on a military plane. You'll get there faster. Much faster."

She grinned. "For a minute there, I was expecting you to say you'd fly me yourself."

He grinned back. "I let my certification for the big stuff go after I retired, but I still piddle around in the smaller twin engine jobs and jets."

"Egypt aside, you do need to talk with Brice," her mother said.

"What about letting the man lead?" Julie countered. "I

reached out to him; he responded and kind of kicked the door shut in my face."

"What do you want?" Ariel answered with a question of her own.

"I don't know," Julie replied. "Some days, I want what he and I used to have. Others, I recognize we're different than we were as college undergrads. Really different. We'll have to figure out who we are today and forge new ways of being together."

"You have history," her mother insisted.

"Common ground," her dad chimed in. "It's worth a lot. Kind of a souls-singing-to-each-other maneuver."

"Why, darling." Ariel gazed fondly at her husband. "What a fanciful, romantic thing to say. Other than the word maneuver, that is."

"I try." He scooted next to her and draped an arm around her shoulders.

Julie stood. "I'm going to stop by Sarah's room, and then I'm going home. See you both tomorrow."

"Same time, same location, soldier," her father quipped as if he were issuing orders.

"I love you guys."

"We love you too," Ariel said. "We try not to be intrusive, but we decided Brice was the man for you long ago."

"You got lucky," her father said.

"Yeah? How's that?" It was impossible not to excuse her father for damn near anything. He was so forthright and sincere, and he meant well.

"For whatever reason, you have another shot at this."

"Don't blow it," Ariel tossed in.

"Geez. Don't know if I can take the pressure." She stooped to kiss her dad on the cheek, her mom on the forehead, and then shouldered her bags and walked back inside.

She was well on her way to the ICU before she realized

her dad had loaded his pipe but never lit it. Either the conversation had distracted him, or the pipe had provided a convenient prop to move her to a location more conducive to private conversation.

Her dad was nothing if not a shrewd tactician, so anything was possible.

She entered the ICU and set her things near the door. Erika nodded pleasantly, and Julie gowned up to see her sister. Once she got close to the room, she saw the Scottish doctor sitting on the edge of Sarah's bed, holding her hand.

Who was this Angus MacDuff? Why hadn't Sarah ever mentioned him? She'd had years to talk with Julie but chose not to. Why? More importantly, clearly the doctor had known about her sister for eleven years, give or take. Why show up now? She'd had brushes with death before. What was it about this one that flagged his attention?

"Are you planning to go inside?" Erika's voice next to her made her jump. "Sorry, didn't mean to startle you."

"Yeah, I am. I was thinking."

"About what?" Erika's question was commonplace yet held worlds of significance.

Julie shrugged. "Lots of things. Sarah never told me about him."

"Maybe it hurt too much to talk about."

The words hit Julie like a fist to her midsection. She understood things being so painful you did your damnedest to distance yourself. She also appreciated that the technique didn't work worth a crap.

"Maybe so," Julie murmured and reached for the sliding door.

Erika wrapped a hand around her arm. "He's a talented healer. I've worked with him on patient care over our telemedicine network."

"If he weren't, my sister wouldn't let him within ten feet

of her. She's always had a sixth sense about things like that. You know she's a nurse, right?"

Erika nodded. "Yes, I do know. If the last few days are any indication, she'll be back to work before long—presuming she wants to go."

Julie walked into Sarah's cubicle. "Hey there. I wanted to stop in before I left for home."

Angus stood and angled his head her way. "I was just going to see to our dinner arrangements. Bet you'd like a word with your sister without my mangy presence hanging about."

Maybe it was the words. Maybe the brogue, but Julie broke into a hearty laugh. "I think I'm going to like you."

"Excellent. Because I plan to be a permanent fixture."

"Permanent is relative." Sarah tried for a sober note but didn't quite manage it.

"Not in my case, it's not," he retorted and aimed his next words at Julie. "Lovely to see you again. Looking forward to getting to know you better."

"Me too," Julie answered automatically, surprised she meant the words. Usually, it took her years to warm to anyone.

"Back soon, darling." Angus waved and left Sarah's room.

Julie stared at her twin, not sure where to start.

Sarah saved her the trouble. "I never told you about Angus for two reasons. The first was I was really, really sick. It was the first time I expected to die. By the time I clawed my way back, I was in such sorry shape, I was convinced sending him away had been right thing."

She stopped long enough to take a breath. Julie listened for the characteristic rattle. It was there, but not as pronounced. "Go on," she urged.

"Getting there." Sarah took another breath. "Damn, but breathing is finally getting easier. Anyway, what man would want to saddle himself with an invalid? Angus called. He wrote. I ignored him. Eventually, he gave up."

"I'm still not getting why he wasn't worthy of a mention. Even in passing. You know. Something like, 'I met this guy. Really liked him, but it didn't work out.'"

"It was easier if I didn't talk about him. When I did, I thought about him and second guessed myself. Mom and Dad nagged me half to death until I told them to let me be. Then they quit, but I still saw questions in their eyes. And disappointment."

Julie rolled her eyes. "Oh my yes. I just got the full court press from them both."

"About Brice?"

"Uh-huh. Back to you. How's this going to work? Will you be moving to Scotland?"

"He's actually based in Paris, but no. I'm not moving. He is. I guess we'll move into my cottage. Or maybe he'll buy something over here on the East Side. Closer to Overlake and all. He's signed on with their staff, and he and Brice are like the medical Bobbsey Twins."

"You have tenants in the cottage for another six months," Julie pointed out.

"The immediate plan is to move into Brice's house. I guess it's enormous. Angus says no one will even notice us there."

Julie winced. "Crap. It's like I'm on a turnpike where every exit leads to Brice, and I can't pick an alternate route."

"Maybe you're exactly where you're supposed to be." Sarah smiled benignly. The smile of a woman who'd stopped fighting her fate, of a woman thrilled to be reunited with the man she'd loved and left.

"I bet Brice doesn't see it that way," Julie muttered. Sarah opened her mouth, but Julie shook her head. "I'll work it out.

The folks already wrested a commitment for Christmas Eve out of me. Susan McKinnon will be there."

"Perfect." Sarah clasped her hands together. "It'll be amazing. We haven't spent a Christmas Eve together since our undergrad years."

Gazing into her sister's luminous eyes and hopeful face, Julie vowed to do her damnedest to make the event a success. She'd be charming, socially correct, smile in the right places, and make her family proud of her. No matter what it cost on a personal level.

"I love you, twin."

"Back at ya, twin," Sarah countered in a greeting they'd pioneered as two-year-olds.

"I'm heading home, and I will do my best about Christmas Eve. Truly I will, but I already told you about the row with my department head. What you don't know about is the problems I'm having at the dig site." She hurriedly sketched out what was happening and her father's offer.

"Dad said he'd charter you a military jet," Sarah said. "Wow. That's huge. I know jet lag is a bitch, but it means even if you have to go you'll get there fast. No one works over the Christmas holiday, though."

"*National Geographic* does, which reminds me. I need to phone my contact again. See you tomorrow, Sis."

"I'll look forward to it. For a while there I wasn't looking forward to anything. It still feels risky, but it's a chance I'm willing to take."

"Good. I meant what I said about respecting your wishes. All of them."

"I know. And it means more than I have words to tell you. Bye, Julie."

"Bye, sweetie." She walked out of the room, ditched her anti-germ gear, and angled toward the parking lot. A glance at her phone told her it was the 20th. She had a few days until Christmas Eve.

Five nights, counting this one.

Her phone was still in her hand when it vibrated. She glanced at the caller ID. It flashed, *Michael Weiss, National Geographic.* Fingers tightening reflexively around the phone, she clicked accept and said, "Hi, Mike. What's up?"

CHAPTER 15

Brice was sitting on one of the buff-colored leather sofas arranged in conversation pits around his ridiculously oversized living room, nursing a tumbler of port and watching lights twinkle on the tree. He'd had a magical afternoon playing with Timmy. What had begun as an altruistic offer to provide care for the boy had ended up so much more.

Who would have guessed small people had so much wisdom? Or that they were such fun? Timmy's unabashed glee had drawn Brice out of himself and into the enchanted world kids lived in. Somewhere between the swings and the slide, the boy had confided how hard he worked taking care of Momma. A domestic, she cleaned houses, picking locations that allowed her to bring Timmy along.

Timmy told Brice all about how he prayed every night for a daddy, so Momma wouldn't have to worry so much. Or work every day like she did. He didn't trust new places after a man scared his momma by hugging her. Millicent had slapped him, and he'd yelled at her to take her brat and get out.

Brice took a deep swallow of liquor, holding it in his mouth to appreciate its age and flavor. The world could be a harsh place, but if Father John hadn't stepped forward and offered financial assistance, Brice would have found a way to do something for Millie and her boy.

Someone had made certain he was where he needed to be when the accident happened. Now that he knew Timmy and his mom, he couldn't let them flounder. It was irrational. The world was full of unfortunates, and he didn't have the means to help them all, but he'd do what he could.

He thought about Doctors Without Borders. He'd gone on several assignments with them during the latter part of his residency—afterward too—and really enjoyed the sense of accomplishment and purpose. The group traveled where need was greatest, providing medical care under desperately primitive conditions. They emailed regularly. Never pushy, just making certain he didn't forget about them.

Brice got to his feet, glass in hand, and wandered through the lower level of his mansion. What had he been thinking to buy a house with ten bedrooms, a dozen baths, two kitchens, and impeccably manicured grounds? Gardeners cared for the outdoors. A pool service maintained the pool he rarely swam in and the spa he used from time to time. Lupe managed the house.

He returned to the sofa where he'd begun. The house was paid for. He'd long since dispatched his med school loans. He'd bought the house as an outward symbol of his success, but he didn't need it. Success was a mindset, not an extravagant house to prove anything to anyone. Feeling shallow and somewhat embarrassed it had taken years for him to realize he didn't need the trappings surrounding him, he flirted with walking away.

From everything.

And spending the next few years doctoring folk who

truly needed him, instead of the patients at Overlake who had access to first-world medical interventions. Some more readily than others, but in truth emergency rooms couldn't turn anyone in need away. And once they admitted a patient, neither could the hospital. Most of the out-of-the-way spots Juliana's digs were located in needed someone like him.

They'd make a great team. She'd bring needed resources to the area by focusing attention on premier finds, and he'd provide medical triage and care. DWB encouraged them to suggest new places…

"Cheers, mate!" Angus breezed into the room, the usually dour lines of his face creased into a smile.

"Can I pour you a drink?" Brice stood and clasped his friend's hand. Freedom had an allure, but for now he wanted to focus on Angus, find out what had happened with Sarah.

"Sure. Whatever you're drinking will be fine."

Brice snorted. "I highly doubt it. This is port."

"Eww." Angus wrinkled his nose. "I'm a simple man. I'll take a simple whiskey. Single malt anything will do."

"Tell you what." Brice motioned him to follow and slid a polished wall panel aside, revealing a wet bar lined with shelves and bottles. "Pick your poison. I'll be back by the tree."

"Sure you don't want to trade out that overly sweet rotgut?"

"I'm on call after midnight." Brice retreated to the couch.

Angus joined him, a tumbler of something fragrant in hand, and sank onto a seat facing Brice at right angles. "How long before they funnel me into the schedule?"

"Probably won't happen until after the holidays. They'll have to verify your credentials, and the hospital admin center is short-staffed until after the first."

Angus smiled mischievously. "Great. I can devote all my time to Sarah."

Brice wanted to mine for details, but he took a different tack. "You'll want to join my practice group."

"Will I?" Angus raised one dark brow.

"Aye," Brice aped his brogue. "That you will. 'Tis either that or running your own practice, which means you'll be on call twenty-four-seven, three hundred sixty-five days a year."

"You talked me into it, but I swear I miss socialized medicine already."

Brice thought about the poor sod with lung cancer. Coming for treatment sooner would have given him more years of life but probably wouldn't have changed the outcome.

"Will you make this move permanent?"

"I believe so."

"Does that mean you'll go for dual citizenship?"

Angus shrugged. "Haven't worked out the fine points yet, mate. I'll do whatever I have to, so I can work here."

Having pushed the backdoor open a crack, Brice edged it wider. "Aren't you worried Sarah might do the same thing she did before?"

"You mean dump me?" At Brice's nod, he went on. "Life doesn't come tied up in a bow with promises. I'll take each day as it comes. She and I talked about that. And a whole lot of other things too. She's scared. Mostly because she doesn't want to be a burden, but I convinced her she has a right to as much happiness as anyone else."

"You always were a silver-tongued devil." Brice drained his glass. He wanted more, but it wasn't a good idea given his call obligation.

"I'm sure I have no idea what you mean." Angus looked askance at him.

"You've talked patients into treatments that were sketchy as hell and not only convinced them to say yes, you made sure they came through the gates of Mordor alive."

"We're doctors. It's what we do." He nailed Brice with his dark eyes. "So, how'd your afternoon go? You found out about mine."

"It was...different."

"You have to say more than that." Angus took a hefty swallow of whatever was in his glass, sighing with pleasure.

"I had a wonderful time. I went into it thinking I'd be kind of like a glorified babysitter, but the boy charmed the socks off me. He's smart and funny and sees the world through fresh eyes. I could have listened to him for hours, but he fell asleep on me after we came home from the park. Lupe carried him up to bed."

"Aye, children are little miracles. You didn't have brothers or sisters? Not younger ones, anyway?"

"None at all," Brice said. "Unless you count my rotation through Peds as an intern, I've never spent any time around kids." So long as he was on a roll, he kept talking, not censoring his thoughts. "I always supposed I'd have children someday, but it was one of those philosophical assumptions. Like I figured I'd get married because it's what you do once you're finished with your training and are established in your career. Kids come with marriage."

"Aye, and your wife takes care of them?" Angus smiled archly.

Brice felt his face heat. "Something like that. I never counted on feeling so protective of Timmy."

"It's archetypal," Angus murmured. "From an anthropological standpoint, children are helpless. They need adults to want to protect them, fend for them, until they're big enough to care for themselves. A couple hundred years ago that was when they were around twelve and hit puberty."

"Today, it's until they're done with college." Brice laughed.

"Aye, and beyond."

"You look happy."

"'Tis because I am happy. I've dithered back and forth about Sarah for years."

"What made the difference this time?" Brice set his tumbler on a low-slung glass-and-brass coffee table and leaned forward. The parallels between his situation and Angus's were disturbingly similar.

"Lots of things. A collection of small items, though, rather than one big one. Of course, her illness played a role, but she's been ill forever. It was more me hitting forty and never finding a woman who resonated here"—he tapped his breastbone—"in quite the same way as her."

He pushed dark hair out of his face. "I had to try one more time." Angus narrowed his eyes. "You look like a ghost just walked over your grave."

"You Highlanders with your ghosts and leprechauns and little folk." Brice attempted to gloss over Angus's hyper-sharp insight with a stab at humor.

"Nay, there's more to it than ye give credit for." Angus lapsed into Gaelic.

"Did you bring your bagpipes and kilts?"

"I do have my family's ceremonial tartan. 'Tis what I'll wear for my wedding, but we'll wait till Sarah is strong enough to enjoy it. 'Twould be a terrible shame if the bride couldn't dance at her own nuptials."

Brice stood. He was happy for Angus, but his friend's joy underscored his own loneliness. And his indecision about his future. "I'm off to bed. See you in the morning. Want to plan another run?"

"Wouldn't miss it. Wake me a quarter hour before you're wanting to leave."

"Will do. Wish me a quiet night."

"Och, you're on call. I'd forgotten. Tell you what. If you get called in, wake me. I'll tag along. 'Tis the only way I'll get the lay of the land, figure out how your group practice operates."

"Are you sure? No reason for you to join the ranks of the sleep-deprived."

"Aye, sure enough. Don't push it, mate. I'm already kicking myself for being a chump." Angus tossed back his head and laughed.

Brice chuckled and strode from the room, taking the home's main staircase to the upper levels. He stopped by Timmy's room to check on him. The boy clutched an enormous stuffed wolf and was sound asleep. Lupe had left a small light burning. Brice started to turn it off, but changed his mind. If Timmy woke, the light would be a comfort. Dark places were where the bad things hid.

Maybe I missed my calling. Should have gone into pediatrics.

His phone vibrated, and he pulled it to eye level to read a text from his mother.

Leaving early tomorrow. See you soon, son. Can't wait.

He texted back, *Safe travels, Mom. Looking forward to meeting Trevor and Rob.*

She sent him two hearts and a rainbow, reminiscent of the stickers she used to paste on her students' papers in the days before the Internet ruled everything.

It would be great to have his mother here. He'd visited her about a year ago, and always had good intentions to go back, but there'd be a patient crisis or his practice would be shy a doc for some reason. He was the only unmarried partner, so the others looked to him to fill in. At this point, he'd been accommodating so often, the other docs expected it.

"No one takes advantage of you without your permission," he muttered and made a sour face.

Brice shook his head. He had more money than he could spend in two lifetimes, and a pile of off time banked. But no one special to share any of it with. He winced. If his own mother got short shrift, how the hell would he manage a family of his own?

Some things would have to change.

He walked into his bedroom, thinking he'd put the cart in front of the horse. First, he needed a wife. Then things at work could change…

"Nope. I need to practice prioritizing my personal life—before I add a woman to the mix. Rather like I did today with Timmy." Nodding, he tapped his phone's display to bring up his calendar. All his work obligations were there. Using a different color, he penciled in personal time, a little bit each day, over the next two weeks, and made himself a promise he'd keep it going.

Developing new habits wouldn't happen overnight, but if he didn't change something, he'd end up a lonely old man with an overflowing ego wall, a phalanx of grateful patients, and not much else.

He toed off his loafers and carried them to the closet. Like he did every night, he undressed in front of the open walk-in closet, hanging clothes that could be worn again and sorting others into a hamper or the dry-cleaning bin. He pulled on a soft, well-worn T-shirt and a pair of running shorts and ambled into the marble inlaid bathroom to wash up and brush his teeth.

The DWB idea held undeniable appeal. He'd float the idea of taking a bi- or tri-annual sabbatical with his practice group at their next monthly meeting. No reason he couldn't have a foot in both worlds. Hell, he had enough vacation time to cover two years' worth of absences.

The tweet of his phone's text tone drew him back to the antique dresser he'd laid it on. His mom was back. This time, her message read:

Just got off the phone with Ariel Wray. She and her husband are coming for Xmas Eve. With Juliana. I'm thrilled to see her again. One of my best students ever!

The text rambled on, but Brice had stopped reading. Juliana. Here. In his house. Damn. Whose idea had that been? Had his mom and Ariel hatched this up?

He narrowed his eyes and forced himself to finish reading her text.

Don't worry about decorating or cooking. I'll get hold of your housekeeper, and she and I will handle everything. I do need her cell number, though. Please send it my way.

Another string of hearts interspersed with plates of food and cakes followed.

His stomach twisted into a knot, and he recognized the one-two punch of adrenaline as his fight-or-flight reaction kicked in.

"Christ." He fisted a hand and brought it down on the nearest piece of furniture. It should have hurt, but he barely felt the impact.

He was a damned coward, but he wasn't ready for Juliana to invade his turf. Bolting across the room, he pulled the door to a veranda open and let the chill night air wash over him. He was primed to talk with her, but he'd envisioned neutral ground.

Not. His. Home.

His mind pedaled in frantic circles. Christmas Eve was only four nights from now, five counting this one. No time at all. He strode back to where he'd left the phone and typed:

Aw, Mom. Sweet of you, but it's a lot of people. How about if we all go out? I can have Lupe hunt down reservations somewhere close first thing tomorrow.

He read it over and cringed but tapped send anyway. Angus had come all the way from Europe. Father John showed up, probably within minutes of Millie's phone call. What on earth was wrong with him? He should welcome the opportunity for an entire evening with Juliana present, but it scared the shit out of him.

Susan didn't make him wait long.

Don't be ridiculous. I love cooking for you, and Ariel will help too, although she never was much good in the kitchen. No worries. I do need Lupe's number though.

More hearts.

Brice dutifully offered up his housekeeper's number, adding she was asleep now but was an early riser.

He set the phone down and returned to shut the patio doors. The temperature in the room had dropped a good ten degrees, and what had felt bracing before just felt cold. Turning in a full circle, he regarded his bedroom, his sanctuary, with as impartial an eye as he could muster.

Furnished with late-nineteenth-century antiques, the oak headboard was intricately carved and rose six feet. The curved footboard was over two feet tall, giving the bed the appearance of a ship. Dressers and a towering armoire matched the bed. In another corner sat a polished roll top desk, also fashioned from oak. Shelves piled with medical reference texts were arranged nearby.

The overall effect was masculine but sterile. He'd always been neat, and everything was put away. Brice shook his head. He was wasting time. The odds of Juliana making it as far as his bedroom were slim to none.

How the hell would he get through several hours of small talk? Doctors Without Borders was looking better and better, but the reality was he'd still be here, front and center on Seattle's East Side, four nights hence.

He inhaled deeply, blew it out, and did it a few more times. He'd figure things out. It was bound to be awkward, but there'd be enough people milling about to smooth things over.

He hoped.

After a stern lecture to man up, he cut the lights and crawled into bed, propping his pager on a bedside table. The call schedule would be another agenda item at January's practice meeting. He'd taken all the extra call duty he planned to, and the other docs would have to suck it up and get used to it.

He shut his eyes, willing sleep to shut off his restless mind, but it was a long time coming. Julie, a naked Julie, teased him. Bouncing breasts, slick labia, the scent of her, the feel of her silky skin beneath his fingers. The tug of the sheets against his painfully erect cock created a cascade of sensation every time he turned over. His determination not to jack off again vanished when a particularly erotic image of Julie, fingers buried in her pussy, rubbing herself, drove him onto his belly thrusting against the mattress.

So close to release he couldn't stand not to come, he moved a pillow beneath his restless hips. The added stimulation of foam gripping him pushed him into a climax so intense he lay panting and gasping afterward, but at least he felt the tightness leaving his body.

Damn. Damn. Damn. What the holy hell am I going to do to fix this?

Telling himself he'd come up with something first thing in the morning, he finally fell asleep.

CHAPTER 16

Juliana waited, phone clutched so tightly her fingers began to cramp.

"'Wanted to check in," Mike said. "'Fraid it's not the best news, but not the worst, either."

"You saved me a call," she murmured. "You were next up on my list."

"Mmph. You might want to look into connections back to Cairo." He cleared his throat. "Don't leave yet, I'm still working a few angles, but the Smithwick fellow got hold of my boss—"

Julie groaned. "Crap on a cracker. That old bastard."

"He is, indeed. Does U.W. have an ethics committee? If so, have you spoken with them?"

"Yes to the first question. No one to talk with until after the first. I did file a written complaint with my field notes as backup."

"Apparently, your colleague is claiming they're his notes. That you stole them and ran back to the States."

She slumped against a nearby wall. "I 'ran back to the

States' because my twin sister nearly died. She has cystic fibrosis, and this last flareup was really, really close."

"I suppose that's something that could be verified."

"Of course. Her name is Sarah Wray, and she's in the ICU at Overlake Hospital in Bellevue, Washington."

"I'm sorry about Sarah. How's she doing?" Mike's rich baritone reflected genuine concern.

"Better. They tried immune modulators as a last-ditch effort, and she's improving. Her lungs have significant scarring, though. And now her pancreas is involved. The next step will be gene remodeling to give her body a boost, so it can do some healing."

"You must be relieved. Uh, no PC way to say this, but isn't she kind of old to…"

"Yes, she is," Julie replied. "We never expected her to live past her twenties, and she's given us a bunch of scares over the years. Hell, I spent something like thirty hours on planes and in airports between Cairo and London and Seattle expecting to turn on my phone at the Seattle end and find out she was gone."

"Does Dr. Conom know about your sister?"

"You bet he does. So does Smithwick."

Mike blew out an annoyed-sounding breath. "I'll be back in touch. Like I said, don't pack a bag quite yet." He paused a beat. "When you do return to the dig site, though, I get an exclusive, right?"

"You bet, Mike. Anything I find is always yours first. You're a genius at showcasing my work for the public."

"That's my girl. If I wasn't already married, I'd want a wife just like you."

Julie swallowed a snort. "Thanks. I think."

"Signing off for now."

Julie dropped the phone back in her pocket and covered the remaining distance to her 4Runner. Given the latest developments, why hadn't Katie called her? A marathoner, Katie Johnson was lean and strong and fit. More than capable of taking care of herself. Maybe she had no idea Orestes was claiming Juliana's field notes belonged to him.

Or maybe she kicked up a huge fuss, and Orestes removed her from the dig site. As senior researcher *in situ*, he had the final say on everything including personnel decisions.

When she got home, she'd figure something out. It was the middle of the night in Cairo, given the ten-hour time difference. Even if she did ping the dig's satellite station, no one would be awake to answer.

She made an effort to clear her mind of everything except the endless stream of cars leaving Bellevue and driving across the bridge. Getting into an accident was an additional layer of complication she didn't need. Between clutching the phone and squeezing the steering wheel so hard her knuckles were white, her hands ached by the time she pulled into her driveway.

A car she didn't recognize was parked across the street, and a tall, lanky man emerged. He had the easy, fluid build of an athlete. She pegged him as a runner or a climber. Julie got out and stood next to her car, waiting while the man caught up with her.

"Yes?" She angled her head to one side, watching him.

He extended a hand. "Dr. Wray. I'm Doug Johnson, Katie's husband. Nice to meet you."

"Please, call me Julie."

"I'm afraid this isn't a social call. Kate would kill me if she knew I was here, but I don't know where else to go. I tried the U.S. Embassy in Cairo—"

"Hold up." Juliana cut him off because she had a bad feeling about what was coming next. "Come inside. I suspect you'll be here for a while. At least until it's six in Cairo and we have a prayer of trying to reach the dig site."

She reached back inside the car to collect her things, locked it, and led the way up her front steps. "Would you like some coffee or tea?" she asked.

He made a gruff noise, somewhere between a snarl and a growl. "What I'd really like is a stiff drink, followed by about five more, but it's not a good idea. If I'm drunk, I won't be any good to anyone."

Julie set her things on a small bench in the front hall and turned to face Doug. At least six feet six, he had a mane of straight blond hair that fell to shoulder level, keen blue eyes, and the angular facial structure that screamed Scandinavian. His chin and cheeks were dusted with a couple days' beard growth.

"Tell you what," she said. "I'm putting on the electric kettle, and I'm going to brew some nice strong black tea. You can have it straight or with cream, sugar, or whiskey."

He smiled, displaying straight, white teeth. "Tea and sugar sounds wonderful. I haven't had much of anything these past two days."

"Can I make you a sandwich to go with it? Or maybe crackers and cheese? Or tea biscuits?"

His smile widened. "I can see why Kate thinks so highly of you. Biscuits would be perfect, and they're easier for you. Can I do anything?"

She shook her head. "Make yourself at home. I'll join you in the living room once the tea's ready."

He nodded his thanks, and she moved across the open downstairs to the kitchen side of things. After she'd piled butter biscuits on a plate, she took them to where he'd settled in an old Adirondack chair that had been one of her father's favorites.

"Thank you."

"Back in a flash with our tea."

She settled across from him, fingers cradling the warm ceramic of her handmade mug. She'd brought the set of six mugs back from a dig site in central Bolivia. The rug gracing the floor had come from the textile market in Otavalo, a small town outside Quito, Ecuador.

Doug sipped his tea. "I'm not sure where to begin, but I'm worried about Kate. Really worried, and equally helpless. It's not a good combination. I'd hop on a plane, but I'd be worse than useless once I got to Cairo. Even if I could find your dig site, what would I do once I got here—?"

"Whoa. Back up. Start at the beginning. When did you first start feeling worried about Katie?"

He took a deep, steadying breath. "I've been worried about her for at least a week. Ever since you left, and she told me the shenanigans that dickwad— Oops, excuse me, I wasn't very respectful."

"Go on. Orestes Conom is the worst kind of scumsucker."

"Kate and I are close. Really close. Some of it is probably because we haven't been married very long, but we've known one another since we were five years old. She's always been the only one for me, and vice versa. Anyway, we talk every day, and—"

"When's the last time you spoke with her?" Anxiety twisted Juliana's stomach into a tight, painful knot.

"Day before yesterday."

"Hmmm. Same time she reached out to me. I think. The days have been flowing together since I got here."

"She said she was scared. She stood up to that Conom dude when he claimed you'd absconded with his field notes. She sang out loud and clear that they were your notes, and her own documentation would bear it out."

"Oh-oh." Julie closed her teeth over her lower lip. "She said she was scared. Then what?"

"I told her to call a cab and leave."

A corner of Julie's mouth twisted downward. "She refused. Not that it would have mattered. Getting a taxi that far out in the bush is damn near impossible."

He grunted derisively. "Aw hell, she was like a goddamned lion sitting over a litter of kits, convinced if she left for ten seconds some other predator would move in and eat them."

"Not far off the mark." Julie pinched the bridge of her nose between a thumb and forefinger.

"Anyway," Doug went on. "Nine at night is our normal time to talk—except it's seven in the morning where she is. She didn't call last night. I waited until nine thirty and called the dig site." He clenched his jaw into a tense line. "A man who barely spoke English answered. Luckily, I'm finishing my Ph.D. in linguistics with a focus on ancient languages, so we had a conversation in the Egyptian dialect of Arabic."

"And?" Julie set the tea down, afraid if she held onto it she'd crush the mug between her hands, and leaned closer.

"He said Kate must have left during the night. She wasn't in her tent this morning, and all her things were gone." Doug twisted his hands together and said, "What can we do? Is there a government agency we can get hold of? I tried the American embassy in Cairo. They were very politically correct and absolutely not helpful."

Julie held up both hands. "Hold up. I need to think. And there's someone I need to call."

"Can I stay here, or is it private and I need to wait outside?" He set his mug down gently, gaze never leaving her face.

"You can stay," she said. "I'm calling my dad. He's a retired Marine general, but he still has connections. I figure we could use his advice. They have boots on the ground in the region, and they're much closer than we are. Even if I left for the airport this second and took whatever flights I could grab, it would still take me two days to get back to Cairo and another couple hours to locate transportation and travel to the dig."

She stood on legs that felt shaky and went to get her phone. One thing was certain, if anything happened to her graduate student, she wouldn't rest until Orestes Conom was stripped of his university appointment and warming a cell in a federal prison.

She tapped her father's number into the display. He picked up on the first ring. "Princess, what a pleasant—"

"No. It's not," she spoke over him. "I've got problems, and I'm hoping you have ideas."

"Shoot. I'm listening."

She could visualize him, iron-gray brows drawn into a thick, intense line over his blue eyes. "Remember that professor who was trying to take credit for my dig?"

"Sure do. What's the bastard done now?"

"Two things. He's claiming I left Egypt with his field notes and that my supporting documentation I filed with the ethics committee aren't my notes at all, but the far bigger problem is one of my grad students seems to be missing. She spoke up in support of me when he said I'd stolen his field notes, and now she's gone."

Chris Wray whistled long and low. "Oh honey, that's not good. Those North African countries can be real snake pits."

"The woman's name is Katherine Johnson," Julie went on. She's twenty-eight years old. I can get you her passport number and other ID data if it will help. Her husband is with me right now. He was waiting for me when I came home. Last time he talked with his wife was two days ago. When they missed their daily phone call yesterday and he contacted the dig site, they told him she'd left."

"Any chance it might be true?" Chris used his calming tone, the one he'd soothed her with since she was a baby.

"No. She'd never have left a find like that. It was her dissertation. Hell, I wouldn't have left if I wasn't certain Sarah might not make it."

"Okay. I need copies of her driver's license, passport, recent photos, everything you can send me."

"Hang on. I'm going to switch to speaker. I have a feeling Doug has all that, and he can scan and email or fax them to you." She clicked a button and centered the phone between herself and Doug.

"Hello, sir," Doug said. "Doug Johnson here, and I'd be very grateful for any assistance."

"Marine General Christopher Wray," her father responded. "Retired, but I worked intelligence, and I still know folk. Get me copies of her ID documents pronto, son. Can you do that?"

"Sure can. I have them in my phone. Where do I send them?"

Julie jotted her father's cell number down for Doug and he went to work tapping his phone's display.

"Got 'em," Chris said. "Okay. I'll let you know how things are unfolding."

"What are you going to do, sir?" Doug asked.

Juliana anticipated her father's reply. Chris said, "Better if you don't know. I have your number, I'll be in touch." He disconnected.

Doug swallowed the last of his tea and got to his feet. "You've been more than kind. I'll get out of your hair. I won't be much good for anything until I hear something. Not even fit company for myself."

Julie stood as well. "I'm worried about her too."

"I'm more than worried." His voice cracked, but he kept talking. "I can't imagine my life without her. I—"

Julie patted his arm, feeling helpless. She wanted to tell him everything would be all right, but she wasn't at all sure it was the truth. Women disappeared every day from the hinterlands of non-Westernized countries. She might have been sold or traded or shot, her body dumped where no one would ever find it.

She swallowed around a thick place in her throat. "Let's keep the faith, huh?"

"Yeah. It's pretty much the only avenue open to us." Dragging a hand through his hair, he shambled out the door, pulling it shut behind him.

Because she didn't know what else to do, she ferried the mugs and plate back into the kitchen and washed them, keeping an anxious eye on her phone, but it remained stubbornly silent.

She'd just decided to go out for a walk to burn off a bad case of nerves when her phone trilled. Snatching it up, she saw Ariel's number. "Yes, Mom?"

"Your dad doesn't know anything yet," Ariel said. "I'm calling to see how you're holding up."

"Not well. Katie is a wonderful person, a talented athlete, and a gifted researcher. She—"

"It's never fair," her mother interrupted. "Dad is doing all he can. We have…friends not far from your dig site."

"How do you even know where it is? We kept it secret for a reason."

"Oh, honey, nothing is secret from satellite surveillance. Your dad's been keeping tabs on you ever since you started working there."

As bad as things were, Julie smiled softly. "God but I love you both."

"We love you too. Try to get some rest tonight."

"Do you suppose I should alert the media about Katie being MIA?"

"Media as in? I'm not sure the Egyptian press would care," her mother replied.

"*National Geographic.* I've been in touch with a photojournalist there, but he'll know folk at NBC, CNN, and the other networks."

"Let me ask your dad. Hang on."

Julie waited as one minute ticked past, followed by two or three more. She could picture her parents, their heads bent together, as they debated the pros and cons of Katie's disappearance hitting the national news.

"All right. I'm back." Ariel's crisp, no-nonsense military voice blasted though the phone. "Dad says hold off for now. We're working a covert angle, and if the girl's disappearance expands into something huge, whoever has her might panic and kill her."

"You believe she's been kidnapped?" Julie's stomach clenched until she was afraid she was going to vomit.

"We're not sure," her mother replied in a carefully neutral tone. "We'll be back in touch with you when we know more."

The call ended icon danced across her screen.

Julie considered jumping in her car, driving to her parents' house, and peppering them with questions, but it wouldn't do any good. They wouldn't tell her anything until they had solid intel.

Back to Plan A, which was a brisk walk. She dropped her phone into a pocket, put on a jacket, and left her cottage. As she executed one of her many loops around the neighborhood, Doug's haunted eyes kept forming in her mind.

That poor, poor man. He'd have a hard road ahead if Katie never came home. Julie fisted both hands. This was her fault. She should have anticipated something like this. She'd seen the desperation—and avarice—sheeting off Orestes. He needed a find—a big one—or the university would drop him from the faculty.

Sarah's illness had provided just the opportunity he'd been waiting for. Damn, but she'd been a fool to believe he'd play fair.

"Focus," she hissed to center herself. Right now, the important thing was getting Katie back. She could reprimand herself later. If anyone could turn this around, it would be her dad. Relentless, driven, wise. Men gave him the best they had in them because he inspired that level of devotion.

In her opinion, the Marines had lost their best general when he retired.

Juliana turned toward home, still antsy but drained. She knew enough from eavesdropping on her folks through the years to understand if they didn't locate Katie soon, they wouldn't find her at all. Tracks grew cold fast in places like Egypt.

Brice joined the cavalcade marching through her mind. She wanted to talk with him, tell him about Katie. He was wise and had a cool head. He'd hold her, comfort her. Or he would have, once upon a time.

She unlocked her front door and walked inside feeling empty. No Brice. No dig. The find that would have set her up for life had turned into such a boondoggle, she was sorry she'd stumbled across it. Nothing was worth the life of one of her students.

Nothing.

The only bright spot was that Sarah was better.

Julie plodded to her desk and booted up her computer. She'd been staring at the screen for god only knows how long before she brought up her email, determined to accomplish something tonight.

CHAPTER 17

*B*rice pulled his mask aside and stripped off his gloves as he walked out of a room at University Hospital. The sun was just breaking through a pallid, gray dawn. His pager had gone off around three, summoning him to intervene with a COPD patient. He and his partners covered several hospitals, and this call had come from one across Lake Washington in Seattle's University District.

Behind him, Angus droned on lecturing the medical students and residents who'd sat in on the patient's struggles and eventual death. He should have remained behind, answered questions from the next generation of doctors, but he was tired.

Not that it constituted much of an excuse. He'd called time of death and walked out of the room. Unlike the lung cancer victim, tonight's patient would have had a different outcome if he'd quit smoking twenty years ago. Even ten would have helped.

"All done." Angus ran up to him. "We can leave."

Brice nodded curtly and strode toward the exit and the physician's parking lot.

"What's wrong?" Angus asked once they reached the car, following it with, "We can't save everybody."

"No. We can't, but he could have saved himself," Brice mumbled.

"Och, and 'tis beside the point. They never see that part, do they? 'Tis the hardest part of our job. Patient non-compliance."

Brice didn't feel like an excursion through that particular minefield, so he asked, "Feel like coffee or breakfast?"

"Both would be splendid. How about a quick jog first?"

"Sure." Brice popped the trunk and traded his lab coat for a windbreaker. The emerging morning was crisp and damp, but it wasn't raining.

Angus rummaged in a small duffle and pulled a well-worn fisherman's knit sweater out, trading it for his white coat. He rubbed his hands together. "Positively balmy this morning. You should come home with me. Scotland has some frosty mornings. Freeze the balls off a skunk."

Brice shot a meaningful glance his way and slammed the trunk. "Paris isn't home, eh?"

"Never." Angus sounded shocked. "Not to a Scotsman. Now this"—he spread his arms wide—"comes closer. I'm looking forward to making a home here with Sarah."

"It will be nice to have you on this side of the pond."

"You do know no one on my side of 'the pond' calls it that, right?" Angus took off at a brisk pace.

Brice ran beside him. They covered a few miles up through the center of the University District, ran through campus with its old, intriguing buildings, and circled back to the BMW chatting about this and that.

"This was a good idea. Thanks." Brice opened the car and got in.

"Always helps my perspective," Angus agreed as he buckled into his seat belt.

"Another plus is the worst of the morning traffic should be done, although I'm not certain of that. Off on a tangent here, you'll want to apply for a post as adjunct faculty at the university medical school. In case you want to teach a class or two. Or mentor residents."

"Technically, I was teaching this morning," Angus said.

"Yeah, I know. We need to formalize everything, though. One of the big differences between practicing here and 'across the pond'"—he grinned—"is our malpractice policies and the insurance industry that's grown fat suing doctors and hospitals. Last place you want to be is on the receiving end of a patient who feels wronged."

"Aye, wronged and entitled." Angus ran a hand through his dark hair.

"Something like that." Brice guided the car into moderate traffic, pleased his prediction was bearing out. "Is the hospital cafeteria acceptable for breakfast?"

"I have no bloody idea, mate. You tell me. Is their food edible, or does it drive the patients to get well faster, so they can escape to their own kitchens?"

"It's surprisingly good, but we can hit Starbucks instead. Their coffee is better, and they have breakfast sandwiches and fruit and yogurt, that type of thing."

"Let's do that. I'll bring Sarah a cup of dark roast. She used to live on it."

His mention of Sarah brought Brice's Juliana dilemma roaring to the fore. He'd come to the inescapable conclusion he had to carve out time to talk with her before Christmas Eve. Since they were running out of opportunities, he'd call her once he got to his office.

Establish a mutually agreeable time and a neutral location. Not the hospital. Not his office. Maybe a quiet restaurant. He knew several within easy reach of Overlake.

"You're quiet," Angus observed as they exited the freeway

and turned toward the hospital. "Losing that man still bothering you?"

"Yes and no. I've always thought we should point more resources toward prevention, but that's a topic worthy of a dissertation."

"Indeed, it is. Something's eating at you. What?"

Brice shrugged. He wasn't about to disclose his pathetic, long-ago saga with Juliana and Sarah. Especially not to Angus who'd soon be Sarah's husband. He didn't need to know his wife-to-be had been involved in an on-purpose, mistaken-identity seduction scheme.

Maybe if he came up with part of the truth, though, Angus would stop staring at him with a gimlet gaze.

"'Tis all right, mate. Your guilty secrets will be safe enough with me. Who would I tell?"

Brice tried for a disarming smile. "This doesn't quite rise to the caliber of a guilty secret. I've been taking stock of my life, and I work way too much. I'll be taking more time off and spending some of it with Doctors Without Borders."

Angus clapped him on the shoulder. "Stellar organization. I've done a few tours with them. Maybe if Sarah improves enough, she and I could go somewhere not too third-worldish and work as a medical team."

"Maybe so." Brice turned into the Starbucks lot and parked in a corner where the odds of someone scratching his paint job would be less. "Come on." He opened his door. "Breakfast is on me."

"Good thing. All I have is Euros—and plastic. I do plan to stop by a bank today sometime, though."

BRICE HUSTLED into his office and shut the door. He'd left Angus at the bend in the corridor leading to the ICU with a cup holder with two coffees and a bag full of goodies he'd selected to tempt Sarah. Tilting his cup, he took a brisk swallow of tepid coffee, followed by another, and waited for the caffeine jolt to hit. He had to call Juliana.

Now.

Before something happened and the day got away from him. He was on call until midnight, which meant he was fair game for being pulled in a million directions.

He dug out his phone and looked at her text, ostensibly to get her cell number. Except he'd memorized it when the text came in. It wasn't quite nine, which meant she should be home or in her office. She generally hadn't come to the hospital much before noon.

"For Pete's sake, I'm making excuses, putting this off."

Disgust turned his stomach sour. Or maybe it was the coffee without much else beyond half a croissant. He could do this. Hell, it wasn't any harder than marching out of the operating room and informing a family their loved one hadn't made it.

He fell heavily into his overstuffed desk chair. Out of all his doctorly tasks, that had to be the hardest. Next in line was telling a patient they were likely terminal. It never got easier, no matter how many times he did it. When he entered the exam room, lab results in hand, patients looked at him with hope in their eyes.

Hope it wasn't as bad as they feared.

Hope that he could wave his white-coat wand and make them well again.

Knowing his next words would make the light in their eyes flicker and die, but he had to utter them anyway, was gut-wrenching. He'd developed stock phrases like, 'hope for the best but plan for the worst.' They always stuck in his craw. When only a handful of patients with a certain condition were alive five years hence, the odds weren't good, but he always opted to be as honest and accurate as he could.

He set his paper cup down and picked up the phone. He'd get through this. Worst thing that could happen is she'd tell him to pound sand, that she was coming to the Christmas Eve party to see his mother, not him."

He tapped his display and dialed her number. She picked up on the first ring. "Brice. What do you want?" She sounded as friendly as a feral cat guarding a newly dead mouse."

"If this isn't a good time—" he began.

"Sarah's still all right, isn't she?" Julie cut him off.

Understanding hit him between the eyes like a lightning bolt. He was her sister's attending physician. It was a logical reason for him to be calling. "Sorry. Sarah's fine. Improving beyond my expectations. I should have said that straight away."

"How? I didn't give you an opportunity. I'm the one who should apologize. Didn't get any sleep."

He wanted to ask why, but it wasn't his place to intrude. "Like I said, if this is a bad time, I can call back later." He uncurled his other hand—the one not holding the phone— from where he'd been gripping the edge of his desk.

"There may not be any good times," she muttered. "Not anymore."

Her tone tugged at his heart. She sounded broken, defeated. Nothing like the Juliana he'd always known. She'd had the world on a string. Always sure of herself. Grounded in her competence and skill.

He inhaled raggedly. "What's wrong, Julie?"

"What's right?" she countered. "Other than Sarah, and for a minute there I was afraid you were going to tell me she'd relapsed."

"Granted we haven't spent any time together since, well in a long time, but I've never heard you sound so overwhelmed."

"Aw geez. I was such a stupid ass. This whole mess is my

fault." Her voice broke and a sob rattled against his ear, followed by another.

"Julie. Breathe. Whatever this is, it can't be as bad as all that."

"Trust me. It is." She snuffled noisily.

He wished he was close enough to wrap his arms around her, comfort her. "How about if you tell me. Let me be the judge of how devastating this thing is."

"Aw crap. Last night, I—" She dissolved into crying that tore at his soul.

"I'm here, Jules. Take your time." Protectiveness surged to the fore, shocking in its intensity. Maybe if he didn't push, she'd talk with him. Whatever this was, she shouldn't be facing it alone.

"Egypt," she croaked.

"Yes. The dig site there. Was it promising?" He fed ideas, hoping she'd pick up on them and it would help her, loosen her tongue. She'd always been so damned strong. An entity unto herself who hadn't needed anyone or anything—except him and her twin. And then she'd decided he was too much trouble.

"Promising? Hell, it was the find of a lifetime. Or two or three. It would have set me up forever. I could have written my own ticket. Taught at any university in the world. Had my expeditions sponsored with premiere equipment…"

"A whole lot of past conditional verbs there," he said. "Did the dig not pan out as you'd hoped?" He leaned back in his chair. Was a dry hole the source of all this angst? That wasn't like Juliana, either. She was a pick-yourself-up, dust-yourself-off gal.

"Crap. I may as well tell you. I've gotten this much out. It'll be jumbled, but let me get through it. Do not interrupt."

He bit back a grin. Finally, she was sounding like the

woman he used to love—and probably still did. Pushy. Bossy. Bitchy.

"I'll do my best," he said.

"The site is the best-preserved one from its time period, which is somewhere between Egypt's Middle and Old Kingdoms. We'd unearthed a very promising layer. When we were done examining it and packaging items to move back to the university, I saw something that led me to believe another level lay beneath."

She stopped to snuffle and blow her nose. "*We* included another professor, junior to me, and assorted grad students and field staff. The other professor argued with me, said I was wasting university resources and we should be happy with what we'd found and go home.

"I understood him well enough. We'd been squatting in tents for six months at that point. Everyone dealt with intestinal issues from bad water and crappy food, and the locals were tired of us. They'd gone from welcoming to making it clear they wanted us gone."

She chuckled, but without much warmth. "I've always been a brassy bitch, and I pulled rank on him. We opened the dig farther, and I swear it was like finding another King Tut exhibit. Wonders atop more wonders. We worked four more months, and then my parents called about Sarah."

She took a measured breath, but at least she'd stopped crying. "Sorry. This is getting long, but I do better when I tell things in order. I was no sooner gone than Orestes Conom, the other professor, declared going deeper had been his idea, and the finds were his. He accused me of stealing his field notes, but that was after I'd filed an ethics complaint with the university—"

"Hold up." Brice took a chance and interrupted her. "How'd you find out about all this?"

"Oh yeah, that's right. You'd have no way of knowing.

One of my grad students, a woman developing her dissertation research on our find, called me. She was panic-stricken that Conom would strip her of her research topic and hand it to one of his students. That was before the stolen field note allegation.

"I went to my department head and told him what was happening after Katie—that's my grad student—got hold of me. I also told him I'd filed a complaint with ethics."

"Let me guess. He wasn't pleased."

"Oh hell no. He all but told me to stand aside and give this find to Orestes. I'd shoot myself first, and I'm not the suicidal type."

Brice smiled to himself. This was definitely the woman he knew. She had a firmly ingrained sense of right and wrong and would go to the mat if her rights were being trampled on.

"Seems manageable. All you need to do is go back to the dig site. You have your notes, and—"

"You haven't heard the bad part yet."

His eyes widened. "This gets worse?"

"Much. Katie stood up to Orestes after he claimed I'd absconded with his field notes. Told him her notes would corroborate what was in mine. And now she's missing. Her husband came to see me yesterday. Poor guy. He was in tears. He's afraid his wife is dead. He raised the dig site via its sat phone and talked with a local who said Katie vanished during the night, along with all her things."

"Jesus." Breath rattled through Brice's teeth. "I take back what I said about this not being as bad as you thought. That's rough. What are you going to do?"

"I got hold of Dad. He still has plenty of connections, and they have boots on the ground over there."

"Good call."

"I thought so at the time, but it's been almost fifte

hours since I phoned him, and I haven't heard anything back."

"Waiting is hard."

"No kidding. I swear, if Katie's hurt, held against her will —or God forbid, dead—because that bastard sold her to a slave auction or to some caravan leader, I'll strangle him."

"How could he finesse something like that?"

"Easily. It's a patriarchal country. Especially in the bush. Women have zero rights. Orestes speaks fluent Arabic. I do too, but it's beside the point. Katie's husband is close to a doctorate in linguistics. If he hadn't had a grasp of the language, he'd never have been able to communicate with the flunky who picked up the phone. Damn it."

Brice could picture her, hands balled into fists and color high on her face. "What?"

"It's exactly what Orestes was counting on. Why he had the Egyptian field flunky sitting over the phone. He assumed Katie's husband might call, and figured it was safe enough since phone-boy didn't speak much English."

"Maybe—"

"Hang on. It's Dad. Let me call you back."

The line went dead, leaving Brice staring at his phone. Despite the hideous news and Sarah's rightful despair and angst, they'd actually talked for the first time in fifteen years. Even better, she'd trusted him enough to open up about her pain and panic and fear.

The world felt right in a way it hadn't since she'd shooed him out of her apartment. He set his phone aside and went to work on his coffee. If Hippocrates, the ancient Greek who kind of watched over those like him, was kind, the hospital wouldn't require him over the next half hour.

Juliana would call him back. He was certain of it. Depending on what news her father had, Brice would help any way he could, even if it meant accompanying her back to

Egypt. Given the circumstances, he wouldn't let her go alone. It was too dangerous.

Besides, if she was correct about her student being abducted, having a doctor along could be critical. He stared at his phone, willing it to ring.

uliana switched to her father's incoming call. "Yes. I'm here."

"Somehow, I didn't doubt that for a moment." Chris sounded like he always did. Calm. Reassuring. "How well do you know the region around the dig?"

"Really well. I spent a month mapping a twenty-mile swathe in that area before selecting a location. Even then, my first guess wasn't good, and we moved to my second."

"Next question. Do you speak Arabic?"

She nodded. "Yes, both Arabic and the Egyptian dialect. Why is it important?"

"You'll see. The plan we came up with is this."

"Who's we?" she cut in. "You and Mom?"

"Hell no, princess. The less you know about the people I've been dealing with, the better. Are you ready to listen without asking questions every thirty seconds?"

"Yes. Sorry." She closed her teeth over her lower lip. No wonder she had such a peremptory manner. She'd inherited it from her father.

"I need you at Boeing Field at noon sharp. I have an aircraft ready to go. Or it will be by then. This missing grad student knows you, which is why it makes sense to bring you along. I'd considered including her husband, but his emotional ties run too deep, and I have no idea what we'll find. Or how he'd react if his wife is too badly mutilated."

Julie's mind stumbled over the word *mutilated*, but she remained silent.

"A local operative tracked Katie to one of the buildings a few miles northeast of Cairo where human traffickers store their goods. As of an hour ago, she was still there. My guess is she's raising hell, which wouldn't make her worth much on the auction block."

Chris inhaled noisily. When he blew the breath out, he sounded stoic. "Usually, in these instances, they hang onto the noncooperative ones. Starve them. Flog them until they realize their only option is to play nice."

Julie closed her eyes, sick to her stomach at her father's description. "Jesus, Dad. How do you know so much about human trafficking rings?"

"I can't answer that. Besides, it's not relevant. Back to listening mode, please."

"Got it," she muttered through clenched teeth.

"The plan is to make certain she's still there once we're in position. Assuming she is, we'll move in with a small unit, blow the lid off that location, and free whoever else is being held there along with Katie. Then we get back on our plane and fly home."

Juliana could almost see her father dusting his hands together. "Any chance of me staying?" she asked.

"No. It won't be safe for a while. Your site is in the middle of nowhere. International crime syndicates are behind human trafficking, and whoever's underwritten this operation will be furious. Why would you want to remain?"

"To secure the artifacts at my dig site." She shook her head. "Never mind. It's not nearly as important as Katie's life."

"It should be safe enough. Someone well above me in the food chain talked with the Egyptian government. They've cleared everyone from the area pending the investigation of Katie's disappearance. I was promised they'd keep it pristine for you."

A low, rattling breath bubbled from her lungs. "So that means my two other grad students are on their way home?"

"Yes. And the bastard who's behind all this. He'll have a spot of explaining to do."

"He deserves to rot in a cell."

"First, we need to extricate Katie. She can testify against him. It should do the trick."

"Do I need to bring anything?"

"A backpack with a change of clothes. Dress the way you would in the field. Sturdy, practical clothing. Nothing that would stand out."

"Thanks, Dad. Not that I'm looking forward to another thirty hours on planes, but—"

"We should be there in twelve hours. Maybe thirteen."

"That's all?"

"Nothing like private jets and direct routes. We'll be in one of the long range, business-class jets the military maintains for situations rather like this. You'll find it quite comfortable. I still have a lot to do. See you soon."

"Can I tell her husband what we're doing?"

"No. Not one word. Promise me. This is as black ops as they come. Under the radar."

"I promise."

Her father disconnected.

She ran to her bedroom and collected her duffle from the closet, stuffing a few things inside. She wouldn't need much but made certain her passport and ID were in her bag, along with her laptop. She was on her way out the door when she thought about Sarah.

And Brice.

She'd promised him she'd call back. The Sarah part was easy. She phoned Ariel. Before she could even say hello, her mother chirped, "No worries. I'll handle everything with your sister and that Scottish doctor. I also talked with Susan, and she's good with extending her stay for however long it takes before you return. But I don't believe she'll need to. These types of operations never take long. You'll be back before you know it, but you need to get moving. See you on the other side."

Juliana smiled grimly, parroted, "See you on the other side," and hung up. It was an old exchange between her parents when one or the other was going into a dicey situation.

Before she could talk herself out of it—after all, she'd told him she'd call back—she dialed Brice's number.

"Julie. What'd your dad cook up?"

"How do you know he 'cooked-up' anything?" she countered, not sure how much she could tell Brice. Her father had been most emphatic about not talking with Doug Johnson.

"Because he's a resourceful kind of guy."

She waited, but Brice didn't say anything further. "I'm kind of in a hurry," she said. "We can talk in a few days."

"Aha! You're going back to Egypt. Don't bother denying it. Juliana. Take me with you. If your student is injured, having a doctor along will be important."

"What are you, psychic?" she sputtered. She'd always been a lousy liar, and he'd see right through her if she told him he was wrong.

"When are you leaving?" he pressed. "And from where? I can call your dad, but I'd rather you told me."

Her temper flared. "I have enough problems right now. You can't just muscle your way back into my life after—"

"I'd never have left if you hadn't been too stubborn to believe me," he countered. "Look. This isn't about you and me. It's about what's best for your graduate student. For Katie."

Julie sat heavily, falling into a nearby straight-backed chair. "You're not playing fair."

"Since when is stating the truth not playing fair? Put me on hold. Call your dad. Please."

"How can you possibly leave? What about your patients?"

"I'm part of a group practice, and every single one of those bozos owes me. Your father?"

"Hang on."

Feeling like she should have just said no, stuck by her guns, and hung up, she ground her teeth. She could tell Brice her father said no and walk out the door. Problem was, she wanted Brice to come along. Craved the time with him and his steady, imperturbable presence by her side. Anxious about what they'd unearth, and apprehensive about coming anywhere near a human trafficking den, she was scared.

Yeah, imagine how Katie must feel. She's caught up in the middle of an unimaginable hellhole. Because she stood up for me.

A glance at her display told her two minutes had ticked by while she stewed in her own guilt and ambivalence. She called her father.

"Yes? Did you get cold feet? If you did, it's all right. I don't blame you. We can manage without—"

"Can Brice come?" she blurted, cutting off her father's words.

"Funny, but that's the angle I was just working on. We

need a doctor. In case Katie's been tortured and is in bad shape. Sure. Love to have him, but he cannot disclose the nature of where he's going to anyone. Not the hospital. Not whoever he practices with."

"I'll let him know."

"Call me back with a firm yes or no. I'm curious as hell why the two of you are talking again, but it's all for the good."

Her father hung up, and she clicked back to Brice. "Sorry you had to wait—"

"Never mind. Am I going?"

"Yes. Boeing Field. Noon. You cannot tell anyone where you're headed."

"Give me credit for a little sense. I'll be there with medical supplies. Thanks for not stonewalling me."

She shouldered her duffle and her bag and tucked the phone between her jaw and shoulder. "I should be thanking you for volunteering. What we're heading into won't be pretty."

"I gathered as much. We'll talk more when I see you. I have to get moving."

He clicked off before she could say goodbye. Juliana locked her house and hustled her things into the 4Runner. She'd be a little early, but it was all right. If she stuck around, Doug might stop by again, and she didn't trust herself not to slip up.

She texted her father to let him know Brice was coming, and drove toward the interstate entrance that would lead her south to Boeing Field. It surprised her when her father commandeered her to help. He hadn't been kidding about the black ops part. Apparently, the military wanted distance between it and whatever they were about to do.

Her phone signaled an incoming call, and she switched to Bluetooth to answer it. "Hello."

"Juliana. Thank God. What the hell is going on?" Mike Weiss demanded.

"Um, hi Mike. I'm kind of swamped right now."

"The Egyptians have shuttered the dig site. Cleared all the personnel. Obviously, I'm not there, but I have spies everywhere." He laughed uncomfortably.

Julie bit down on her lower lip. "I'll be back at the site just as soon as a misunderstanding gets cleared up. Once I'm back, I'll alert you and you can show up with your camera."

"Yes, but what's going on now?" he pressed. "My person said it looks like a crime scene."

"I can't disclose anything, Mike. I'm sorry."

"Even to me?"

Yeah, especially to you. You're the media.

She organized her thoughts. "I value our professional relationship, but this is one instance where I truly cannot say anything. If I do, I might jeopardize someone's life."

"Fascinating. Damn. I want to know everything. Maybe I'll hop on a plane."

"Not a good idea, Mike. Please. It could be really dangerous."

"Which means I might capture the shot of a lifetime. I was an Army Ranger. I—"

"You have a wife and two children." Her tone was sharper than she meant it to be. "In the end, you'll do what you want, but please wait on this. I'll get hold of you as soon as I can."

"I'm trusting you mean it."

"I do. Why would I want to burn a bridge with you? You're my favorite photog."

"Any idea how long before—?"

"None. Might be a few days. Might be a week. Or two or three until the Egyptians deem it's safe for me to set up shop again."

"How do you know thieves won't make off with the artifacts?"

She bit back a snort. "You sound just like me. I don't, but there are some very old universities in Cairo that have exceptional antiquities departments. I'm going to assume their scientists are involved at least peripherally in the lockdown."

"Okay, Juliana. Gotta run. I'll look forward to hearing from you. Merry almost Christmas."

"Back at ya," she said and disconnected.

Traffic thickened as she traveled through exits serving Seattle's downtown area, but she had over an hour before she had to meet her dad. Using her voice-activated Bluetooth, she texted her father:

Where at Boeing Field?

He texted right back:

Tell the gate guard you're meeting me. He'll direct you. I've already alerted Brice.

Brice.

A welter of confused emotions threatened to swamp her. Excitement. Anticipation. Fear they'd lost their special connection—because of her stupidity. None of them had a place right now. Brice had been dead on when he'd said this was about what was best for Katie.

Except she couldn't stand to think about Katie. It tore her heart out. Especially after her father's graphic descriptions about starvation and flogging. Thank God, he hadn't gone into any further details about methods of torture. If he'd worked to stymie human trafficking, she bet he knew a whole lot in Technicolor detail.

Photos from some *National Geographic* articles flashed through her mind. Emaciated humans, some with body parts that had been severed.

Back off. Stop, she ordered herself.

Katie had only been missing for a short time. It took far longer than that for short rations to take a toll. She reminded herself of the "Rule of Three." Humans could survive three minutes without air, three days without water, and three weeks without food.

Her thoughts circled back to Brice. It had felt almost normal to talk with him earlier. He'd listened in his usual, thorough manner. He'd always had a way of focusing his entire attention on her, of making her feel heard in a way no one else had ever come close to. Most people—including her sister and parents—listened until they figured they had the gist of something, and then their attention wandered as they assembled their own ideas about the topic *du jour*.

Not Brice. He gave you his full and undivided awareness until he was certain you'd said whatever was on your mind. At that point, he'd ask a few questions for clarification. She cringed as she replayed his many attempts to talk with her about the episode with Sarah.

He'd tried to explain that day in her apartment. When she refused to listen, he'd called, but she hung up. Next, he'd written. She'd burned the letters without reading them.

"Goddammit," she muttered. "I cannot believe what a sanctimonious bitch I was. People make mistakes, but I couldn't offer him any latitude. Not an angstrom."

"Because if I had," she answered herself, "all that anger would have transferred to Sarah."

Forgiving her twin had been easy sitting on her hospital bed, fifteen years after the fact. Finding compassion for her illness and recognizing the harsh impact of chronic, debilitating disease was a no-brainer today. When they were twenty, though, she'd been in full denial about the seriousness of her sister's condition.

Damn me. No insight. No compassion. Just a pile of hubris.

Julie exited the freeway and drove onto the grounds of

Boeing's vast campus south of Seattle. Crossing an enormous parking lot, she rolled to a stop at the gated entrance to the airstrip and rolled down her window.

After a quick conversation with the guard, she drove toward a bank of hangars. A sleek Gulfstream sat on the tarmac. To avoid thinking about what she was about to embark on, she admired its lines. A man in coveralls balanced on a ladder, futzing with the craft's tail numbers.

Her eyes widened as she realized he was altering them. She was pretty sure it was illegal, but she'd keep that opinion to herself. Her father strode out of the hangar, dressed in military fatigues, and pointed to where he wanted her to park.

She put the 4Runner in the indicated spot and got out, going around to the back to gather her gear. She'd just slammed and locked the car when her father walked up to her.

"Hi, Dad."

He nodded curtly, back in full military operations mode. "I'll take your kit. Step inside the hangar."

She furled her brows his way, but he shook his head and gave her a small shove toward the open hangar door. Julie hurried inside and blinked to adapt to the sudden dimness.

"Over here, Dr. Wray," a man's rough voice ordered.

She angled toward a bald man. Medium height, with keen blue eyes, he wore a Marine uniform. "Remove your coat," he said, and then added, "Please."

"Why?" She stared at him, mystified.

He reached down and grabbed a Kevlar vest, waving it her way. "The general says you need one of these. Got to get the right size, or it won't do its job."

"B-but it's a bulletproof vest," she stammered. "Surely, that's overkill."

"Juliana Wray." Chris's voice boomed from the hangar

doorway. "If you can't follow orders, immediately and without question, you can't come."

Her temper had always been quick to ignite, and a rush of white-hot anger flashed through her. What the hell? She wasn't one of his men.

Her father stood still, staring at her, his eyes cold and his face impassive. This was a side of him she hadn't seen before.

She slid out of her jacket and took the proffered vest, fiddling with the fastenings.

The Marine said. "Nope. It's too big. Try this one."

She traded hers for his next guess at size. This one passed muster, but it was snug enough it bordered on uncomfortable. "It feels tight," she said.

"You'll get used to it," the Marine said. "It has to stay put if you're running or crawling or engaged in any type of activity. The larger sizes have a nasty habit of twisting and leaving a vital area exposed to gunfire."

She started to unfasten it.

"Leave it on," Chris said. "It needs to become a part of you, so it doesn't divert your attention when we get to the place where you might actually require its protection."

"One more thing," the Marine said and handed her a large-bore semiautomatic pistol in a shoulder holster.

"Any chance I could have a revolver instead?"

The Marine exchanged a pointed look with her father, who nodded.

She traded guns, figured out the shoulder holster, and picked up her jacket along with two boxes of shells.

"Come on," Chris said, his demeanor much less forbidding. "I'd forgotten how bad you were with semiautomatic weapons."

"Bet you haven't forgotten what you used to tell me."

He grinned. "You better nail 'em with the first bullet because after that you jammed the gun."

They walked outside, and she scanned the tarmac. Where was Brice?

Her phone jangled; she dragged it out of a pocket. A text from him scrolled across her display.

Almost there. Caught in traffic. Let your dad know, please.

Chris read the text over her shoulder. He motioned her off to one side. "This mission is far from a sure thing, and we're off normal radar. Once Brice gets here, you'll both leave your cell phones with the master at arms inside. We'll all have burner phones. Untraceable," he clarified.

Her mouth grew dry, and sweat formed in her armpits. "Serious stuff."

"Very. It's why you must do exactly as I say. No second guessing. No questions."

"Is anyone else coming?"

Her father nodded. "An old colleague of mine. You won't know his name, but trust he knows his stuff. He's already inside the plane. He and I will be flying it."

"I thought you let your certificates go."

"I did, but this is a Gulfstream G650, long range. As jets go, it's on the smaller side, and I'm still qualified to fly them. Thanks for asking." His words were so droll and so typically Chris, it reassured her.

"Will four of us be enough? I'm scarcely mercenary material. Neither is Brice."

"Half a dozen hand-picked men will meet us near our target." He looked straight at her. "Neither you nor Brice will go inside." His eyes developed a pinched aspect. "I don't want you to see what's probably in there. It would give you nightmares for the rest of your life."

A shiny, black BMW slewed around the corner and headed right toward them. Must be Brice. Her heart did a funny little flipflop. She shouldn't be thinking about him, but she couldn't help herself. They'd have hours to talk and catch up and…

She cut her thoughts off at the roots. The time in the plane should be spent strategizing, developing several alternate plans to rescue Katie. If she and Brice had any kind of a shot at a mutual future, it would have to wait.

rice parked where General Wray indicated and got out of his car after popping the trunk. By the time he walked to the hatch to collect the three bags of gear he'd thrown together—two medical, one personal—the Wrays had joined him.

"Were you able to get everything on the list I sent?" Chris Wray asked.

"Yes. Apologies for being late. Traffic was a beast coming from the east side. Be sure to thank your wife for running interference with my mom. Saved a whole lot of time when I called her because she already knew something had come up."

"Ariel's always been good at thinking on her feet." Chris smiled. "We'll have to find out what story she concocted, so we're all on the same page after we're back."

Brice began gathering things from the car, but Chris waved him aside. "Julie and I will move your kit to the plane. You need to head into that hangar. How long since you've fired a sidearm?"

The question caught him off-guard. "Maybe six or seven

months. I still enjoy hunting, and I try to hit the range occasionally."

Chris keyed a mike clipped to his collar. It was so small and unobtrusive, Brice might not have noticed it otherwise. "Last man headed your way," he said. "Send him to the plane once you're done."

Julie dragged one of his bags out. "Wow. What's in this one? Rocks?"

"I'll get it." Her father slung the strap over one shoulder. "Get moving, son."

"On my way, sir. What will I be collecting in the hangar? A gun?"

"And a Kevlar vest." Julie tendered a gritty smile that spoke to just how out of her league she was feeling.

He wanted to offer support, but they needed to get moving. Besides, he felt awkward with her father standing there. "Just close the trunk when you're done," he said. "Everything's already locked."

"Hold up a second." Chris extended a hand, and Juliana gave him her phone, which he handed to Brice. "Give this and your cell phone to the master at arms inside. They'll be waiting for you when we return."

Brice wanted to protest. Instead, he asked, "How will we communicate?"

"Burner phones. Get moving. We'll have hours to talk on the plane."

Brice loped for the open hangar door. After a short session with the absolutely humorless Marine who outfitted him with a gun and vest, he ran to the plane and up its steps. He and his practice partners had sprung for a plane to make it easier to provide service to locations east of the Cascades, but theirs was a plain Jane workhorse compared with this beauty.

He'd always appreciated fine machinery. He'd acquired

the BMW roadster direct from the factory in Munich because that particular model wasn't available in the United States. He wanted to comb through every inch of the Gulfstream, starting with its power plant, but he recognized it for a diversionary tactic. Being fitted with a bulletproof vest had been sobering, and it added a whole new angle to what lay ahead.

The Wrays stood just inside the plane. Its interior surprised him. He'd expected luxury to match Gulfstream's reputation as a premier private jet manufacturer. Instead, the passenger compartment was spartan. Seats that looked as if they'd come out of a military transport were arranged in four rows, one on each side of a center aisle. The back of the plane was devoted to storage; his duffles had been secured by straps along with several others.

General Wray hit a button, and an electric motor whirred as the steps rose and locked into place. The whine of turbines made the floor vibrate beneath Brice's feet.

"Prepare for takeoff," an unfamiliar male voice called. "Need you in the cockpit, General."

"Be there in five," Chris replied.

"Roger that. Full power run-up in progress."

The engine noise grew much louder.

Juliana's father narrowed his eyes. "Grab these two seats." He jerked his chin at the first row. "You'll wear headphones, so we can communicate. They're tucked into pouches along the wall."

"You'll be flying us?" Brice asked.

"You have a problem with that, son?" The corners of Chris's mouth twitched but didn't make it to smile position.

"No. Not at all. Who was that other fellow?"

"Mystery man," Julie spoke up. "We won't know who he is."

Her father offered her an approving nod. "Once we hit

cruise altitude, you'll be free to move about. Head's in the back. So's a small galley with snacks, water, and maybe fruit juice."

"What? No booze?" Julie waggled a finger her father's way.

"We can pop the champagne after we're back stateside. I'll continue this briefing once we're upstairs." Chris ducked through the open cockpit door, dragging it shut behind him.

Julie took the seat on the left side of the aisle, so Brice settled into the one across from her and buckled what turned out to be a shoulder harness. He found the headset and settled it into place.

Julie did the same and keyed the push-to-talk switch. "Can you hear me?"

"We all can," Chris's voice crackled through Brice's earpieces. "Quiet until we're off the ground."

Brice unplugged his headset and gestured for Julie to do the same.

"But Dad said we should wear them," she said.

"Yes, but that was so he could communicate with us, something he won't be doing for at least the next twenty to thirty minutes. Right now, they have an open channel to the tower," he told her. "Once we leave the ground, they can set the system so it's only the four of us."

"Why wouldn't the plane have a PA system, independent of headphones?"

"Probably to avoid anyone intercepting what's said. I bet they have some way to scramble the electronics. Maybe it works better with individual units than a PA system."

"I'll ask Dad later." She clasped her hands over the headset in her lap.

"How are you doing?"

She shrugged. "Scared we won't get there soon enough. Dad gave you a list of supplies, huh?"

"Enough to outfit a small field hospital. I had kits still packaged from my DWB tours, though. Made it easier, but I still had to detour through the hospital pharmacy for some of the drug items."

"DWB?" She raised one dark brow into a question mark.

"Doctors Without Borders. It's essentially an international medical aid society."

"I know about them. Just didn't recognize the acronym straight off. Did you run into problems getting here?"

"You might say so. I was hoping your father wouldn't ask for a blow by blow, and he didn't."

The plane started down the runway, moving fast. It rose smoothly into the air, much more quickly than Brice anticipated it would, and climbed steeply. He whistled long and low, appreciating the plane's abundance of power.

"What?"

He shrugged, feeling uncomfortable. "I've always loved machinery. You know. Fast cars."

"And loose women?" she quipped.

"I wouldn't know. None ever threw themselves across my path."

"Maybe they did, and you were too preoccupied to notice. What happened to slow you down getting to Boeing Field?"

"I chose the south bridge route and took a chance with the carpool lane since it was moving much faster than the others."

She made a face. "Oh-oh."

"Yeah. Predictable, huh? A cop pulled me over. I flashed my medical creds and mostly told the truth. Said I was heading to Boeing Field, and I was late for a life flight plane leaving the country. Don't know if you noticed, but all my medical bags carry the DWB logo, so he waved me through and told me he'd radio his buddies not to stop me again.

Even though the episode ended decently, it cost me almost twenty minutes."

She rolled her eyes. "Your MD credentials go a whole lot further than my archaeology ones. Last time I was speeding —on my way to present an academic paper, mind you—the Highway Patrol guy could have cared less who I was or where I was going. Ended up costing me over three hundred bucks."

"Not too late to go to medical school." He smiled.

"I'd make a crappy doctor, and both of us know it. Never had the aptitude for smoothing over cranky, sick people. Hell, I was in denial about how sick Sarah was until very recently."

"Be a surgeon. Their patients don't talk much."

"Yeah, because they're asleep." Julie laughed.

Damn it was good to hear her rich, throaty laugh that had always reminded him of a rambunctious kitten, purring. He struggled for words to describe how much her happiness meant to him. Before he settled on something that was neutral and didn't presume too much—or anything at all— the cockpit door flew open.

"What part about headphones on escaped the two of you?" General Wray scowled. "If we weren't already late, I'd be tempted to circle back to the strip and leave you there."

"Sorry, sir. Julie was compliant. I'm the one who suggested she and I talk while the plane—"

Chris made a chopping motion. Brice dropped his headset back into place. Julie's already circled her head. "Better." Chris's voice crackled through the electronics. He went back into the cockpit, but left the door open.

Brice watched him settle into the copilot's seat and waited for the promised briefing.

"Conditions are favorable," the other pilot said. "We should arrive in just shy of twelve hours."

"Will we stop somewhere to refuel?" Juliana asked.

"No." The pilot paused for a beat. "I recognize you weren't trained by the military, Dr. Wray, but trust we will tell you what you need to know."

"If that's a roundabout way of instructing me not to ask questions, you can just come out and say what you mean," she replied.

"Fine. If the general and I open the floor to questions, you'll be the first to know."

Brice couldn't see the other man since he was turned toward the windscreen, but his words held the slightest hint of an accent. Perhaps Russian. Maybe Eastern European. Possibly Scandinavian." A wool watch cap covered his head with a headset perched atop it.

Juliana reached across the aisle and rested her fingertips on Brice's arm. He glanced at her, and she rolled her eyes and mimed a salute.

Brice grinned. Before she could take her hand away, he placed one of his over it. Touching her, any part of her, was exquisite. He savored the silk of her skin, the line of her long, tapering fingers. Her nails were short and blunt cut, which pleased him. He'd never had any use for long fingernails on anyone.

"Listen up." General Wray was all business. "The most likely scenario is our target is still at the identified location. It is possible they will have transferred her, though. Or that someone will have purchased her. Healthy white women command high prices. A ground team will be moving into position in roughly two hours to keep an eye on the location."

Brice had questions. Like why wasn't the team already in place? How many men were on the ground team, and did the human trafficking den have more than one entrance? He'd come across one with an underground tunnel affair attached to it during a medical cleanup operation.

"Another possibility"—the general cleared his throat—"is our target escaped."

"Sorry. I know you don't encourage active dialogue." Juliana's tone was carefully neutral. "How likely is that?"

"If she's anything like you," her father retorted, "I give it better than fifty percent, but you'd better hope she stays put. One of the best ways for her to end up with a bullet through her head and dumped where we'll never, ever find her is for her to run. They have dogs, and her captors will be extremely motivated to make certain she doesn't reach the American embassy in Cairo."

Pain and horror washed over Julie's expressive features. Brice tightened his grip on her hand.

"Transport will be waiting for us at the airport," the pilot added. "Depending on intel from the ground team, we'll select our route."

"We'll be landing at an unmarked, currently unused, strip in the desert. Originally, it was built by the Russians, but they abandoned it years ago," Chris said, and then added, "It will expedite things. Less air traffic. No customs. No issues with our guns. If we get very lucky, no one will strip the plane while we're gone."

"I'm leaving two men with it," the pilot said. "Sorry, I thought I'd mentioned that."

Chris made a noncommittal sound that could have meant anything, followed by, "Once we reach the target, you two will remain with the car and driver. In the event we develop unexpected problems, the driver will take you directly to a safe location. I'll join you as soon as things are mopped up."

Julie frowned and captured her lower lip with her teeth. Brice could almost see wheels turning in her head. He covered his mouthpiece and hissed, "Follow orders."

She flashed a determined grin, mouthed, "Bite me," and said, "Dad. You always told me how important it is to deploy every resource at your disposal."

"I know where you're headed, and you can stop right there," Chris growled.

"First off, trust I'm not stupid enough to get caught in the middle of a major firefight," Julie replied. "Second, sending Brice—our team doctor—to a location where he can't do any good makes no sense."

He liked the sound of *our team doctor* because it made it clear he and Juliana were playing for the same side. Finally.

"This is why we do not place family in a direct line of command," the pilot sputtered. "Dr. Wray. When things turn to shit, it happens fast. Far too fast for you to get into an argument over orders. If the general's attention is split too many ways, he might end up shot."

"You can't bully me," she retorted. "Threats never had much impact, either. Brice and I will stay out of the way, but we're not leaving unless we have to. I'm afraid Dad will be conservative."

"Damn straight, I'll be conservative." Chris left his seat and stomped to where he stood over them. He ripped off his headset and jerked Julie's off her head, unplugging it from its socket. She pulled her hand out from beneath Brice's and clasped it with the other one, regarding her father.

Before he could launch into a parental lecture, Julie said, "You brought me for several good reasons. I fill multiple roles. I know Katie. She trusts me. I speak the language, and I'm familiar with the Nile Delta region. And Cairo. None of those reasons have gone away."

Chris dropped to a crouch between their seats. "I promised your mother I'd bring you home safe, and by God, I will."

"Fine, but I'm not flying halfway around the world for

you to shuttle me off to the side. Why outfit me with this"—she tapped her Kevlar vest—"if you didn't expect me to need it?"

"Standard field gear. Juliana. You have a temper. When it's activated, your ability to reason is impacted."

"You think I don't know that about myself? I'm not fifteen anymore." She glared at her father. He glowered back.

Brice recognized a standoff and removed his own headset. It was as good a time as any to jump in. "I agree with your daughter about not moving me off the field. If Katie—or anyone else—is injured, the first few moments can be critical. If I'm in a safe house miles away, I won't be any good to anyone. Plus"—he leaned forward in his harness—"I'm a decent shot."

Chris shook his head. "You medical types balk at shooting people. Goes against the grain."

"You trusted me enough to bring me. Don't second guess yourself," Brice countered, certain if it was a "me or him" situation, he wouldn't hesitate to shoot.

"What he said," Juliana chimed in.

Brice could have hugged her. They were definitely playing for the same team again. God how he'd missed her presence and her support. And a whole lot more he couldn't let himself think about. Not until Katie was safe.

Chris pushed heavily to his feet. "We'll see how things unfold once the field team sets up shop and the plane is on the ground. Meanwhile, try to catch some sleep, so you're not zombies when we get there."

"What about you?" Brice asked, concerned about General Wray.

"The pilot and I are trading off four-hour rest breaks. Mine begins in about thirty minutes. There's a seat in the back near the duffles. Once we're in Egypt, you'll receive specific orders. You cannot question them, no matter how stupid or ill-conceived you think they are. Am I clear?"

Julie nodded. So did Brice.

Chris softened his tone. "I would never dream of telling you how to conduct a dig," he told his daughter. "Nor would I presume to tell you how to care for your patients," he said to Brice.

"Point taken," Brice said. "This is your area of expertise, and we have to respect that."

"Sorry, Dad," Juliana said. "I'll rein in my opinions and be a good soldier."

Relief etched into his features, and he returned to the cockpit, closing the door behind him.

Julie put her headset back on and reached across the aisle. He laced his fingers with hers. Even if they didn't have a future together as a couple, they were friends again. She clearly saw him as a source of comfort and support, and it warmed his heart.

He wanted to pull her into his lap, slash his mouth down on hers, but now wasn't the time. If she was still as conflicted as he about their relationship, furtive kisses would add an emotional overlay neither of them needed until this mission was over.

uliana was keyed up enough about the phalanx of unknowns ahead, she didn't expect to fall sleep, but the flight was so smooth, it lulled her. Having her hand clasped in Brice's helped. It felt normal. Right. Like they were settling back into a familiar place, one that had brought them both joy.

Before she'd allowed her temper to rule the day.

Maybe she should apologize. Again.

Or maybe they could let the past die, the bad parts, anyway, and pick up from where they were. It felt like a wiser course.

His eyes were closed, head tilted against the seat back. She studied him with his mop of blond hair that never stayed put and his Greek-god build. And his eyelashes. No man had a right to eyelashes like that, so long and thick they almost brushed his cheeks. It took discipline not to extricate her hand, so she could run it through his hair.

Her father emerged from the cockpit, stopping where their joined hands blocked the aisle. He raised a gray brow, and a knowing smile played around his mouth, but he didn't say a word.

Julie untangled her fingers from Brice's, and her father walked past them, probably on his way to the seat in the back. Brice opened his eyes and regarded her with his direct, appraising gaze. He removed his headset. "We probably won't get in trouble again while your dad is resting."

She tugged her headset off and unplugged it. "Hope not. The pilot seems like a real badass."

"He's not that terrible," Brice replied. "He's a competent field operative, and they're not particularly flexible about how they want things done. I've worked with men like him before. They've secured sites, made them safe enough for me to provide medical services."

She smiled, feeling a soft, vulnerable place deep inside crack open. She'd locked it up tight after catching Brice with Sarah. "You always wanted to be a doctor. Is it anything like what you thought it would be?"

He drew his blond brows together. "Yes and no. If I was twenty-two again, though, I'd choose the same career. Never really saw myself doing anything else."

"Kind of like me and archaeology. I couldn't wait to get to graduate school so I could lose myself in ancient worlds, pick through what our ancestors left, and try to make sense of it."

"You always loved to dig. Hell, we'd go clamming, and you'd dig way below the clams."

"You used to tease me about leprechauns and the pot of gold. Or finding a secret path that led to China."

He laughed softly. "I'd forgotten that part." He reached for her hand, and she clasped it. "Thanks for being you. I've missed…everything about us together."

Her heart swelled, the crack in her guarded places widening. "Me too. I was such a stupid—"

"Uh-uh. None of that. No looking back."

"Funny, but I came to the same conclusion. If we have any chance at all, it will be from building on now."

He twisted in his seat so he faced her, his expression serious, eyes brimming with an emotion she didn't have a name for. Hot and intense, his gaze drew her. "We make our own chances. Don't answer me now, but think about what you want. I can't guarantee I won't make another mistake, one where you'll want to strangle me. What I can guarantee is I'll never hurt you on purpose. That was true fifteen years ago too."

Her eyes burned, and she swallowed around a thick place in her throat. Hope burned a fiery path through her, from the soles of her feet to her head. Her father and mother knew. What had her mother said? Something about deciding Brice was the only man for her long ago.

"We can talk after we're back home," she said, but her voice vibrated with longing.

"We can, and we will. It's more than I hoped for, and plenty good enough for now." He smiled, his whole demeanor conveying warmth and promise. "Maybe we should put the damned headsets back on and try to catch some shuteye."

She wanted to undo her harness and wrap her arms around him. The touch and taste of his lips sang to her, lured her, but now wasn't the time or place. They had to get through this mission in one piece, hopefully with Katie still relatively uninjured.

She was smart and scrappy. Resourceful too. All of them were strong assets. Julie blew out a tense breath.

Brice stopped before settling his headset in place. "You're thinking about Katie, aren't you?"

"Yes, but how did you know?"

He shrugged. "I've always read people easily, and I spent years being attuned to your moods. Try not to worry. We'll get her back."

"How can you be so sure?"

"I get feelings about things. It's part of practicing medicine. Not everything is science. Some of it's hunches. Kind of like the one you had that led you to the dig level that's created all the problems. I had no idea you academics were such a bloodthirsty crew."

"We're not usually this overt about it, but theft of original work is enough of a problem, most universities have a mechanism in place to assess culpability and deal with PhDs who steal other researchers' work."

He laced his fingers with hers again. "Get some rest, Julie. Egypt will be here before we know it. I have a feeling this will unfold fast."

"My mom said the same thing."

"I've always liked your mother. She's the perfect combination of tough and maternal."

"Thanks. I'll tell her you said so. It will please her."

Julie plugged her headset back into the jack and shut her eyes. Excitement she and Brice might have another chance rippled through her, heady as a fine, old wine. It almost displaced her anxiety about what lay ahead, but not quite. Her father was right to chastise her. This wasn't a university field trip where everyone was deluded enough to believe they had equal rights and an equal voice.

She vowed to be a good soldier, just like she'd told her dad. He'd brought up a good point about not fancying himself an archaeologist—or a doctor.

A HAND on her shoulder woke her. Her father said. "We have

about half an hour before we'll begin our descent. Get up. Move around. Throw some water on your face."

She blinked and shook her head, working to clear the cobwebs from her sleep-fuzzy brain. "Geez. How long was I out?"

Chris smiled. "Most of the trip, but I bet you didn't get much sleep last night. Not after that visit from Doug Johnson."

"You're right, I didn't."

Across the aisle, Brice stood and stretched his arms over his head, pivoting his torso from side to side. "I'm going to troll through the galley. Want anything, Julie?"

"Water, but I can get my own. I need to get up too."

Brice nodded and started toward the rear of the plane.

"Thanks for keeping your headsets on," Chris said. "I'll let you know when you have to buckle in for landing."

"Why doesn't the plane have a PA system?" she asked, thinking back to her conversation with Brice.

"It did. We disabled it. Far easier to scramble the headset electronics than the whole PA system."

"Brice thought it was something like that." She unbuckled her harness and got to her feet. "Would enemy agents actually listen in on planes like this one?"

"You betcha. Modern microprocessors and wireless systems have made it easier than ever. Frequency scanners are always active—and manned. When they zero in on something interesting, they amplify it."

She finger-combed her tangled hair. "There's a whole world out there I don't know much about."

"Yes, there is." He tugged a lock of her hair. "Braid that. Get it out of the way so it won't blow in your eyes or give someone something to grab onto. See you on the ground." Her father vanished into the cockpit, oozing "bring it on" energy. He'd lived and breathed combat and covert operations for a long time, and he probably missed the adrenaline that came from courting danger. She'd always wondered why he retired and suspected Ariel had something to do with it.

She walked to the back of the plane, stretching this way and that to ease her cramped muscles. Bending over the galley sink, she cupped water in her hands and sluiced it over her face.

Brice came out of the head, drying his hands on a paper towel. "All yours," he said.

Julie walked into the neat bathroom, noting it was twice the size of a normal airline lavatory. She dug through drawers until she found a hairbrush and carried it to the galley where she perched on a counter and brushed out her hair.

"You have the most beautiful hair. It's always reminded me of liquid midnight." Brice came up behind her and threaded his fingers through her locks.

She leaned into his touch. It would be easy to pivot and wrap her arms around him and...

She drew away from the magic and promise of his touch. "I need rubber bands. Dad said to tie my hair out of the way."

"I saw some. Hang on." He bent and opened a lower drawer on the other side of the galley. Sure enough, it contained a potpourri of items. Scissors. Sewing kits. A stapler.

Brice handed over a packet of rubber bands with a flourish. "Your wish is my—"

"Knock it off." Grinning, she sectioned her hair and turned it into four braids. Once they were done, she wound them together and secured them at the bottom with another band.

"Wow. You're fast," he observed.

"I should be. It's my hairdo *du jour* for the field."

He stood close to her, so close, she itched to close her arms around him. He dropped his hands atop her shoulders and kissed her forehead, the gesture so sweet it cut through her resolve to keep her distance until after they had Katie safely rescued.

Julie threaded her arms beneath his, splaying her fingers across his back.

He held her close for one, wonderful, delicious moment before letting go. "You feel the same, but different."

"You too, but I need a more comprehensive sample." She smothered a comment about the tantalizing bands of muscles she'd felt running along his back. He'd been kind of a skinny kid, but then so had she.

"A sample, huh? You'll be sorely disappointed I don't date back to the Pleistocene."

"Good thing," she shot back. "If you did, I'd be turning you over to anthropology."

"Buckle in for landing," sounded through her headset.

Brice snatched up two packages of crackers and a bottle of water. "Come on. I located nourishment. I have a feeling we won't be eating much on the ground."

"The food in the Americanized parts of Cairo is safe enough, otherwise—"

"I understand," he cut in. "I'm the one with the background staring through a binocular scope at microbes that make you sick. Got to stick with things that have been well cooked or boiled."

"Ha! Even that won't save you from dysentery some of the time. We were all sick at the last dig." She sank into her seat and reached for her harness.

"Did you take antibiotics?" He buckled in.

"Sometimes."

"Yeah, you probably incubated antibiotic resistant bacteria. They're a bitch to get rid of."

The plane dropped lower until her ears ached with the abrupt pressure change. When she stared out the window, all she saw was desert. Where the hell were they? Come to think of it, neither her father nor the pilot had said boo about the ground team or Katie's whereabouts.

She opened her mouth to ask but was worried they were tuned into some tower frequency like they'd been back at Boeing. It didn't seem likely if they were landing at an abandoned strip, but her father's nonchalant comment about enemy ears being everywhere had been unsettling.

The wheels touched down so gently, she wasn't sure they were on the ground until negative acceleration dragged at her as the jet slowed. They'd arrived. It was game time. The crackers Brice had insisted she eat congealed into a sodden mass in her stomach.

Chris came through the cockpit door as the other pilot taxied; he motioned for them to get rid of their headsets. Once they were unplugged, he sank between their seats and said, "Ground team believes Katie is still in the same spot, so it's where we're heading. It's about a twenty-minute drive from here. Maybe thirty."

He blew out a breath and continued. "Rather than waiting for us, they're going in. If things proceed well, they'll have Katie by the time we get there. We can triage any others who may require care, and turn the Land Rover around."

The plane rolled to a halt, and the pilot killed the engine. Chris moved to the door and unlocked it. The steps deployed automatically. He hadn't asked for her input on the current plan, and she didn't like it. A whole lot of things could go wrong. No reason Katie would trust this new batch of men any more than whoever had kidnapped her.

"Work as a team and hand the gear up this way," her father instructed.

Brice loped up the aisle and bent to undo the webbing

holding the various bags and duffles. Julie ferried items to her father, who dropped them down the stairs. Presumably the pilot—or their driver—was at the bottom, but she didn't hang around long enough to check.

"I'm leaving my personal stuff in the plane," she told Brice.

He nodded. "Yeah. Me too."

"Grab the two long, black ones on the bottom," Chris yelled. "That should do it."

Julie hefted one as she carried it, figuring it had to be some type of rifle. Her father took it from her and gestured her down the stairs. Two men wearing traditional, flowing Egyptian tops called gallibaya, layered over trousers, hurried over. Despite turbans, the men were American—or maybe European. She'd bet her bottom dollar on it. Although they had dark eyes and swarthy complexions, they didn't carry themselves like men in the Arab world did.

"We're here, boss," one said in pure Brooklynese, clinching her impression.

What looked like AK-47s were slung over the men's shoulders. The pilot, still wearing the wool watch cap, handed an envelope to the man. "You get the rest when we return, and the plane is still here and untouched."

The faux Egyptian snapped off a sloppy salute and took stock of what was in the envelope before pocketing it.

Brice trotted down the steps. He had on dark glasses, but he still raised a hand to shield his eyes from the glare. She put on her own sunglasses. They helped but not all that much.

An older Land Rover roared out of nowhere, screeching to a halt next to them and their pile of gear. Another turbaned man—this one Egyptian—jumped out and began grabbing duffles and throwing them into the back of the car.

Julie greeted him in Arabic, but he ignored her. Not a

total surprise. If she'd been male, he'd have greeted her in return.

The pilot got into the front seat of the Land Rover. Chris herded her and Brice into the back before climbing into the front, which forced the pilot to straddle the center hump. She inhaled deeply. The baked clay scent of Egypt was unique. Heat beat down on her, dry and unforgiving. The sky was a brilliant blue without a cloud in sight.

"I didn't miss this part," she muttered. "Damned hot here."

"Yeah, and this is December," Brice said. "Bet it's worse in July."

"Over a hundred every day," she told him. "Doesn't cool off much at night, either."

Their driver jumped nimbly inside, fired the engine, and took off, driving fast. If Julie was a decent judge of body language, he was frightened half to death and wanted nothing more than to be done with this.

Chris twisted until he leaned over the seat back and gave her and Brice phones. "Only use these in an emergency. Numbers are programmed into them. I'm A, the pilot is B, Julie is C, Brice is D, and the embassy is E. They're fully charged. Keep them on and close to you. Call the embassy only as a last resort."

Her mind jumped from topic to topic, which told her how nervous she was. One minute she wondered how much money was in it for the mercenaries if they watched over the plane. The next, she was certain Katie would run from the team breaking into the trafficking den. Brice threaded his fingers with hers, and she held on tight.

The desert gave way to mud huts, and then to more substantial buildings as they hit slums marking the northern outskirts of Cairo. A brown pall clung to everything from chronic air pollution.

The Land Rover took a hard left toward the Nile Delta.

"Is the water as bad as the air?" Brice asked.

"Yup. Plus, they've had issues with mercury poisoning."

The car wove through run down tenements. Garbage rotted beneath the hot sun lending a stench that mingled with broken—or nonexistent—sewers. A distant pop-pop reached her. Gunfire?

The driver hit the brakes and the car squealed to a halt. With a rush of Arabic, he bolted from the vehicle and took off running.

The pilot cursed under his breath, slid into the driver's seat, and the car rolled forward again.

"Where'd you find him?" Chris asked.

The pilot shrugged. "Doesn't matter. He won't get paid."

"What'd he say when he ran off?" Brice turned to Julie.

"Loosely translated, it was that no amount of money is worth getting killed over. That's rifle fire, and we're closing on it."

"Probably the trafficker's den," the pilot said. "Half a mile, and we'll be there."

Chris vaulted into the backseat. Reaching into the jumble of cases behind it, he grabbed one of the long, black bags. He unzipped it and removed the automatic rifle she'd suspected was there, inserting a magazine.

"Yeah. Assemble the other one for me," the pilot said, "and then get back up here."

Her father unpackaged the other rifle and slid both across the back of the front seat before clambering over himself. Brice pulled his weapon from its holster. She reached for hers, but her hand shook so badly, she couldn't unsnap the piece of leather holding the revolver in place.

The sound of gunfire had grown so loud, she wished for earplugs. The men seemed on edge and excited. She wanted to crawl under the seat and hide.

She inhaled deeply, and wished she hadn't. The reek of

raw sewage and rot burned the back of her throat and made her eyes water.

"One more block," the pilot said. "Get ready."

The Land Rover skidded around a corner on its outside wheels and came to a stop behind a line of six hard-bodied, flinty eyed men with rifles trained on a long, low, concrete building that looked like a bunker. Volleys of bullets rained from the bunker, and the mercenaries fired back. Chunks of the building sloughed off, turning into projectiles of their own.

"Get down," Chris instructed. He and the pilot leapt from the Land Rover, rifles firing almost before their feet hit the ground.

Brice pushed her into the footwell, throwing his body across hers as added protection. Her heart ratcheted into hyperdrive, and her tongue flooded with the sour taste of adrenaline.

"I can't see what's happening," she protested, writhing beneath him.

"Maybe not, but you're safe. I can't see anything, either."

Her ears rang; her head throbbed. The proximity to Brice would have been exciting in almost any other circumstance, but he was providing something far more precious than sex. He was shielding her, offering the ultimate proof he still loved her. In the midst of the heat and noise and stink of gunpowder, she fought the quick, hot bite of tears. She didn't deserve him. Not the way she'd acted.

He heaved his weight off her, and she realized everyone had stopped firing. She unfolded from her crouch in time to see Brice scrambling through their gear for one of his bags. Once he had it in hand, he bolted from the car.

She scanned the cracked, dry earth in front of the bunker, noting it was littered with bodies. The front door cracked open, followed by a flash of something white. More of it emerged, and she recognized a torn strip of cloth.

"No more gunfire," Chris yelled. "They're surrendering."

One of the mercenaries—this batch garbed in Western clothing—trotted to Chris. He touched the tip of his ball cap. "General. Do you trust these yahoos? Because I sure don't."

"Of course I don't trust them," Chris growled, "but I bet they ran out of ammo, which would explain why they quit firing on us. Use the bullhorn. Tell them we want the slaves out in the open. Pronto."

The man nodded and directed a few words of horribly bad Arabic at the bunker. A stream of emaciated bodies stumbled out the door, lining up in the yard. Scraps of cloth had been knotted into a semblance of clothes. Everyone was barefoot with matted hair and open, running sores. Some of the people couldn't walk unassisted.

"Goddammit," Brice cursed from where he knelt next to a fallen man dressed in Bedouin robes. "Those poor bastards."

The cavalcade of human misery continued, but Katie wasn't among them. Julie got out of the car and hurried to her father, grabbing his shoulder once she reached him. "She's not here."

"Yes. I have eyes."

"Who are all the bodies?" She gritted her teeth, swallowing back revulsion at the carnage spread before her.

"The bad guys. Save your pity. They don't deserve it."

The mercenary who'd approached them before trotted close. "I have no bloody idea what happened to the target. I swear, she was inside. Hold up. I'll conduct a search."

"Can I ask the ones in the yard about her?" Julie tightened her grip on her father's shoulder. "Please."

He nodded. "Yes. I'll be right next to you."

She waited for Chris and his automatic rifle before walking closer. Using the Egyptian dialect of Arabic, she greeted the people milling about. Then she asked about her friend, her sister, who was missing. Tears gathered in her eyes at the misery surrounding her.

A man shuffled forward. Iron bands circled his ankles with a chain connecting them. He didn't look at her but said Katie had escaped through a little-used tunnel the previous night. When she asked how he knew, he switched to English and said, "I help."

"Why didn't you run too?" she asked, also in English. He pointed mutely at his hobbled ankles.

Julie bowed her head in deference and thanked him. She turned to her father. "What happens next?"

"Help for these people should be en route, and we need to update our game plan."

The mercenary emerged from the bunker and called, "She's not here, General. I checked all the cells. The keepers aren't here, either, but I figured they'd run before the authorities showed up." He gave a short bark of a laugh. "Maybe we got lucky and killed them all. Fuckers."

"Did we sustain any casualties?" Chris asked.

"They winged Joe, but it wasn't bad." He pursed his lips into a thin line. "Figured out how the target escaped. There's a tunnel, probably part of an old sewer system."

"No, it's not," Julie said. "This area has been inhabited for thousands of years. People lived underground as a hedge against the heat. There are grottos down there. Whole towns, like as not. It's how Katie found a way out. She's studied the history of this place, so she knew what to look for."

Chris turned his steely blue gaze her way. "Put yourself in Katie's place," he instructed. "Where would you go?"

Brice was moving from one person to the next, sorting them into groups.

Juliana got her bearings. They were miles from the more civilized part of Cairo. She shut her eyes and did her damnedest to reconstruct what her student would do. When she opened them, she said, "I bet she headed back to the dig site. It's maybe five miles that way."

"Why the hell would she do that?" her father asked.

Julie skinned her lips back from her teeth. "To confront Orestes about what he did to her. She'd have no way of knowing he's not there."

Cars were pulling up, and a variety of officials had gathered. Brice latched onto one man and was gesturing, no doubt explaining how he'd triaged medical needs. A black flatbed truck backed into the crowded courtyard. Two men piled out and began tossing corpses into the truck's bed.

"Brice. Back in the car." Her father raised his voice to be heard over the din.

He nodded and ran to them. "Did the best I could. The man I was talking with assured me they'll transport the sickest people to local hospitals, but I'm not sure I believe him."

"They'll provide a cursory level of treatment," Julie murmured and left it there. No reason to go into how limited any type of medical or social services interventions would be.

They drove away from the bunker, following a series of smaller and more deeply rutted roads until they turned onto a track she recognized. "One more mile," she told the driver.

He waved his satellite phone in her face with a mapping program on its display. She wanted to ask if he'd always been a know-it-all, but bit back the words. They rolled into the clearing where she'd lived for ten months. Yellow tape hung from shrubs and bushes, and a dark-eyed, slightly-built man ran toward them screeching in Arabic that the site was off limits. He wore Western field garb comprised of tan trousers, a white shirt, and a floppy sun hat.

She jumped out of the car before her father could stop

her. "I'm Dr. Wray. Did Katherine Johnson show up last night or today?"

The man drew himself taller and replied in British-accented English. "Dr. Wray, the pleasure is mine. I have read—"

"Katherine Johnson," she pressed. Interrupting a man was the height of rudeness, but she'd apologize later.

"Of course not. I'd have alerted the embassy, the authorities."

Julie had always trusted her instincts, and every single one screamed Katie was in the bush somewhere between here and that godawful bunker. Or between here and the river. They'd have to search on foot.

Her father would give her nine yards of hell, but she marched back to the Land Rover. "I'm going to traverse the most likely route on foot," she announced.

"I'll come with you," Brice got out of the car and shouldered one of his medical bags.

"It's not a bad idea," the pilot said. "I'll carry a rucksack with water."

The man who'd warned them to stay away walked to her. "I called the embassy. She isn't there."

"Thank you," Julie told him. "We'll be back before dark."

"Best of luck." The man bowed formally, and she bowed back.

Her father had extracted a device and turned in a circle, holding it in front of him. Something must have alerted him because he took off at a fast lope on a diagonal in the direction of the river.

"What is that?" Brice asked the pilot.

"Thermal scanner. Damn if the general didn't lock onto something." He bolted after Chris with Brice right behind him.

Julie trotted after them. Thermal meant heat, so her

father could have picked up on anything. Or was his device sophisticated enough to sort human emanations from those belonging to animals? She'd never been the praying type, but she offered up a plea her father was on a track that would lead to Katie Johnson. She'd been missing long enough that she was running out of time.

CHAPTER 21

Brice moved the duffle of supplies he'd slung over a shoulder, so it didn't bang his hip with every step. Whatever whiz-bang device Chris was using apparently wasn't foolproof. The general had changed directions a few times. Julie ran alongside Brice. The pilot trotted next to Chris a few feet ahead.

"Watch out for snakes," Julie said. "The afternoon's moving along. Once the heat of the day ebbs, they come out of their nests."

"Any particularly bad ones?"

Breath hissed from between her teeth. "Yeah. Cobras and black mambas are the worst. Several types of cobra—" She stopped talking and extended an arm.

He followed the angle she was pointing toward and spotted a flock of large, dark-colored birds. "I see them. What's the significance?"

Instead of answering him, she called out, "Dad. Look up at about fifteen degrees."

"Good eyes," Chris muttered and altered course toward the birds.

"Are they vultures?" Brice asked.

"I believe they're a type of raptor, and it looks to me like they're waiting for something to die. No other reason for so many of them to have collected in close proximity. I've never been much for bird identification—unless it's bones and they're underground."

Chris had stepped up the pace. Brice welcomed it. Moving dissipated the disappointment of not finding Katie at the sad human slave encampment. He worried they wouldn't locate her at all—until it was too late. Every person in the bunker had been malnourished and dehydrated. Several had the deep, rattling cough that probably meant they suffered from tuberculosis.

Katie hadn't been a prisoner long enough to run a serious risk of catching anything, but dehydration would weaken her. If she was dressed the same way as the other detainees, she'd be barefoot. Not a good bet traveling through snake country.

He had antivenom in his kit, but there was a specific window where it was effective. If they found Katie more than a short time after exposure, it wouldn't do much good.

The flock of birds squawked, not pleased by their approach. Insects whined and buzzed, and the distant chitter of monkeys and small rodents rose and fell. Julie dashed around her father, straight for the protesting birds.

"Juliana. Behind me," he yelled after her, but she ignored him and kept on running.

When she got to the thicket supporting at least twenty birds, she ducked beneath a luxuriant growth of some spiny plant.

"Brice!" she shrieked. "Hurry."

He sprinted for the spot he'd last seen her, with Chris and the pilot close on his heels. Thorns stymied him, snagging on his clothing as he worked his way deeper into the hedge from hell. "Where are you?"

"Middle of this hedge. I found her, but she's barely breathing and burning up."

Brice followed the sound of her voice, but muscling his way through endless thorns meant he moved at a snail's pace. Noting space below, he dropped to his belly and crawled. It worked. In about twenty feet, he entered a rough opening a few feet across.

Julie knelt next to Katie Johnson, cradling her in her arms. The woman's blonde hair trailed in the dirt. Her face was streaked with grime, and her exposed skin bore marks from being whipped.

"Move over," Brice said. Grabbing a pair of gloves, he started a quick assessment.

"How can I help?" Julie asked.

"Open my bag. Get my stethoscope and the BP cuff."

She handed them over.

"Good. Go through the medication vials. They're in a padded leather case."

"Found it. Which one do you want?"

"Hang on. I'll let you know. Meanwhile, locate the syringes. They're individually wrapped. I'll need an eighteen-gauge, three milliliter, with a one-and-a-half-inch needle."

Chris and the pilot slithered through the same low tunnel Brice had used. "What the hell is this place?" the pilot asked. "Never seen anything like it."

"Exactly what it looks like." Juliana's words were terse. "A natural shelter, which is why Katie crawled into it. Before she passed out."

Brice examined Katie's bare feet and sunburned legs. The bottoms of both feet were abraded and blistered. Assuming she pulled through, she wouldn't be walking for a while. Her lower calf bore telltale viper marks, only one set, though, which might bode well.

"I need the antivenom and that syringe and an alcohol wipe."

Julie gave them to him and looked at Katie's legs. "Her poor feet. I'm blown away she made it this far, but that woman always had guts and nerves of steel." She fluttered one hand over the bite mark. "I'm pretty sure a cobra did that."

"Then this should work. The antivenoms are specific, and this one is SAIMR polyvalent, the one your father told me to bring." Brice made a guess at Katie's weight and drew an appropriate amount of drug into the syringe.

"It works on mamba snakes too," Chris said, his voice gruff. "While I'd love to take credit for the roster of supplies I gave Brice, the military maintains medication and supply lists specific to geographic locations."

Brice cleared a spot on Katie's thigh and injected the substance slowly, watching her. A whole lot of things could happen. Antivenoms could be brutal. "Julie. Dig out the epinephrine and another syringe."

"Sure, but isn't that for severe allergic reactions?"

"Exactly. I have no idea how her system will react to what I just gave her, and I want to be ready." He craned his neck around until he saw the pilot. "I could use a bottle of water."

The pilot removed his rucksack and located one, dropping it next to Brice.

"How long before we know if this is going to work?" Julie had moved back to Katie's side and was cradling her head in her lap.

Brice took her vitals again. Not much had changed, but her heartbeat was a little less thready. He had Ringer's solution and IV equipment. He turned toward his bag and dragged it closer. He'd just pulled out a sterile packet with an IV needle and fresh gloves when Katie moaned.

"It's okay, sweetie. I'm here," Julie crooned, bending close and smoothing tangled hair out of her face.

"Julie?" Katie's voice came out in a croak that sounded like long-dead leaves rustling in a brisk wind.

"Yes. It's me."

Brice uncapped the water and got an arm around Katie's shoulders, supporting her in a more upright position. "Take a sip. Not too much."

Katie opened bloodshot green eyes, squinching them against the light. "Damn. Everything hurts."

"Water," Brice urged.

Katie swallowed but then coughed and coughed, struggling for air.

Brice turned her to one side and waited until she caught her breath before offering more water. "This time it will go down easier," he promised. "You have to drink. You're dehydrated."

She swallowed obediently. "Who are you?"

"An old friend of Julie's. And a doctor. Concentrate on taking nice, deep breaths. You're going to be fine."

"Thank Christ for that," Chris muttered.

"I'll bring the Land Rover," the pilot said. Dropping to his belly, he started out of the thicket.

"Doug." Katie struggled against Brice's hold on her. "Got to call Doug."

"We'll let him know we found you," Julie reassured her. Her blue eyes glistened with tears that spilled down her cheeks. She brushed them away.

Brice offered water again. Katie drank and sagged against him. "Thought I was a goner. I saw one cobra, but when I was avoiding it, another one got me." She flexed her feet and groaned.

"We'll get you home and to a hospital," Julie said.

Katie transferred her gaze to where Julie knelt. "Aw geez. You're crying. It's okay."

Julie shook her head. "No. It's not." She gripped Katie's hand. "Orestes Conom will pay for what he did, and we're going to salvage your dissertation project."

Katie nodded, tears sheening her eyes too. "Most important is you found me, saved me. I get to go home to Doug. Everything else can wait. I did a number on my feet. Bet I won't be able to walk for a month. And I won't do Boston this year."

"You're a marathoner?" Brice asked. At her nod, he said, "Me too. At least I used to be. You'll run again, and sooner than you might think. Your wounds are superficial."

At least the ones to her body were. How quickly her spirit would rebound from being abducted and tortured depended on her, but Brice had a feeling Katie Johnson wouldn't let the horror she'd lived through slow her down.

The sound of an engine grew louder.

The Land Rover.

He took one more set of vitals. They were moving in the right direction. "Do you have any idea how long ago the snake bit you?"

Katie narrowed her eyes and glanced at the angle of the sun. "Maybe an hour. Maybe a little less. I was headed for this thicket when it got me. I planned to tourniquet my leg, but I must have passed out."

"Why the thicket?" Brice asked.

"Dig site was cordoned off. I had no idea why, but it didn't feel safe. Thickets like this one have provided protection for thousands of years. This type of plant has water in its root system. Figured I could go to ground here, rest my feet. I'd almost made it when the snake came out of the blue."

"We can talk in the truck," Chris said. "Let's get you out of here."

"Drink the rest of this." Brice waggled the water bottle, and Katie finished its contents.

"Can you crawl?" Julie asked.

"I think so. It's better than you dragging me."

"What do you think?" Julie asked Brice.

He grinned and dropped things back into his duffle. "Absent a machete to carve a path, it's a grand idea. If Katie bogs down, we'll help."

Relief he'd gotten the antivenom on board in time thrummed through him. Cobra venom was a neurotoxin that caused respiratory paralysis, which was why she'd been unconscious when they found her. He helped her roll onto her stomach, and she slithered toward the path leading out of the thicket with Julie right behind her.

Brice zipped his duffle back together.

Chris crouched next to him. Keeping his voice low, he asked, "How close was it?"

Brice met the other man's unwavering gaze. "Close. Another half hour, we'd probably have had a different outcome."

Chris scrubbed the heels of his hands down his face. "Thank Christ I had the thermal scanner. Almost didn't bring it."

"Yeah. Julie would have headed back toward the bunker, which is the route I'd have selected too."

"Makes a hell of a lot more sense than this no-man's-land." Chris's voice was laced with relief. He shook his head. "Damn. Julie was so smart, she could have done anything. Why in God's name she picked a profession where she ends up stuck in spots like this is beyond me."

Brice didn't bother to point out both Chris and Ariel's

life's work had landed them in similarly primitive, godforsaken locations.

He held out a hand. Chris shook it. "We had a good outcome. I've found it's best not to dwell on the might-have-beens," Brice murmured.

"One of my favorite take-home messages as well." Chris's weathered face split into a smile. "So will I finally end up with you as my son-in-law?"

"Hope so, sir. We'll see." Brice crawled out of the thicket, pushing his bag ahead of him.

Katie sat in the back of the Land Rover with Julie's arm firmly around her while she talked on one of the burner cell phones. She was crying, so presumably, she'd called her husband.

"It'll be a bumpy ride until we reach better roads," Chris said, "but we'll manage." He transferred his attention to the pilot. "Is our bird refueled and ready?"

"Indeed, it is."

Brice tossed his bag in the back and slid in next to Katie, sandwiching her between him and Juliana. Chris got into the front and laid one of the rifles across his lap. The other one was wedged between him and the pilot.

"I told the watchdog guarding the dig site we'd found Ms. Johnson," the pilot said. "I swear, he was as delighted as if I'd told him Allah was primed for a second coming."

Chris slugged him in the arm. "You old fucker. Your lack of political correctness never fails to stagger me."

The pilot slugged him back. "Yeah, but you love me anyway." He turned the key and guided the Land Rover back toward the dig site. No roads meant a lot of twists and turns to avoid vegetation and holes.

"Doug wants to know where he can meet me," Katie spoke up.

Chris twisted, extending a hand for the phone.

"I have to go, love. A man wants to talk with you. I'm sorry, but I don't know who he is."

"He'll remember me," Chris said. "We've spoken before."

Katie gave him the phone and glanced at Julie. "Who are they?" She tilted her chin toward the front seat.

"The man in the passenger seat is my dad."

Katie's mouth rounded into an oh. "He's like a bigwig in the Marines, right?"

"Used to be. He retired."

Chris shot her an exasperated look, probably because of the "used to be" comment, and bent over the phone. "Mr. Johnson, it's Chris Wray. You cannot ask how we managed it, but we have your wife. We'll be flying her home."

He hesitated, listening to Doug, and then replied. "No. You can't meet the plane. We have an MD with us. He'll escort your wife to a hospital to make certain she's stable."

"Tell him, I'll call him as soon as I can," Brice said. Assuming Katie didn't decompensate between here and the States, he'd transport her to the hospital closest to her home. If he told Doug that, though, the man would probably camp out in the visitor's lounge.

After Chris disconnected, Brice turned to Katie. "Which part of town do you live in?"

"Queen Anne."

"Any preference on hospitals?"

She shrugged. "Swedish or maybe Virginia Mason. I'm actually feeling better. Not sure I even need a hospital."

Brice nodded, not wanting to argue with her but unwilling to turn her loose without lab work. "We'll figure it out once we're closer. I have privileges both places."

The Egyptian guarding the dig site waved them down when they got close and ran to the Land Rover with a shiny hardcover book and a pen. He handed both to Juliana, who opened the book and signed her name and the month and year.

"Thank you, Dr. Wray." The man bowed and took her book back.

"Thank you. It's wonderful to know people are still reading it."

Brice caught the title. *The Sign and the Seal: Mayan Culture Revisited.*

The Land Rover lurched onto a rutted track, but at least it was a road, as opposed to their journey from the thicket.

"How many books have you published?" Brice asked.

Before Julie could answer, Katie piped up, "Ten, with an eleventh in the works. Best day of my life was when she accepted my application to work under her." Pride was laced into her words.

"The book I just signed came from my dissertation research," Julie explained. "It's been out a long time."

"I want to visit that site," Katie murmured. "The one from *Signs and Seals.*"

"It's in the Guatemalan Highlands," Julie said.

"I know that." Katie rolled her eyes.

"Rather than revisiting my triumphs," Julie said softly, "blaze your own trail. You're a brilliant researcher."

"Awww, you're just saying that because I'm hurt."

"No. I really mean it."

Brice listened to the exchange, love for Juliana swelling through him. She could be short tempered and abrupt, but she was also compassionate, with a big heart. He'd tell her how he felt as soon as he could. No more beating around the bush. She'd always been the only woman for him.

Katie's eyes fluttered shut for a moment before she pried them open. "I'm so tired."

"You would be. You've been through a lot." Brice turned in the seat and dug through the luggage pile behind the back seat until he came up with the pilot's rucksack. He extracted another bottle of water and gave it to Katie.

"Thanks. I am thirsty."

"Bottoms up, and then you can take a nap until we get to the plane."

She took a few swallows. "Geez. I'm not sure I can walk. Bet there's a wheelchair somewhere at Cairo International. Dammit. I don't have a passport. They'll never let me on the plane."

"We came by private transport," Chris told her. "Outside of your husband, it would be best to downplay that part, as in do not mention it at all."

"We knew you wouldn't have ID," the pilot said. "You won't require any for this jaunt."

"Who are you?" she asked.

"Even we don't know his name," Julie replied. "Close your eyes, sweetie. Lots of strong men are guarding the plane. Someone will carry you inside."

"Oooh, sounds decadent." She leaned into Juliana.

Brice kept a close eye on her as she drifted off. She'd probably moved out of danger, but it paid to be vigilant. Once they were in the plane, he'd work on her feet and dress her wounds from where she'd been whipped.

Julie caught his eye and mouthed, "Thank you."

He placed an arm over the one she had around Katie. The Land Rover had reached the paved road leading toward the airport. Chris and the pilot were still alert, which might mean they expected problems.

"Is everything okay?" he asked softly.

"We're not sure," Chris answered carefully.

"Airport in ten," the pilot said, followed by, "Fuck. We have company after all."

The Land Rover sped up until its aging engine squealed in

protest. Brice twisted around and spotted a black car closing on them. "Give me one of the rifles," he said.

"What's happening?" Katie asked, her voice thick with sleep.

"Keep your head down," Julie said. "We'll be all right." She shielded the other woman with her body.

Chris handed one of the automatic rifles over. "Ever fire one of these?"

"I can figure it out." Brice turned and knelt on the bench seat, stabilizing the rifle against his shoulder.

"Get down lower," Chris instructed. "Lay the gun across the seat back."

Brice slid into the footwell. The Land Rover was one of the ancient safari models. If it ever had a back window, it was long gone, so he didn't have to worry about shooting through glass.

"Wait until they're fifty feet away," the pilot's words were terse.

"And then hit them with the entire magazine, but in short bursts. If you try to empty the magazine all at once, your aim will go to hell," Chris said. "Julie, here's a spare."

Out of the corner of his eye, Brice saw Chris toss something into the back seat. It gave him an idea. "Do we have grenades?"

"Yeah, but no launcher," Chris said.

Brice watched the Mercedes sedan get closer and closer. He eyeballed fifty feet and engaged the trigger. Chris had said sort bursts. He aimed for the windshield first. When it dissolved in a spray of shattered safety glass, he switched to one of the front tires. The acrid bite of propellant and gunpowder filled the cab as he fired, and the gun warmed in his hands. Before the first tire went totally flat, he shot the other one. The Mercedes slewed sideways, obviously well beyond the driver's control.

"Aim for the front side window," Chris said. "Nice shooting. I'm impressed."

Two more bursts emptied the magazine. The Mercedes skidded to a halt. No one got out. Brice had half expected men in black suits with sidearms. He turned back around and handed the rifle to Chris who ejected the magazine and slammed in another.

"We should be home free," he growled, "but I like to be ready."

Five minutes later, they pulled up next to the plane. The pilot and Chris piled out and began emptying the Land Rover, dragging gear toward the steps.

One of the turbaned faux Egyptians trotted down the steps. "All safe and sound. Full tanks. Ready to roll." He held out a hand, and the pilot dropped a thick envelope into it.

"Could you help get everything inside?" The pilot asked.

"Sure." The other guard slung sacks over his shoulders and hucked them into the Gulfstream.

Brice got out of the Land Rover, intent on helping Julie move Katie inside.

"Move aside," the mercenary who'd taken the money said. "I'll get her." Lifting Katie easily, he carried her up the steps.

Brice hefted a medical bag lying on the tarmac. Julie grabbed the pilot's rucksack. Brice planted himself in front of her. "Not quite the romantic setting I'd hoped for, but this needs saying. I love you, Juliana. I never stopped. There. Short. Sweet. Simple, but you're everything to me. Just like you always were. We can go inside now."

A bright smile began in her eyes and spread to her mouth. "Good because I love you too. Watching you work was amazing. You've always had this quiet competence. Nothing rattles you. I remember—"

"Inside," Chris yelled. "Now. We need to get this bird upstairs."

"To be continued." Brice brushed his lips over hers in a quick, sweet kiss.

"Gosh, we sound like a romance serial," she joked.

"I'll give you romance beyond your wildest dreams, wench." He stood aside, and then followed her up the steps.

"I'll hold you to it," she called over one shoulder.

"Katie's in the seat in the back," Chris told Brice as soon as he was in the plane.

"Perfect." Brice headed for the rear of the aircraft to sit with his patient, warmth spilling through him. The rest of the world would fall into place. Julie still loved him. It was the only thing that mattered. Hunkering next to Katie, he stripped off gloves that smelled like gunpowder and dug in his bag for a fresh pair.

"We're out of here," one of the mercenaries said.

Chris tossed him the keys to the Land Rover. "You might want to select an alternate route."

The man smirked. "Yeah. We heard gunfire. Never fear, we have our exit all planned out."

The Gulfstream's steps locked into place, and the turbines whined. The pilot didn't bother with a full power anything this time, just nosed the craft down the runway and took off.

CHAPTER 22

Juliana opened the driver's window on her 4Runner. Rain spattered in, but at least the cold air would keep her awake. It was past nine at night, and amazingly it was only December twenty-third. Hard to believe she'd traveled through so many time zones—twice—in a period of about fifty hours.

The same master at arms had been at the airport. He'd collected their burner phones, vests, and firearms and returned their personal phones.

Brice had left with Katie, en route to Swedish Hospital. Julie had helped him clean and dress her wounds during the flight. It had taken a couple hours. Brice was thorough, and some of the abrasions had begun to fester. According to him, she was out of danger from the toxins in the snakebite, which was a huge relief. Julie had been concerned some type of delayed reaction might create issues. A bigger problem had been moving her into Brice's car since he didn't want her walking on her bandaged feet. Between the four of them, they'd managed it.

Her father and the pilot had taken off, moving the plane

elsewhere, probably to a military base. Brice had hugged her briefly before leaving, and they'd made plans to meet at Overlake around noon the following day. She'd bring work with her and find a place to hang out until evening and the Christmas Eve festivities. She'd toyed with showing up at Brice's early to help Susan in the kitchen, but she'd only be in the way. Fancy food preparation wasn't one of her strengths.

Despite being weary and bleary-eyed from being on the move for two days straight, happiness seared her, made her spirit light. It wasn't too late for them, after all. Brice still loved her. And she'd never stopped loving him. Not really. He'd matured into an amazing man. All the attributes he'd possessed as a youth had grown richer, deeper. He was competent, patient, compassionate. Medicine was far more than a profession for him. It was a calling. He was a natural healer. She'd watched him as he worked on Katie, reassuring her with both voice and touch.

He had a way of looking directly at you that was supportive and comforting. She had a feeling his patients loved and trusted him because he was a straight-shooter. If the way he'd been with Katie was a bellwether, he told the truth and worked with his patients to develop an action plan. Katie hadn't wanted to go to the hospital, but Brice had charted the advantages. His line of reasoning had been he needed the reassurance of another set of eyes and lab work to confirm she truly was on the mend.

Katie may not have wanted to go, but she'd agreed because she believed Brice's assessment and didn't want to cause him worry. Julie smiled to herself. In addition to being a stellar MD, he'd developed a few psychological tactics along the way.

She squinted against the glare of oncoming headlights and flashed her brights at the other driver, who retaliated by flashing twice back at her—and leaving his high beams on.

Julie shook her fist his way, more amused than annoyed. Compared with Orestes Conom, the dude with his brights on was a piker.

Her phone trilled. She debated not answering it, but a quick glance at the display convinced her to pick up. Her stomach tightened as she clicked accept. "Hello, Dr. Smithwick."

"Dr. Wray. So glad I reached you."

She tightened her grip on the steering wheel. Was this when he tried to sack her? She was almost certain he couldn't, but she wasn't looking forward to the ensuing fight as she tested how solid her tenured status truly was.

"Sounds as if you're in a car," he went on. "Do you need to pull over?"

Damn it. He is going to fire me.

"No. The phone is on Bluetooth. What can I do for you?"

May as well get this over with. In truth, she could probably snag another faculty job, but it added a layer of inconvenience to her life.

Could be a plus. It would give Brice and me freedom to settle wherever we want.

Dr. Smithwick blew out a noisy breath that crackled against her ears. She moved the volume indicator down a couple of notches, waiting.

"I regret our exchange in my office the other day, my dear. I wanted to let you know Dr. Conom is no longer associated with our faculty."

Her jaw dropped open. "W-what?" she stammered. Out of all the things she'd expected when she'd seen Smithwick's name on her phone, this was at the very bottom of the list.

"Do we have a faulty connection?" he inquired. "Should I call back?"

"No. I thought I heard you say you'd terminated Orestes Conom."

"I did say that, although it's counter to personnel regulations to discuss one faculty member with another. In this instance, I've made an exception because of your graduate student, Ms. Johnson. Anecdotal evidence suggests Dr. Conom may have been behind her recent abduction. He'll be facing criminal charges."

Anecdotal evidence, my ass.

"Thank you for letting me know."

"Oh, I'm not quite finished. I've been in contact with Ms. Johnson's husband. You may not know, but he's also a graduate student in our linguistics department. In any event, Dr. Reinwall's been involved as well."

"Who's he?" Julie spoke up, swallowing reflexively to move saliva down her dry throat.

"She. Elizabeth Reinwall heads up our linguistics department. She's also my wife."

Julie sputtered, at a loss for words. Who would have guessed a dried-up stick-in-the-mud like Smithwick would be married? Maybe her assessment of how he viewed females in academe had been way off base.

He chuckled. "Yes, well, we keep our relationship quite low key. In any event, you'll be relieved and pleased to know Ms. Johnson has returned to the United States. I believe she sustained mild injuries, but she'll be back working for us in no time."

"Wonderful news," Julie managed, determined not to disclose her role in the rescue. Smithwick might find out soon enough. Or not. It depended if he had access to the same contacts her father had leveraged to cordon off her dig site.

"Yes, it is, isn't it? All's well that ends well. Will we see you after the first, or will you be returning to Egypt right away?"

"Not until after the first of the year. I'll be celebrating the holidays with my family this year."

"Excellent. Excellent. I've worried you had no personal life."

Yeah, I'll just bet you have.

If I was a man, you'd never mention my personal life.

She smothered her annoyance. He was trying. It must have cost him to reach out to her after his earlier stance about giving Orestes credit for the dig. "Thank you so much for getting hold of me, Dr. Smithwick. Have a merry Christmas."

"You too, my dear. You too. After the first, Elizabeth and I would like to have you and the Johnsons over for dinner one night. We'll come up with something that works for everyone." He disconnected.

She inhaled, blew it out, and did it twice more. If she discounted the *my dears*, it was the best conversation she'd ever had with Smithwick.

She pulled into her driveway, surprised to see lights on in her house. What the hell? She hadn't left anything on. She was certain of it. She'd departed in broad daylight, for one thing. And she hated to waste anything, including electricity.

She got out of the 4Runner, pulled her duffle and computer bag out of the back, and locked everything up before running lightly up her front steps. The door was locked, but while she fished for a key, it swung open.

"I was just beginning to get worried." Ariel beamed at her. "Come on in, sweetie. Let me pour us a drink."

Julie dropped her gear in the spot where she usually left things to the right of the front door beneath an antique oak mirrored hall tree. Too tired for subtlety, she asked, "What are you doing here, Mom?"

"Come on in. We can sit at the table and talk for a bit."

Julie rounded the corner and stared at a huge bouquet of flowers resting in the middle of her dining-room table. "They're beautiful, but—"

"Doug Johnson delivered them," her mother said. "They are lovely. He stopped by a little bit ago on his way to the hospital to meet Brice and his wife." She pushed a glass of amber spirits toward Julie.

Hooking her foot around a chair's leg, Julie pulled it out enough to drop into it. She curled her hands around the tumbler and took a deep swallow, savoring the burn of what turned out to be Irish whiskey as it traveled down her throat.

"I'm here," her mother said, "because Chris and I decided we'd do everything we could to maintain the illusion you never left the country. I've answered the door, pretending I was you, kept the lights on, and done what I could to make it appear you were here."

Julie set the glass down and raked her hands through her hair until her fingers tangled in the braids she'd forgotten about. "How will that work?" She stared at her mother. "People saw me over there."

"Really?" Ariel quirked a dark brow. "Who?"

Julie thought about it and gave her parents points for shrewdness. "I'm guessing the slaves won't say anything. Even if they did, they don't know me, and who would believe them?"

"Exactly. The mercenaries know how to keep their mouths shut."

"Oops." Julie closed her teeth over her lower lip.

"What?" Ariel leaned forward.

"The man guarding the dig site. He had one of my books, and I signed it for him with a month and year."

"Eh." Her mother shrugged. "Nothing to worry about. You were at the site early this month. Beyond that, he's another mercenary. Not all of them run around wearing bandoliers and brandishing sabers." She offered a toothy grin.

Julie laughed. "You're impossible. How's Sarah?"

"Really good. Out of ICU. Should be coming home with

Angus tomorrow. To Brice's. Another reason I'm in this neighborhood is to check in with her tenants and see if there's any way we can cut the lease off a bit early."

"What'd they say." The whiskey buzzed pleasantly, humming along her tense nerves, relaxing her.

"Haven't gone yet. I'll take care of it tomorrow. Your dad should be home by then."

"That long?" Surprise ricocheted through her. "Where'd they fly the plane to?"

Ariel waved a finger at her. "Classified information."

Julie rolled her eyes. "Stupid of me to ask."

"No comment." Ariel poured another finger of whiskey into her glass. "Before you turn in, how are things with Brice?"

Warmth rose from her chest in a wave that washed over the top of her head. "Good. Exceptional. I'll see him tomorrow."

Her mother nodded knowingly. "Don't give me an answer right now, but think about it. Sarah and Angus are planning a mid-March wedding—"

"And you want to make it a double." Julie finished her mother's sentence.

Ariel clasped her hands together, dark eyes shining. "It would be perfect. Both my girls. But no pressure."

"Yeah. None at all. I like the idea. When Sarah and I were little, we used to playact getting married at the same time. It's a twin thing."

"I know. I was there. Finish your drink and get some rest. I'm bunking on the couch in your guestroom."

Julie drained her glass. If nothing else, the liquor would knock her out. "Is Susan here yet?"

"Not quite. She and her fiancé and his son are in Portland. They made good time. She said they'll be here midmorning. Lupe's already bought enough food to feed an army, and as soon as Susan arrives, they'll dive into cooking."

"I still can't believe I went through all that in Egypt, and it's not Christmas Eve yet."

Ariel reached across the table and placed a hand over hers. "The world's not all that big. Nothing like fast planes and hardy men to pound that home."

Julie stood, surprised she hadn't pitched head down on the table. "Oh yeah. Another piece of good news. Smithwick called while I was driving here. He fired Conom, and he apologized. Even invited me for dinner—along with the Johnsons."

"Doesn't surprise me. I did a little digging and figured out the Reinwall woman was married to Smithwick. I'm the one who told Doug to go to his department head."

Julie tossed her head back and laughed. "Mom. You're amazing."

Ariel got to her feet and made a self-deprecating gesture. "Once a tactician, always a tactician. I shouldn't admit this, but I've had more fun these past couple of days than I've had in years."

"Fun, huh? Maybe you should have gone with Dad."

"Nope." Ariel shook her head emphatically. "If I'd done that, you wouldn't have had an opportunity to mend fences with Brice."

"Did you mastermind that too?"

"No, sweetie. Whatever happened between you and Brice is all on you."

"Really?"

Ariel patted her arm. "Really. I'm thrilled though. A double wedding…"

"I thought you said I had time to think about it."

"You do. Now, off to bed with you."

Julie was still chuckling when she shambled to her

bedroom and fell heavily onto her bed, not bothering to do anything beyond unlacing and toeing off her boots. She'd lived in the clothes she was wearing for two days. What was one more night?

~

BRICE WAS SO TIRED he couldn't remember the gate code. He stared stupidly out his open car window, willing the string of numbers to materialize so he could drive the remaining few feet to his home. He'd waited at the hospital until the ER doc verified Sarah was stable and didn't require being admitted.

Doug had shown up within minutes of their arrival, and his reunion with Katie was so tender, Brice fought against very unprofessional tears. Love shone from the Johnsons, palpable, tender, all-consuming. It was the same way he felt about Juliana.

It had been hard to leave her at the airport. He'd selfishly wanted her to come along with him and Katie, but she'd looked trashed with dark circles beneath her eyes. He'd told her to go home and get some rest. The hug and kiss they'd shared had been fraught with promise. And he'd see her soon.

Very soon.

He gave his fingers free rein, and they tapped the succession of keys to open the gate. Brice snorted. Once he'd removed his tired brain from the equation, muscle memory had taken over. He nudged the car into the driveway and shut off the engine, collecting his thoughts.

The medical bags could wait, but he gathered his personal items. A glance at his phone told him it was just past eleven. Morning would come soon. Julie had promised to be at Overlake by midday.

An idea struck him and made him smile. He'd have plenty

of time in the morning to stop by a jewelry store. He knew what she liked, at least he had once upon a time. He'd buy her an engagement ring. She'd have to have it sized, but he'd pick something lovely and old-fashioned, reminiscent of the antiquities she loved so much.

He'd just pushed his car door open when light spilled down his front steps. It took him a moment to understand someone had opened the door.

Angus ran down the steps and across the driveway to his car. "Welcome home, mate. What was all this hush-hush stuff? Where the devil were you?"

Brice reached across to snag his duffle and got out of the BMW, shutting the door behind him. "How's Sarah doing?"

"She's fine. Out of ICU. Where were you? You've been AWOL for two days."

Brice shook Angus's extended hand. "Remember how you couldn't tell me exactly what you did that earned you a private jet ride?" At Angus's nod, he went on. "I can't disclose anything, either. But things worked out. My patient is alive and well."

Angus's gaunt face split into a smile. "Grand news. I figured it was one of those QT military operations when Sarah's mom went around sowing bits and pieces of a story."

"Ariel? Usually she's so smooth, you'd never suspect a thing."

"Most wouldn't, but I have a background in covert ops." He pried the bag from Brice's hand. "Come on in. We'll have a nightcap and drink to your success."

Brice walked up the stairs and into the house, pulling the door closed. Lupe would have long since gone to bed, or he'd have bid her a good evening.

Angus dropped Brice's bag at the foot of the stairs, and they walked through to the living room. The tree smelled wonderful. Brice stood for a moment, inhaling the pine scent and thinking how much better it was than gunpowder.

Angus thrust a glass into his hand. "Have a wee nip. 'Tis good for your heart."

Brice snorted. "Oh really? Not what I hear from cardiology." He took a sip, rolling the mellow liquid around in his mouth before he swallowed it. "Thanks. That's good."

"Should be. 'Tis Scotch and more than thirty years old."

Brice sank onto a nearby sofa. "Is Timmy still here?"

Angus shook his head. "Nay. His mum and the priest came for him early today. You should have seen the wee laddie's eyes. He was so excited to be going home."

"So, you met Father John?"

"Aye. Seems a solid chap. He held out his arms, and the boy ran right into them, nattering away a mile a minute. Blood comes through, every single time."

"Not every time," Brice said, "but I'm very glad this worked out." He drank more of the Scotch. Now was as good a time as any to come clean about Julie. Especially since Angus was marrying Sarah, he had a right to know.

"Aye." Angus cocked his head. "Your mind is busy."

"Were you a psychic in another life?"

"I've been accused of it before. I chalk it up to being raised in the magical, mystical Highlands."

Brice snorted. "I won't go into detail. It's late, and I'm tired, but Juliana and I were a couple long ago. We began dating in high school and continued through two years of college. A misunderstanding drove a wedge between us."

"I know about the wedge." Angus skewered him with his keen, dark gaze. "Sarah told me."

"Good. Couples shouldn't have secrets, and I wasn't planning to out her. The important part is Julie and I found our way back to each other. I plan to ask her to marry me tomorrow, and we can't have the wedding soon enough to please me. We've lost fifteen years. I don't want to lose another day."

"Fantastic news!" Angus plopped next to Brice and slapped his shoulder. "Make it a double wedding with Sarah and me."

"When?"

"Middle of March. Sarah will be strong enough by then."

"So long as Julie agrees, I love the idea." He drained his glass and set it on a table. The alcohol made his head spin pleasantly.

"Sure you can't offer any clues about the mystery mission?" Angus cast an appraising look his way.

"Yup. Very sure. See you in the morning. If I'm not too rummy, we can run."

"I've set my clock for five. I'll wake you."

Brice stood. "Deal."

"Sleep well."

"You too." Brice climbed the stairs to his room. Tired, but happy in a way that had eluded him for years. His mother would be thrilled too. She'd always loved Juliana.

For once, he dropped his clothes over a chair, too tired to sort or hang anything. He considered a trip back down to the spa, but discarded it as too much work. Lupe had turned his bed down. He crawled into it and was asleep as soon as he shut his eyes.

CHAPTER 23

Juliana woke surprisingly refreshed. Maybe jet lag wasn't bad because she hadn't been in Egypt long enough to adapt to the ten-hour time difference between there and the West Coast. Her mother, always an early riser, was already gone, but she'd left a note saying she'd see her at Overlake.

Ariel had made coffee and laid toaster pops and a couple of cereal boxes on the table. Julie rolled her eyes. No wonder she couldn't cook. Look who she'd grown up with for a role model.

After a shower and clean clothes and coffee, she felt more or less like herself. She was in the car backing out of the driveway before she realized she needed something fancier for tonight. Returning inside, she perused her closet. Not only was she not particularly domestic, she avoided events requiring anything more elaborate than dark slacks, a white blouse, and a jacket. She'd almost given up when she came across a sealed garment bag holding a simple black sheath she hadn't worn in years.

Among dust bunnies in the bottom of the closet, she

located a pair of black pumps. She'd need nylons, but she could pick them up at one of the big drugstore chains. Satisfied she'd done as well as she could, she walked out her front door for the second time and headed toward the hospital.

Even with her hunt for party clothes, she arrived just before eleven. It took her a few minutes to find out where they'd moved Sarah, which was a bed in Med-Surg, one floor down from the ICU.

"Hey there!" She breezed into Sarah's room to find her sister sitting up in bed working a crossword puzzle.

"Hey, yourself." Sarah laid the puzzle aside. "Good to see you." She smiled. Her color was almost normal, and she no longer had that "at death's door" look about her.

"You too." Julie pushed the door shut. "Aren't you going to grill me about where I've been?"

Sarah shook her head. "Nope. Mom told me enough I've been worried, though."

Julie perched on the edge of the bed. "You shouldn't have been. Dad was there."

"He's a force to be reckoned with, for sure. Your student?"

"She's fine." Julie didn't tell her sister what a close call Katie had. No reason to. Her sister's plate was full enough.

"I'm glad. I get to leave later today. I'm excited."

Julie took her hand. "I'm excited for you. This hospital stuff gets old."

"You have no idea."

After a brisk knock, the door opened, and Brice strode in. "Morning, ladies."

Julie's heart did a funny, little flip-flop, making it hard to breathe. He could have doubled for a Hollywood star with his mop of blond hair and hazel eyes. As usual, he was dressed in his doctor outfit. The long, white lab coat with his name embroidered over a breast pocket and teal scrubs might have looked scruffy on someone who wasn't tall and lean with impossibly broad shoulders, but they made him even more appealing.

"Did you sign off on my discharge?" Sarah asked.

"I did. It's what I came in here to tell you. Angus will stop by to collect you very soon."

Sarah clasped her hands together. "Thank you. I understand you bent a few rules so I could be at the party tonight."

He waggled a finger at her. "I'll be there too. So will Angus. Between us, we plan to keep close tabs on you."

"That's okay. It's good to be loved, especially when I was certain I'd be dead before Christmas."

Sarah's words were so matter-of-fact, Julie felt proud of her and a little in awe. If her sister could address her illness so directly, Julie would too. "I'm very glad you're still on this side of the veil. Remember what I said about death being pretty damned permanent?"

"I do."

Brice walked to where Julie was still sitting on the bed. "Ready to leave for a few minutes? I made us reservations at a restaurant not far from here."

"Sure."

Sarah shifted her gaze from one to the other of them. Her breath gave an odd little hitch. "Are the two of you back together? Oh, please *please* say you are."

Julie nodded. "Yes. We figured things out. I—"

Sarah's eyes filled with tears, and she clutched Julie's hand. "Thank God and all the blessed saints—and a few pagan goddesses to boot. I can't tell you how long and hard I've wished for this." She choked back a sob. "Don't you see? What happened was my fault. I always felt like I ruined things for you. And then I was too big a chicken to set things right."

She rushed on, forcing words out between sobs. "I've felt guilty about being so happy with Angus. Like I had no right after what I did to you two."

Julie's eyes burned, and she wrapped both arms around her sister, holding on tight. Sarah was still far too thin, but her skin no longer had the translucence where her veins and arteries were visible.

"It's okay, sissie. Truly it is. Twins forever."

Sarah wormed out of her embrace and made shooing motions. "Twins forever. Go on. Get out of here and enjoy each other. You just gave me the best Christmas gift of all."

Julie kissed her sister's forehead. "See you later today." She got to her feet.

"I'll look forward to it. Mom is coming up with something for me to wear tonight."

Julie snorted. "I had a few problems in that department myself. Maybe I should ask her to wave her mom wand and bring two dresses."

"I can do that," Sarah said.

"It's okay. I found something. I'm not the dress-up type. Actually, neither is Mom. It will be interesting to see what she brings for you."

"I'd thought the same thing," Sarah replied, smiling wryly.

"Fingers crossed it's not one of her leftovers from the seventies." Julie cast a knowing look her sister's way.

Sarah shrugged. "Anything would be better than this." She tugged at the neck of her hospital-issue gown.

"It's you I want"—Brice focused his words at Julie—"not a piece of clothing. You could wear nothing, and it would be fine."

Julie shot him a look, and they all burst out laughing.

"Sorry." Brice's cheeks developed a rosy tint. "That didn't quite come out right." He draped an arm around her waist, and she leaned into him as they strolled out of Sarah's room.

"Can we walk to the restaurant?" she asked.

He nodded. "Before we go, though, come by my office for a second. I want to show you something."

"Gee, after that comment about me not wearing anything, you're not planning an assault on my virtue, are you?"

His eyes twinkled mischievously. "I'll never tell. If you want to find out, you'll have to take a chance."

He guided her through back corridors until they came to his office.

"I always wondered how you guys got around the hospital," she said. "Who would have guessed there's a warren of secret passageways?"

"Ssht." He put a finger over his lips. "Don't tell anyone."

"Your secret is safe with me." She followed him into his office, taking in the large desk and stacks of books and journals. "Never made the digital transition, huh?"

"Nope. Not totally."

Julie leaned close. "So long as we're trading secrets, neither did I, but I have a good excuse."

He furled his brows. "And that would be?"

"I read a lot of source documents. Scrolls, tablets. Original writings. At least, so far, they haven't been digitized, and I hope they never are. It would ruin the specialness of touching something that's hundreds or thousands of years old and considering what the writer's mindset was when they penned whatever words they wrote."

"Or chiseled them into stone?"

She looked down, her cheeks warming beneath his scrutiny. "You're making fun of me."

"No. I'm not." He turned until he stood facing her and wrapped his arms around her.

She hugged him back, loving how he felt in her arms. She'd never forgotten the sense of well-being, of everything being right in the world, his proximity provided. Leaning her head back, she hoped he'd kiss her. Surely, this was why they'd stopped here before lunch. To have an island of privacy. Her breath came faster as she anticipated the touch of his lips for more than the nanoseconds they'd kissed at the airport.

"Open your eyes, Juliana." He placed an index finger beneath her chin, tilting it upward.

She hadn't realized she'd closed them.

"You're lovely," he said. "I always enjoyed looking at you, but your beauty has grown richer, deeper. You were a girl when I fell in love with you, but now you're a woman and so stunning you take my breath away." He moved his hand to cradle the side of her face, tracing the line of her cheekbone.

"I was thinking something similar about you," she said. "You're so striking, it's hard to tear my eyes away, but beyond that, I love what's inside you. You're kind and smart and funny and compassionate."

The corners of his mouth twitched. "And you can be a ball-busting bitch, but I always liked women with spirit. When we were in the Land Rover and you told Katie to blaze her own trail, I fully understood what a big heart you have. And why you've been so successful."

Bending closer, he brushed his lips over hers, a gentle tentative kiss. One that gave her permission to pursue it or not. Julie kissed him back. His lips hadn't changed at all. They were firm, beautiful, perfect. They clung together, kissing one another as if they were the only two people in the world.

Brice pulled his mouth away, eyes brimming with warmth and love. "I remember kisses like that. We did a whole lot of kissing before we did anything else."

"We did. I never forgot anything about how we were. No other man came close to measuring up. It's why I'm still single."

"I could say the same about you." He moved his arms from where they curved around her and fumbled in a pocket. Offering a boyish grin, he sank to one knee. "Hope I do this right. It's not the type of thing where you get much practice. I love you, Juliana Wray. Would you do me the honor of becoming my wife."

He held out a small, black velvet box. Her fingers shook as she opened it and gazed at an intricately modeled gold ring with an exquisite pear-shaped diamond nestling in its center.

"It's beautiful," she said, and her eyes flooded with tears. "Of course, I'll marry you, Brice. If I hadn't been such a fool, we'd have married years ago."

"Uh-uh. None of that. No looking back. Go ahead. Try it on. We can have it sized, but maybe we won't have to."

She tugged on one of his arms. "Get up off your knees, Sir Lancelot. The lady said yes."

He rose and stood close, clearly waiting for her to try on the ring. It was so delicate and so obviously expensive, she treated it like a precious artifact as she removed it from the velvet-lined case. "Here." She held out her left hand and gave him the ring. "You put it on for me."

"Kind of like handfasting or carrying you across the threshold?" His eyes sparkled with happiness and a fierce longing.

"Something like that, but don't forget the salt."

"What's it for?"

"To discourage evil spirits from intruding on brand-new marital bliss."

Brice slid the ring onto her finger. "Wow. Between the jeweler and me, we guessed right."

Julie held out her hand, watching light glint off the diamond as she tilted it this way and that. "I don't have words for how incredible this is, but you always had superb taste."

He nodded sagely. "I do, indeed. I picked you, didn't I?"

She mock slugged him, but he ducked. "We picked each other," she said. "Is that lunch offer still on?"

"Certainly is. There's a matching band to add to the ring once we're married. Speaking of which, I was talking with Angus last night."

Julie laughed. "Yes, and I was talking with Mother. I'd love to do a double wedding with Angus and Sarah."

"Perfect, because so would I. Even though if it were up to me, I'd spirit you before a justice of the peace tomorrow."

"Good luck finding one," she countered. "Tomorrow is Christmas."

"So I'd wait until city hall is open for business." He slipped a hand beneath her elbow and guided her out of his office.

"I love it that you're determined and persistent." She smiled up at him as they walked out of the hospital into a day where a weak sun was trying to break through a layer of gray clouds.

He snorted. "Yeah, both of us can be pretty bullheaded at times, but we have a whole future to plan."

"The house in the suburbs and two point five children." She hesitated. "You still want kids, right?"

"You bet I do. My brief stint with young Timmy Davidson hammered that point home. Hey. Maybe I can get Father John to officiate at the double wedding."

"That would be nice. Who's he?"

"Oh, that's right, you'd have no way of knowing. He's Timmy's father."

"From before he became a priest?"

Brice shook his head. "Nope."

Julie angled her head to one side. "Bet there's an interesting story behind that one."

"Yup. Sure is. Remind me to tell you sometime." He guided her into a small café where a table was ready for them near the back. "I took the liberty of ordering for us. Hope that's okay." When he looked at her, he was so earnest, she could have kissed him all over again.

"Yes. It's fine. Perfect. I could get used to being taken care of. I do need to go back to Egypt, though. I have to finish up there."

"I understand. Maybe I'll come along. For some of the time, anyway."

"Wonderful. We've never had an onsite doc."

A smiling waiter left bread and a Caesar salad fragrant with fresh grated cheese, garlic, and anchovies. The sat close together, on the same side of a small booth, and shared bread and salad. After a while, a creamy pasta dish materialized.

Happiness thrummed through her. They had their whole lives ahead of them. To live and plan and love.

He smoothed a tendril of hair behind one of her ears. "After lunch, why don't you go right to my house. Mom is anxious to see you, and Sarah should be there by then."

"You're worried about her, aren't you?"

"Not in the way you mean. But I don't want her to overdo things. It could set her remission back a few days."

"Sure. I'll head over there and show off my ring. Anything to keep me out of the kitchen." She nudged him. "Are you going to pony up an address, or will I need to ask my mom?"

"Give me your phone. You'll need the gate code too."

She handed it over, and he put his address and a string of numbers—presumably the code—next to his name in her contacts section. When he gave it back, he said, "Better watch it. There's no escape."

"I don't want there to be." Setting her fork down, she launched herself into his lap and kissed him.

~

BRICE PULLED into his driveway around five. The afternoon had passed in a blur. Julie had agreed to be his wife. A lifelong dream was finally, finally coming true. He'd done his doctor gig for a few hours but couldn't remember who he'd seen or what he'd ordered.

His mother ran down the steps, her blonde hair longer than he remembered, and her brown eyes shining with happiness. Curvy and medium height, she wore a long cream-colored skirt and a colorful tunic. Brice got out of the car, and she hurtled into his arms, hugging him tight. A tall, slender man with dark hair going gray and dark eyes stood behind her with his arm around a gangly teenaged boy.

Susan disentangled herself. "Sorry. Sorry. I'm just so happy to see you. This is Dr. Trevor Wilder and his son, Rob."

Brice extended a hand, and both Trevor and his son shook it. "It's quite a pleasure to meet you," Trevor said in a deep, musical voice. Dressed in a gray woolen suit with a tasteful blue-patterned tie, he carried himself like a Marine. Straight and proud.

"The pleasure is mine," Brice said, and meant it.

"I'm hoping while I'm here, we can spend some time at your lab," Trevor went on. "I've read about your pioneering research with immune modulators and gene remodeling, and I'd like to see some of the experiments."

"Of course we can do that."

Rob rolled eyes that were dark like his father's. "I need a dictionary to understand you."

Susan ruffled his shaggy black hair. "While they're doing that, you and I will go down to the waterfront. Seattle has an amazing aquarium."

"Really?" Rob's eyes lit with enthusiasm.

"I said so, didn't I?"

"I'd love for us to catch a ferry out to the islands," Bride said, adding, "We'll pick the most promising day in terms of the weather forecast."

"We'd love that too," his mother said.

"Back inside, everyone," Brice urged. "I want to change out of my scrubs. Usually I leave them at the hospital, but today's a red-letter day, and I was in a hurry to get home."

Susan hugged him again. "We saw the ring. Congratulations, son. I'm very, very happy for you. I used to worry about who you'd marry since I'd set my heart on Julie for my daughter-in-law before you finished high school." She moved back a couple of paces, still grinning.

"I heard my name," Julie called from the door. "Why are all of you outside?"

"Aye," Angus joined her in the doorway. "Come on in and save a bloke from getting drunk by himself."

Brice closed up the BMW and followed everyone into the house. He'd just crested the stairs, intent on changing into something more appropriate for a party when Lupe darted out of a side hallway and grabbed his arm.

"Yes? Did I do something wrong?"

Lupe smiled broadly. "No. Something right. I like Julie. Good woman. Happy for you. Very happy. I dance at wedding."

Brice swing her around and set her down. "Wouldn't dream of getting married without you, Lupe."

"Come downstairs. Lots of food."

"I will. Just as soon as I change."

She patted his arm and bounded down the stairs humming a song in Spanish.

He put on tweed slacks and a pale-green cashmere sweater over an ivory silk shirt. The sound of another car in the driveway brought him to a window wondering how the hell anyone had gotten in without the gate code. Chris and Ariel Wray got out of black SUV, and he shook his head. The general and his colonel wife were more than capable of defeating something as trivial as an electronic gate.

Working with Chris Wray had been a real wakeup call. The man was sharp and skilled. He'd finessed a complex operation and seen it through to its end.

Brice slid his feet into loafers and walked down the winding staircase, anxious to greet his guests. Christmas was a magical time. A time for families and love.

"There you are." Julie smiled up at him from the bottom of the stairs. A simple sleeveless black dress hugged her like a second skin, ending just above her knees.

He whistled, long and low. "Wow! You're quite a knockout."

"You're not bad yourself, Doc. Not bad at all. Come on. Mom and Dad just got here."

"I know. They jimmied the gate."

"No, they didn't. I gave them the code, silly."

Threading an arm around Juliana's waist, Brice walked toward the sound of voices where everyone was gathered in the living room. They weren't just joining the party, though, he and Julie were transitioning into a whole new life.

He bent so his mouth was close to her ear. "I love you."

"Not as much as I love you." Leaning closer, she rose on tiptoe and kissed him once, hot, brief, and brimming with promise.

"I can't wait until I have you to myself," he murmured.

"I want to run away with you too, but we've waited fifteen years. Let's enjoy tonight. We've made our families very happy."

"Oh hell, Juliana, you've made me the happiest man in the universe."

Chris and Ariel caught up with them on their way in from

outside. Chris dropped a hand onto his shoulder. "Right this way, my boy. We have years of toasts to catch up on."

"Indeed," Ariel chimed in. "You can snuggle later. You're not kids anymore. You have a whole house to cavort in, not just the downstairs hallway." A rich, rowdy laugh punctuated her words.

Reluctantly, Brice let go of Julie.

She flashed him a grin worthy of Aphrodite. "Hang onto those thoughts."

He smiled back, bursting with love. "Every single one of them."

CHAPTER 24

*A*ngus had long since taken Sarah upstairs. Susan, Trevor, and Rob had retired to the downstairs suite Lupe had prepared for them. Julie and Brice walked her parents out onto the front porch.

"We want to come along on the daytrip to the San Juan Islands," Ariel said.

"Should be fun," Chris seconded.

"I'll call and let you know as soon as we get it scheduled," Julie promised. "Night, Mom. Night, Dad."

"Night, honey." Ariel hugged her, and then she hugged Brice. "Welcome to the family. Better late than never, I always say."

"Mom." Julie elbowed her, disconcerted by her propensity to say things out loud that most people only thought.

"What?" Ariel quirked a brow. "You have a problem with the truth?"

Chris shook Brice's hand for the millionth time. "Pleasure working with you, son. You might consider signing on. We always need medical personnel."

"Do you mean enlisting in the Marines?" Brice smiled warmly.

"Not exactly. This is more of a private list we keep. Of civilians willing to help out from time to time. The pay is good." He released Brice's hand. "Think about it. You'll receive a check in the next few days for what you just did."

"What about me? Do I get paid too?" Julie asked.

Chris snorted laughter. "Nope. Sorry, honey, archaeology isn't one of the specialties the service is willing to reimburse." Still laughing, he looped a hand beneath his wife's arm and guided her down the front steps and to their car.

Brice stood by Julie's side, and they watched her folks turn the car around and drive away. "It's a nice night," he said. "Would you like to go for a walk down by the lake?"

"Sure, but I need a coat." Nice was relative in the Pacific Northwest and usually meant it wasn't raining.

"Hang on, I'll get you one." He ducked back inside, returning a moment later with an insulated jacket that he draped over her shoulders. It smelled like him, musky and masculine, and she snuggled into its folds.

He held out a hand; she clasped it, weaving her fingers with his. They walked down the brick steps in front of his house and followed a path inlaid with paving stones around the house. He'd been right about it being a lovely evening. Crisp and clear, the sky was alight with thousands of stars.

"Tonight was magical," she said.

"I thought so too. Which parts did you like best?"

Julie thought about it, and for once words didn't come easily. "I may make a botch of this, but tonight felt right. Like you and I were exactly where we were supposed to be—after a very long time. Sarah and Angus and your mom and her honey were icing on the cake."

"I'm still in awe you agreed to be my wife. I've felt like I was floating ever since you said yes."

She tossed her head back and laughed. "The trick will be if you're still floating a year from now. It's not going to be easy living with someone like me."

"Why?" Genuine curiosity underscored his question.

"I'm addicted to being in the field, and when I unearth something, I can hunker over it for hours. When I get like that, I shut the rest of the world out."

"Only because there wasn't someone you valued enough to share your treasure with." He paused long enough to take a breath. "Sheesh. If your colleagues are anything like that Conom bastard, I'd keep a pretty low profile about my finds too."

"Oh, come on." She leaned closer, loving having him by her side again.

"Oh, come on, what?"

"Surely, you're not going to go all gaga over thousand-year-old etchings."

"Maybe not," he replied, "but I'm plenty gaga over you. When we were patching Katie up, you did a credible job assisting me. No reason I can't help in the same way. I have good hands and a deft touch. Couldn't do surgery without them."

"Is that an oblique way of telling me you'd take good care of my artifacts?"

"The best."

"Speaking of best," she murmured. "You are the best, most wonderful, most amazing person. I'm honored you still want me in your life."

They'd reached a short pier jetting into Lake Washington, and Brice closed his arms around her from behind as they looked out on flickering lights from boats and neighboring houses. She leaned back against him, enjoying the long, lean lines of his body pressed close to hers.

"A lot of love stories have come full circle," he said, his

tone thoughtful. "Ours isn't the only one. We were blessed to share two others tonight. I never thought Mom would fall in love again, but I really like Trevor."

"Me too. He's solid, and his boy is a gem."

"My stepbrother." Brice chuckled. "That's going to take some getting used to."

"That's right." She turned and threaded arms around him. "You were an only child."

Brice cradled the side of her face in one hand. "You're so beautiful."

Breath caught in her throat. "So are you. I'm happy. So happy it hurts."

He ran a hand down her back, cupping the curves of her ass and making a decidedly masculine purring sound. "I am too. Did I ever tell you your ass is amazing?"

"Yours is pretty spectacular too." She gripped it and pulled him closer. A growing erection pressed into her belly, and she felt aroused and shy at the same time. He hadn't seen her body in years. She wasn't exactly young anymore.

"Tell me what you want." His voice rasped with desire. "How you want us to come together for our first time."

She recognized the way he sounded when he wanted her, and a quiver of heat skittered down her spine. "But it isn't our first time."

He nuzzled her neck, warm breath tickling her sensitive skin. "Yes, it is. We're starting over, you and me. We can go back inside and upstairs to my bedroom. We can drive into Bellevue and check in at a fancy hotel. We can sit in the spa if you'd like or take a dip in my almost-never-used pool. We can drive across the bridge and go to your house. You call it."

"It's you I want. Not a glitzy hotel room."

He nodded. "I feel the same way, but we're going to talk, Juliana. A lot. About everything. We're going to make certain we don't have any more misunderstandings. I want to protect you. Take care of you. Give you everything you want."

"What if the only thing I ever really wanted was you?" Her throat developed thick places from the emotion sluicing through her, and her chest constricted, suddenly not big enough to hold her heart.

"Really?"

She nodded and blinked back tears that threatened to spill over. "I've spent the last fifteen years buried in work so I wouldn't have to dissect what happened." She tilted her chin upward. "In grad school, they used to call me the Ice Queen. I hardly ever dated, and when I did, the guys never lasted past one or two evenings." She held his gaze, liquid in moonlight trickling from the waxing moon.

"Why not?"

"Because they weren't you."

He tightened his hold on her. "That's the sweetest thing anyone's ever said to me." Angling his head, he brought his mouth down atop hers. The kiss was slow and lazy, an all-the-time-in-the-world kiss. Stubble from today grazed her cheek as he licked and sucked and teased her lips. He bit her lower lip and soothed the sting with his tongue.

She laced her fingers into his hair, delighting in the blend of silky strands and rough curls as she explored his lips and mouth with her tongue. He tasted sweet from a cinnamon-y dessert Lupe had made combined with sharp overtones from the aged port he'd always enjoyed. He strung kisses down her cheek to the hollow in her throat, moving her jacket aside for better access as he darted little jabs with his tongue.

The sensation of hot breath and firm lips made her gasp. Her nipples formed peaks where they pressed against his chest, and heat engulfed her nether regions, startling in its intensity. She'd decided sex was overrated and she could live without it, but she'd been dead wrong.

Brice opened channels in her that had been dammed up for years. Channels carrying love and hope and tenderness. Sensitivity and compassion.

She wanted to take her time.

She wanted to rip his clothes off and inhale all the wonderful maleness that was Brice right here on the pier.

He lifted his face from her neck, breath coming fast. "I want you, Julie. Need you." Without warning, he moved an arm downward and beneath her knees, sweeping her off her feet and into his embrace.

"You don't need to carry me." She laughed, not trying very hard to break free.

"Maybe I want to." He laid a hand over her head, tucking it against his shoulder.

"Where are we going?" Letting go of her need to always be in charge was easier than she'd have thought possible.

"Closest place is the pool house, but the house will be warmer, at least until I get the brazier lit."

"Close is good." The nearness of him combined with letting him carve out the next piece of their future was intoxicating.

He turned away from the lake and its gently lapping water and walked slowly toward a structure she hadn't noticed in the dark. Sitting partway between the house and the lake, it reminded her of a geodesic dome.

He stopped next to a door and let go of her head long enough to punch a series of numbers into a keypad. The door sprang open, and he carried her inside. Muted light illuminated a patio with soft outdoor furniture artfully arranged around a center pit containing a brazier. Beyond stretched a pool with a gurgling hot tub off to one side.

"I hate to let go of you even for an instant, but I need to light that." He kissed her forehead, her cheeks, and her lips before setting her on her feet and bending to an igniter.

The gas-powered fire blazed to life, looking incredible realistic.

"This is lovely," she said. "Bet you spend a lot of time down here."

"No. All I do is work, but I've always had plans for it. In the summer, the top of the dome rolls back and the sides come up, so it's like having an outdoor pool."

She gazed at him, drinking him in. "Yeah, I work all the time too, but you're going to save me from a spinsterhood where the only thing that keeps me warm at night are my cases of artifacts."

"Maybe we'll save each other." He slid her jacket from her shoulders and placed his hands on her upper arms.

Shivers cascaded down her spine. She wanted him to touch her, stroke her, kiss her. Extending a tentative hand, she pushed his sweater off his shoulders and went to work unbuttoning a cream-colored silk shirt. He groaned at her touch but remained still as she worked the shirt off him and laid it over his sweater.

Breath hitched in her throat at the beauty of his naked chest. Muscles curved around his shoulders and down his arms, but he had the lean build of a runner, rather than the bulked-up look of someone who lived in a gym. A dusting of blond hair circled bronze nipples. Bending close, she licked one, and it hardened instantly beneath her tongue.

"Aw, Jesus, you're amazing." He grappled behind her back, hunting for the zipper holding her dress in place.

The fabric loosened and slithered from her shoulders and then to the ground where it puddled around her feet. She stepped out of it and her shoes at the same time and took a deep, shaky breath. Would he still find her attractive?

Brice reached around and undid her lacy black bra, tossing it aside. A harsh intake of breath was followed by him surging forward and filling his hands with her breasts before he angled his head and traded his mouth for his fingers. Sensation shot from her nipples to her crotch, and liquid added to the heat throbbing between her legs.

She reached for the tented-out front of his trousers and wrapped a hand around the cock she remembered so well, it invaded her dreams.

He pushed into her hand, making wonderful male noises. Encouraged, she undid his belt and the button and zipper holding his trousers up. They slid down his legs, leaving silk boxers. Too aroused to bother with dragging them down, she reached inside and drew his cock out.

Hard, proud, thick, wonderful. She fell to her knees and took him into her mouth, working him between her hands, lips, and tongue. They'd spent a lot more time pleasuring one another this way than they had having actual sex. They'd only had intercourse a handful of times before she had her hissy fit and kicked him to the curb.

He thrust into her mouth a few times before placing his hands on either side of her head and pulling free. "I'm too close. And you still have clothes on."

"Not technically," she managed through a haze of desire that clouded damn near everything. "Pantyhose aren't clothes."

He gripped the form-fitting nylon and worked it down her hips and legs, steadying her while she stepped out of them. Stumbling slightly, he worked himself free of trousers and loafers while she divested him of his shorts.

The vista of him naked almost made her come. The cords of muscle marking his upper body continued along his slender stomach and down powerful legs. The cock she still held firmly in one hand rose from a mat of blond curls.

"I can't believe how beautiful, how perfect, you are." His voice came out in a low growl. Fierce and protective. "Don't know about you, but my legs are shaky." He held out a hand.

She clasped it, and he led her to an ivory-colored divan right next to the brazier.

The room had warmed considerably, but she was plenty hot from a fire burning within. Sitting, he pulled her across his lap and covered her mouth with his. Unlike his last kisses, this one ran wide open. It said clearer than any words she was his woman.

His and his alone.

She kissed him back, clinging to him as if they were the only two people left in the world. Somehow, they ended up lying on their sides with her breasts crushed against her chest and his cock curved into her belly. She reached between them and positioned him between her legs where she could rub against his hardness.

She'd come that way lots of times before as they'd moved incrementally closer to actual sex. The heat and familiarity were like an aphrodisiac as she writhed against his erection. He moved his hands to her ass, pressing hard. The increased stimulation drove her mad, and an orgasm raced through her, cresting hard.

He waited until her breathing quieted, and then rolled them until he was on top. "I remember you coming like that. It always made me hotter than hell. So hot, I'd almost always come along with you."

"But not tonight?" she teased.

"I'm waiting for the real thing."

Julie wrapped her legs around his waist, opening herself to the thick head of his cock pressing for entrance. Still higher than a kite, drunk on sex and love, she gripped his hips, encouraging him to fill the empty place inside her.

Brice sank into her slowly, stretching her as he went. Once he was fully encased, he stopped moving and looked down at her, his face flushed with lust and love spilling from his eyes. "I'm not going to last very long."

She smiled, slow and lazy. "That's okay, neither am I." She tightened her vault around him. When he groaned, she did it again.

He withdrew and sank back inside, growing stiffer and bigger. She moved one hand from his hips and sank it between her legs, rubbing her clit. After a startled gasp, he pulled out and drove back inside her. Savage. Fierce. Any pretense of lingering, of making their coupling last, fled.

She shrieked, thrilled by being taken. Delighted by his lack of restraint as he fucked her. This was a place they'd never gotten to when they were young. A place where the veneer of socialization dropped away, leaving sheer animal lust.

Another climax hovered. She felt it spool deep inside her, ready itself, and explode in concentric waves of desire and need. He hesitated at the top of the next stroke. She felt tension in every part of his body and understood the slightest motion would drive him into the no-man's-land of male ecstasy.

She rocked against him and pulled him into her, both hands on his ass.

With a low, feral cry that exhilarated her, he let go. His cock juddered, painting her with white-hot gouts of semen. He spasmed over and over, and she held on to him as hard as she could, wanting to enhance his pleasure.

Gasping, panting, they ground against each other as the last of their passion faded. He turned her until they lay on their sides, and smoothed hair out of her face. "I love you, Juliana." A soft smile curved his beautiful mouth into something profane. "I feel like you and I have been linked forever, not just through this lifetime, but like I must have known—and loved—you through many others."

She cupped the side of his face, enjoying the feel of him. "I love you too, darling. Thanks for never giving up on us."

"You're giving me too much credit."

She shrugged. "Don't complain. I'll retract the praise."

"No, you won't." He held her tight. "We should get dressed and go back inside."

"Why? We're fine here."

"Really? You're good with a couch and not a bed?"

"More than good. Home is where you are. And right now, it's here. This is luxurious compared with how I live at dig sites."

The steady beat of his heart beneath her ear lulled her. "I wonder if we made a baby just now."

His hands, which had been rubbing her shoulders and back, stilled. "Would that be all right with you?"

She leaned back and gazed at him, loving how the firelight illuminated his features. "More than all right. We're not young anymore, and—"

He smiled, and the fire reflected in his eyes looked like twin flames. "That was the right answer, but we'll see if we can't at least wait until your Egypt project is done."

A chuckle bubbled up, followed by another until she was laughing.

"What's so funny?"

"You've accomplished the impossible, Dr. McKinnon. For a while there, I forgot all about archaeology. All about Egypt. All about everything except you and me."

"That's quite a compliment, Dr. Wray. Keep 'em coming."

Drowsy, happy, content, she let herself drift. When she opened her eyes, the pale light of morning surrounded them, but she lay still, wanting to make the precious moments of her and Brice alone and finally together once again stretch as long as she could. Once they went inside, she'd be surrounded by family. Not that she didn't love and cherish them, but Brice was her everything.

"Hi, sleepyhead," he murmured.

"Hi, yourself."

"Feel like a run?"

"I'm out of shape, but I'd love to come along."

He brushed his lips over hers. "Come on, wench. Let's get moving."

She trailed her fingers over his erect cock. "Are you sure?"

"Mostly sure, but I'm weak where you're concerned, so don't tempt me. We'll save him for later."

Delighted that all the laters in the world stretched before them, she got to her feet and began hunting down her clothes.

❧

You've reached the end of *Since We Fell*. I hope you enjoyed it.

While I'm not exactly known for writing contemporary stories, you might enjoy *Icy Passage*. It's an action-adventure romance with a few paranormal elements. A sample follows.

ABOUT THE AUTHOR

Ann Gimpel is a USA Today bestselling author. A lifelong aficionado of the unusual, she began writing speculative fiction a few years ago. Since then her short fiction has appeared in several webzines and anthologies. Her longer books run the gamut from urban fantasy to paranormal romance. Once upon a time, she nurtured clients. Now she nurtures dark, gritty fantasy stories that push hard against reality. When she's not writing, she's in the backcountry getting down and dirty with her camera. She's published over fifty books to date, with several more planned for 2018 and beyond. A husband, grown children, grandchildren, and wolf hybrids round out her family.

Keep up with her at www.anngimpel.com or http://anngimpel.blogspot.com

If you enjoyed what you read, get in line for special offers and pre-release special reads. Newsletter Signup!

Fresh out of residency, Dr. Kayna Quan opts for a tour in Antarctica. Money is short, so she hires on as medical officer aboard a Russian research vessel headed for McMurdo Station. Primed for almost anything, she plays her paranormal ability close to the vest.

Stationed on remote South Georgia Island for two years, Brynn McMichaels is eager for a change. When cultures of the single-celled organism, archaea, overgrow their bins in his lab and begin shifting into another form, he worries he's losing his mind and talks with scientists at McMurdo, but they have problems of their own—bad ones. Brynn agrees to help. The weather's too uncertain to send a plane, so he hitches a ride aboard Kayna's ship and brings his mutant culture colonies along.

Attraction sparks, urgent, hot and powerful, between Brynn and Kayna, but her disclosure about her magic is a tough nut to crack. It doesn't help that her dead father is stalking her. Lethal cultures, bizarre illness, and McMurdo's refusal to let them land force Brynn and Kayna into an uneasy alliance. Will their fragile bond be enough to thwart the powers trying to destroy Earth, and them along with it?

Micah Greenwich sucked air as he pushed up from his squat, a weight bar balanced across his shoulders. He did one more squat before a wave of dizziness threatened to bring him to his knees. Gasping, he shucked the bar onto pins protruding from the back of the squat rack and grabbed one of the metal stanchions for support. A headache pounded behind one eye, and he felt nauseous.

"What the fuck is wrong with me?" he muttered, still clinging to the metal cage shoved in a back corner of the gym at McMurdo Station, Antarctica. No one was in the gym. Not at this hour. Granted, the perpetual night for part of the year, followed by perpetual day, yielded some odd circadian rhythms, but Micah rarely had competition for any of the gym machines or weight equipment late at night.

He glanced at the weight plates balanced on the ends of the forty-five pound bar, thinking perhaps he'd misjudged and put too much weight on it, but that wasn't the issue. He shrugged. Maybe he was getting sick. Something was going around. So far, he'd been lucky during his brief stint at the southern end of the Earth and had avoided the colds and flus McMurdo residents passed among themselves like candy.

He wiped sweat from his face with a ratty towel and decided to call it a night—at least for working out. He still needed to stop by his lab. Because he was the newest and greenest microbiologist, he'd been assigned archaea, the most ancient single-celled life form on the planet. His cultures had taken a decidedly odd turn, though, a couple of weeks back—growing like mad and not looking like any prokaryote he'd ever seen. While he might have started with archaea, what was in his bins didn't look much like them anymore.

Another wave of nausea battered him, and he folded his arms around his midsection, wondering if he was going to vomit. Saliva flooded his mouth, but he choked it back. Even though he didn't feel like doing anything beyond finding his bed, he left the gym and made his way three buildings over to his lab. McMurdo was a series of prefab buildings with interconnecting doors and insulated tunnel-walkways, so you didn't have to go outside into the weather. Antarctica never got particularly warm, and nights were always bitter.

He glanced out a window at an inky sky shot with stars, and a reluctant smile split his face. It might be minus something outside, but it was beautiful too. He'd always loved wild, remote places, and Antarctica was about as wild and remote as it got—shy of signing up to be an astronaut, which was a long-standing dream of his.

Micah frowned, wondering if the astronaut gig was even possible. The United States had cut their funding for the space program rather dramatically. Besides, he needed more in the way of credentials to even be considered for something like that. With another swipe at his still sweaty face—the more he thought about it, the surer he was he was coming down with the flu—he pushed open the door to his lab and froze, not believing his eyes.

"Britta?" he called. "Marguerite!"

The women didn't answer. They sprawled face down on the floor in front of his main workbench, clearly passed out. Wondering if they'd gotten into the high-grade, ethyl alcohol he used to preserve things, he called their names again, louder this time. The longer he looked at them, the weirder he felt. They were too still. Sudden fear gripped him, making the nausea worse.

"Jesus fucking Christ. Why me?" he muttered, and raced to the women. He bent, grabbed Britta's shoulder, and shook her. When she didn't respond, he flipped her over and stared at her cherry-red face.

Fighting a deeply sinking feeling, he turned Marguerite over. She looked just like her friend and roommate. Micah squatted next to them and laid his fingers across their necks, searching for a pulse.

Nothing.

He placed his ear over their hearts, willing there to be something, anything, before he started CPR. Still nothing. He ground his teeth together, unnerved. How could there possibly be two dead women in his lab?

Even though he was pretty sure it wouldn't do any good, he tilted Marguerite's head back and breathed into her mouth before doing chest compressions. When he looked over at Britta, he understood he had to have help and lurched to his feet. Snapping up the wall phone, he punched in the after hours code for the clinic. As soon as one of the nurses answered, he screeched, "Send help now. Third micro lab."

His headache worsened. So did his twisting, roiling guts, but he went back to the women. He didn't need to be a doctor to recognize death. Despite the futility, he alternated

CPR from one to the next. Five long minutes passed—but they felt like five years—before the door burst open.

"Christ!" One of the docs—Stewart maybe, Micah was too rattled to take a good look—pulled him off Marguerite. A tall, broad-shouldered woman Micah didn't recognize examined Britta.

"Looks like carbon monoxide poisoning to me," the female medic said flatly. "This one's well past CPR."

Dr. Stewart rocked back on his heels. "Yeah, her too." He trained his blue eyes on Micah. "What happened?"

Micah shook his head. "Damned if I know. I just got here. I had dinner in the mess hall, worked out in the gym, and then I swung by here to check on my cultures."

The woman narrowed her eyes and half-crawled to where Micah sat on the floor. She folded her fingers over his wrist and took him in with practiced hazel eyes. Her reddish hair was short, almost in a butch cut. She pressed her lips into a harsh line, frowning.

"I'm Ariana," she said, letting go of his wrist. "One of the nurse practitioners. How have you been feeling?"

"Bad," he admitted. "Think I finally succumbed to the community disease everyone else has."

Dr. Stewart joined them and squatted next to Micah. He ran a hand down the side of Micah's neck and listened to his chest with a stethoscope before exchanging a pointed glance with Ariana. "Where's the CO meter in here?" he asked.

Micah gestured behind him. "On that wall." He twisted to look at it, but the indicator light was green—safe. Maybe it was defective. His scientifically trained mind arranged informational bits into an unpleasant pattern. "The women," he said. "If I'd been firing on all cylinders, I'd have figured it out as soon as I looked at the color of their faces. They died from carbon monoxide poisoning, didn't they?"

"Probably," Dr. Stewart said cautiously. "But it's conjecture at this point."

"That cherry-red color is a dead giveaway," Ariana said with conviction. "Nothing else will do that."

"We'll wait for an autopsy before we make statements like that." The doctor eyed his colleague coolly.

"Yes, Doctor. Sir. King of all things medical." She set her lips in a thin line, clearly biting back further sarcasm. "Meantime," she ground out, "I'm pretty sure he—" she jabbed a finger at Micah "—has whatever killed these two." She stood and punched numbers into the wall phone. "I'm calling security."

Dr. Stewart sifted his hands through his untidy, blond hair. "Tell them to alert maintenance. Until we figure out what killed these two, we've got to get out of here. Now."

Micah straightened. "Wait a minute," he sputtered. "The meter says it's safe. For all we know, Britta and Marguerite got poisoned elsewhere and just happened to be in here cleaning when they collapsed."

Dr. Stewart got to his feet and hauled Micah upright. "For tonight, we'll put you in the infirmary and run tests to check if your hemoglobin's been compromised. I've got to alert the boss and talk with base security. We'll to get to the bottom of this."

"But my lab—"

Dr. Stewart made a chopping motion with one hand, and the rest of Micah's protest died unspoken.

Ariana hung up the phone and nodded at Dr. Stewart. "You take care of the boss. I'll deal with security and maintenance. Need to get the gas sniffer in here to make sure there's not a leak."

Micah tried to focus, but the room spun crazily. He really was wiped out. Much more tired than a thirty-year-old man had a right to feel.

"Can you walk?" Dr. Stewart nudged him.

Micah focused bleary eyes on the physician. "Yeah. I think so."

"How are you feeling?" Ariana asked the doctor.

He shrugged. "Normal. But it takes time for exposure to take a toll. Micah probably lives in this lab, except when he's asleep."

"Yeah, but," Micah pointed out, "those women didn't. They clean all the science labs. Maybe one of the other ones is the problem."

The doctor folded an arm around Micah's waist supporting him, and led him out of the lab. "I'm on it. By the time you wake up, we'll know more."

Micah staggered through the door, flanked by Dr. Stewart and Ariana. "What are you going to do about the women?" he asked.

"You were there when I alerted base security. They'll take care of them," Ariana assured him. "For tonight, focus on getting well."

~

IT HADN'T BEEN JUST that night, though. Micah spent the next three days in the infirmary sucking bottled oxygen. When that didn't clear his red blood cells fast enough, the doctors ordered chelation treatments. In the meantime, he had a chance to think, and he didn't care for what he came up with. Besides, it was so fantastic, no one would believe him.

Maintenance had given his lab, and the other three microbiology studios, a clean bill of health, which meant he could go back to work tomorrow. Even more disturbing, the entirety of the science wing where the dead women cleaned showed zip in the way of evidence of a gas leak. In the interest of thoroughness, maintenance had checked the female dorms too, and found exactly nothing. Autopsy was conclusive regarding cause of death, but no one could figure out how the women had been exposed to a big enough dose of carbon monoxide to kill them.

The same was true for him—major exposure to something pigging up his hemoglobin, but without an identifiable source. Another few hours without medical intervention and he'd have been just as dead as Britta and Marguerite.

Armed with that knowledge—and a phalanx of unanswered questions—Micah spent his downtime in the infirmary mapping out a series of tests to run on his strange archaea colonies. He had suspicions, but needed facts before he presented them to Jack DeVoe, the man in charge of McMurdo operations. If he went to him now, Jack, who had a Ph.D. in biochemistry, would laugh him right out of his office. And there would go Micah's hopes of earning his chops, so he could go on to something more prestigious than working at McMurdo Station.

ICY PASSAGE, CHAPTER TWO

Jack DeVoe sat behind his desk staring at his computer monitor. He snagged a bottle of whiskey from a drawer and belted back a slug, but it didn't make the news any more palatable. Russia and the U.S. were at it again, arguing over Ukraine like a pack of feral dogs battling each other for a juicy bone. The U.S. threatened to send troops, and the Russian president was screaming threats over network news. Unfortunately, Jack was fluent in Russian, and the barrage of words sounded like much more than posturing.

He'd been in Antarctica for years. Maybe now was a good time to go for early retirement—before World War III stranded him at this remote outpost. The more he thought about it, the better he liked the idea, especially in light of the two dead women who'd shown up in the micro lab the other night. Despite him harassing maintenance until they ran the other way every time they saw him, they hadn't come up with a goddamned thing.

He straightened in his chair and rolled his shoulder blades to loosen the tension making his neck hurt. How in the fucking hell could two women die from carbon monoxide poisoning with no leaks? Not just two women, either. The young microbiologist would've been just as dead —but he got lucky. Jack ground his jaws until his teeth ached. He'd figure out what was killing his people. No matter what it took.

Then he'd leave Antarctica.

His phone buzzed, and he picked it up, growling, "What?"

"Hey, boss. Micah here." He hesitated. "Is this an okay time? You seem miffed about something."

Nothing much. The world's imploding and a mystery gas leak is on the loose.

"Nah, I'm fine, Greenwich. You still feeling all right? What do you need? It's ten at night."

Micah cleared his throat. "Thanks for asking, but I made a good recovery." He paused a beat. "I suppose in a backhanded way, I owe my life to Britta and Marguerite. If it weren't for them, I'd be dead too."

"Get on with it." Jack rolled his eyes. "You didn't call to swap philosophies."

"Right, sir. Sorry. I know it's been a while since you did much with your biochem background, but I'd appreciate it if you could stop by the lab."

"Now?" Jack straightened in his chair and screwed the top back on the liquor bottle. "Is the lab on fire or something?" He shoved too-long blond hair out of his face and listened intently.

Micah laughed, but it sounded strained. "I've been running tests on my single-celled samples, but I keep coming up with odd results." He hesitated. "The other problem is a critical mass issue. Something bizarre happens when the colonies reach a certain size."

Jack squeezed his eyes shut. "Bizarre, how? Did you run it

past the other microbiologists?" When Micah didn't answer, Jack prodded, "Well, did you?"

"Yeah. They're so freaked out by this, they don't want anything to do with it. They'd rather chalk it up to me being nuts."

Jack clicked away from Yahoo! News. He couldn't do a damned thing about bad decisions on either side of the political fence. Or dead staff, apparently. Focusing on the phone in his hand, he said, "I still don't understand exactly why you need me," and followed up with, "Can it wait until morning?"

"I really think you should come see this, sir. If you tell me I've spent too much time at this Godforsaken outpost, I'll pick up my marbles, and no one will ever hear another word about my concerns."

Breath hissed from between Jack's teeth. "Fine. Be there in ten."

He dropped the phone into its cradle before the other man said goodbye and pushed heavily to his feet. The cold and isolation of Antarctica did things to people's minds. Maybe Micah had fallen prey to what Jack labeled the, "Aw shit, I'm stuck at the ass end of the world," syndrome.

He flexed his fingers, stretching them after long hours at the keyboard. Maybe a side trip to the lab wasn't a bad idea. He'd worked as a senior researcher in biochemistry at the National Institutes of Health before accepting the job running McMurdo, and he missed being in a lab teasing out thorny problems.

Besides, if he retreated to his quarters, he'd polish off the whiskey. A wry grin split his face. Compared with a lot of McMurdo residents, he was practically a teetotaler. The base went through buckets of booze, but it kept other problems at bay. He booted down his terminal, told the base operator he'd be on the sat phone if anyone needed him, and left his office.

The halls bustled with activity. Between the times when they had twenty-four hours of daylight, and the months of twenty-four-hour darkness, no one kept much of a regular schedule. He nodded to a few folks as he passed them, clapping a shoulder here and punching an arm there as he made his way to the microbiology laboratories.

Located near the end of one of McMurdo's many wings, the labs housed state of the art equipment for studying the rich array of unicellular life forms that inhabited the Antarctic. He pushed the door open and strode inside. Not seeing Micah in the outer room, he yelled, "Greenwich!"

"In here, boss."

Following Micah's voice, Jack walked into one of four smaller rooms that shot off from the main one like wagon spokes.

The other man straightened from where he'd been bent over a binocular microscope. Tall and lanky, he wore hazmat gloves. Blond hair stuck out at crazy angles around the mask perched over a full beard. Bright blue eyes regarded Jack. "Thanks for coming."

Jack grunted and grabbed a mask and gloves of his own. "What's got you so fired up, son? And why the major hand coverings?"

Micah shook his head and twisted his stool to face Jack. "Should I start at the beginning?"

"Just hit the high points and let me ask questions." Jack hooked his foot around a stool and dropped into it.

Micah pulled his mask aside. "Okay. I've been here four months. Because I was youngest and new kid on the block, the others stuck me with archaea, you know the prokaryote colonies."

Jack snorted. "Yeah, no one's ever very interested in

proks, probably because their structure's so simple." He narrowed his eyes. "You never answered me about the fancy hand coverings. Did the little bastards get away from you?"

Color stained Micah's face above his beard. "Now that you mention it, yes. Things were fine until the colonies developed a certain mass, but then things shifted."

"Are you talking about quorum sensing?" Jack asked, referring to a bacterial mechanism of population control based on density and several other factors.

"That's exactly what I'm talking about." Micah exhaled softly, fogging the lab glasses perched atop his nose. "Before we go further, come look at this." He got to his feet and pulled a sample bin across the table. Beige plastic, it was about eighteen inches long and a foot wide.

Jack got to his feet, frowning. The bin was large for bacterial colonies, which grew just fine on agar plates. Micah removed the lid, and Jack's mouth fell open when he stared at towers of cell colonies growing up the sides and along the bottom of the bin. Instead of the gray-green he'd expected, the colonies were violet, blue, red, and bright green.

"Holy crap!" He grabbed a sterile instrument off Micah's tray, pulled the plastic protector off, and gently prodded the mass in the bin. The tower nearest the tip of his instrument recoiled and flowed into a nearby glob of cells.

"I wouldn't get my hands too close," Micah cautioned.

Jack dropped the spatula back on the tray and motioned for Micah to put the lid back on the colony bin. "So instead of limiting their growth in response to quorum sensing, they're going nuts?" he asked.

"That's what it seems like to me," Micah replied. "But it gets worse. You asked about my gloves. I started feeling bad last week—a few days before I came in here and found Britta and Marguerite. Because of them, Dr. Stewart and Ariana caught my downhill slide in time to save me." He shrugged sheepishly. "The symptoms of carbon monoxide poisoning are subtle, and I'm a guy. I probably wouldn't have ever thought to turn myself in to the medics."

He shook his head. "During my stint in the infirmary, I had a lot of time to think, and I figured out what might've happened. It was pretty off-the-wall, though, and I needed to run some tests, first—"

"Cut to the chase. I'm all ears." Jack sat back on his stool. His stomach tightened, and he wished he'd either laid off the booze—or finished it.

"This will sound farfetched—"

"You already said that. Skip the fucking caveats. Just spit whatever it is out."

Micah inhaled sharply, exhaling in a rush before words tumbled past his lips. "You know how some proks have an affinity for iron?" At Jack's nod, he continued, "My best guess is I got sloppy with my gloves, and the proks worked their way through my skin, latched onto my red blood cells, and displaced their ability to bond to oxygen. It's the same mechanism carbon monoxide—and any other toxic gas— uses to kill you. Basically, you suffocate."

Jack felt like someone had sucker punched him. Before he could stop himself, a long, low whistle escaped. "I can see why the other researchers would want to discredit your theory. Distance themselves."

Micah colored again and studied his hands. "Sorry to bother you, sir. Like I said, you'll never hear another word—"

"Shut up," Jack snapped. "I didn't say I didn't believe you. Did you experiment with mice?"

The color mottling Micah's face deepened. "Er, yes. I know I'm supposed to requisition—"

"I don't give a flying fuck about that. What'd you find?"

Micah straightened his shoulders. "I introduced normal proks into a bin with two mice and these proks into a bin with two others. The mice with the normal proks are fine. The others are dead. When I examined their tissues, they died from oxygen starvation. Just like Britta and Marguerite." He stared hard at Jack. "Since maintenance couldn't find any gas leaks, my best guess is the women looked in the sample bins, were fascinated, and touched the colonies."

Jack felt old when he got to his feet and went to look into the bin with the crazily growing bacterial colonies. Micah's theory made a whole lot of sense. Plus it explained why maintenance had come up dry. After he replaced the lid, he gestured to the microscope. "What's under there is stained samples from this bin?"

"Yes."

"What's unique about them?"

"It's why I called you, sir. We finally made it to where I need your biochem background. These don't exactly look like proks anymore."

Jack strode to the microscope, adjusted it, and peered through the eyepieces. What he saw gave him pause. The prok structure was there, but these had more to them—lots more. He straightened slowly. "What happens if you separate the colonies?"

"Funny you should ask, since I already did. After a day or two, they revert to regular proks. My assumption is they'll stay that way until they divide enough to reach whatever critical mass spurs them to shift into that." He pointed at the sample bin.

"Mmph. Let's limit access to this lab to just you and me. For now, keep the colonies small, even if you have to jettison some material."

Micah shook his head. "I don't think tossing anything is smart. These guys thrive in almost any environment including extreme cold and salt water, but I'll do my best to keep the colonies under critical mass."

"Douse the ones you want to get rid of with ethyl alcohol and see how they like it." Jack stripped off his mask and gloves. "I'm going to call a friend of mine, Brynn McMichaels. He's a microbiologist I worked with at NIH. Just so happens he's stationed at South Georgia Island. Proks were a big interest of his."

"What's he doing with them?" Micah perked up, the flat, worried expression leaving his face.

"Building boutique antibiotics or some such thing. It's been a while since we've talked, so I'm not totally certain. Anyway, his contract must be close to up. If he hasn't signed on for another stint on South Georgia, maybe I can talk him into coming here. We might be onto something fascinating with these mutant proks."

Micah smiled for the first time since Jack had entered the lab. "Thanks, sir. I appreciate it."

"Hang onto your gratitude. Let's see if we can get Brynn to come here, first. At the very least, I'm sure he'd be willing to bat ideas around on the phone or via email."

Jack headed out the door before Micah could thank him again. He remembered what it was like to have ideas no one else endorsed. The scientific community could be pretty shitty to researchers they viewed as renegades.

As he walked McMurdo's corridors, he rolled Micah's idea around in his head. Whiskey sloshed in his belly, and for the first time in years, he wished he had a pack of cigarettes. To quell his craving for tobacco, he scrolled through the contacts list on his sat phone on the way to his quarters. He had no idea if Brynn would be up yet, but it was morning on South Georgia, so he punched the buttons to put the call through.

After three rings, a sleepy-sounding Brynn said, "Hello?"

"Hey, old buddy. Jack here."

Sputtering blasted through the phone. "What the blazes

are you doing calling at this hour? Must be the middle of the night there. Did McMurdo implode?"

"No, but the world might. Are you following the news?"

"Yeah, sure, but that's not what you woke me up for. Or is it? Hang on." Something clinked against the phone—probably a glass. "Damn. It's past eight. Time for me to get up anyway. Back to why you called. You speak Russian. Do I need to beat a path home?"

Jack grunted. "I was actually considering that earlier tonight, but no one's declared war—not yet, anyway. The reason I'm calling is we've got an unusual situation in the lab here with proks that've gone wild—"

"Aw, shit!" Brynn cut in. "You're kidding, right?"

"Wish I were." Jack pushed open the door to his small suite of rooms and kicked it shut behind him. Instincts working overtime, he asked, "You having the same problem?"

"Not exactly, but my colonies are acting oddly. Growing like mad. For some reason quorum sensing isn't slowing them down one whit, and once the colonies get to be a certain size, they almost demonstrate a group intelligence."

Air left Jack's lungs in a whoosh. Brynn had always been the most level-headed of researchers. "Are you certain?"

"Of course I'm certain," Brynn snapped. "What I haven't figured out is what to do about it."

"Be very careful while you're figuring it out. It's likely the proks here killed two women."

"What?" Brynn screeched. "They're single-celled life forms. How could they possibly harm a human?"

"This batch has an affinity for iron. Once they drill through the skin and get into the bloodstream, they have a heyday." Jack paused. "I've read about that phenomenon, but never come across it before."

Time dripped by before Brynn spoke again, still sounding agitated. "Maybe mine have a different problem. If they were going to get me, they've had lots of opportunity, and I feel fine."

"When's your contract with that Brit bio firm up?"

Brynn snorted. "Very soon. I already gave notice. I've had it with the southern ocean. Two years was plenty."

"Would you consider coming here and bringing your colonies with you?" Jack forged on before Brynn could protest. "It's good science to look at both mutating colonies side by side. Maybe we'll learn something critical."

A low rumble—maybe compressed frustration—preceded Brynn's next words. "I don't know, Jack. If I don't charter a flight back to Argentina, I might be stuck here if the political mess heats further."

"You could catch a plane from here to Christchurch," Jack pointed out, not bothering to mention he'd be on it right along with Brynn.

"How would I get there? We're heading into winter, and the weather's unpredictable."

"Does that mean you'll come if I can figure out the logistics?" Jack pressed.

After a lengthy pause, Brynn said, "Yeah, I guess that's what it means, but I'll be damned if I know why I just said yes."

"Because we go back a long way, buddy."

"Yeah, we do. Keep me posted. If I don't hear from you in a few days, I'll make arrangements to get to Ushuaia or Buenos Aires."

"Fair enough. One more small favor."

"Hard to imagine it could be any bigger than what you just asked. What?"

"Can I give one of the microbiology staff your number? He'd love to have a blood brother to talk with, and the other three here have pretty much blown him off."

"Sure, Jack. No problem. As long as he waits until a little later this morning to call."

"I won't even tell him how to reach you before tomorrow morning here—and I'll remind him about the fifteen hour time difference. My admin staff will figure out how to transport you and your cultures to McMurdo. Stay tuned."

"Gosh, guess I'll make myself some breakfast now that you've given me something to look forward to. A reason to get out of bed and all that."

"Spare the sarcasm. Talk to you soon." Jack disconnected and booted up the computer in his quarters to check the weather window.

As his fingers flashed over the keys, he kept seeing the bacterial colony with its multi-hued towers of one-celled organisms. It seemed absurd, beyond the pale, that they'd attacked Micah and the two women. Regardless, Jack felt certain that if the young researcher hadn't stumbled over the lab cleaning staff, he'd be just as dead as them—and the mice in his experiment.

An uncomfortable sensation tracked down Jack's spine. It took a moment before he recognized it as fear. Thank Christ he'd warned Brynn.